Thy Will Be Done

by

Richard Davidson

The Lord's Prayer Mystery Series
Volume IV

Richard Davidson

"Thy Will Be Done," by Richard Davidson.
ISBN 978-0-9829160-2-5.

Published 2012 by RADMAR Publishing Group, P.O. Box 425, Northbrook, IL 60065, U.S.A. Copyright 2012, Richard Davidson. All rights reserved. No part of this publication may be reproduced, stored in a retrieval system, or transmitted in any form or by any means, electronic, mechanical, recording, or otherwise, without the prior written permission of Richard Davidson.

Manufactured in the United States of America.

This book is dedicated to the memory of J. E. McClear, M.M. (Padre Mac), a great friend who served as a missionary priest in Guatemala for approximately forty years, educating and making a significant impact on the lives of the rural population. He was also proud of the fact that he had assisted the local people by pulling more than fifteen thousand of their teeth.

Richard Davidson

CHAPTER 1 – FAMILY REQUEST

At the point in the service normally reserved for the closing benediction, Pastor Arthur Blake asked the congregation to be seated for a special message. He then relinquished the pulpit to a first-time visitor to Parkville United Methodist Church.

A blond muscular man with weightlifter shoulders flaring into his neck adjusted the microphone for his greater height. "Good morning. I want to thank Pastor Blake for giving me the opportunity to address you. I'm Ted Karga. My sister, Kristina Karga, worshipped with you for the last six months or so, until she died last week. The doctors still don't know why she left us so suddenly. She was only thirty-two years old."

Several people shook their heads and murmured comments to each other.

"I'm here this morning to ask if any of you may have borrowed or know the whereabouts of Kristina's journals. She maintained those journals for several years, and none of her friends know where to look for them. I need to learn why she died, and I'm hoping that her written entries will reveal key information. If you find the journals, please give them to Pastor Blake; he will get them to me.

"I apologize in advance for what I am about to say. My upbringing makes me tremble, but I can't hold it back any more...God, why did you make her die so young? She had so much to offer you and the world. I stand here in your house in front of your people, and I declare that you are not a God of love. She served you well, but I will no longer be one of your followers! You are no longer my God!" Ted screamed this last declaration and blinked back tears as he ran down the aisle and out of the church.

Pastor Blake's prayed in response to Ted's outburst: *Forgive him, Lord; he can't really mean that.*

The buzz of reactive comments filled the sanctuary. A scattering of worshippers stood and stared at each other and the exit door. Wally Sanborn hastened out, trying to catch up with Ted. Some people stayed in their pews, but others moved around to talk with their friends. A few left the sanctuary and headed for the parking lot in Wally's wake in an effort to keep Ted from breaking his religious connections.

After a long pause Arthur stood and approached the pulpit as though drawn to it by a magnet. "If we ever needed a benediction, we need one now... Lord, your ways are mysterious and difficult for us to accept at times like these. Be with Ted as he struggles with the loss of his only sister. Be with all of us now and in the future as we face our own losses and pain. We know that frustrated people may turn their backs on you, but you will not forsake them. Cherish your troubled children, all of us. And now friends, go from this place, and seek God's meaning in your lives. He will be with you, even in terrible times...Amen.

Hesitantly and sporadically, individuals stood up and moved slowly toward the exits. Most of the older ones left silently, while the chatter of the younger congregants displayed interest and even excitement.

CHAPTER 2 – KRISTINA

Arthur sat with his fiancée, Irma Custis, on their favorite boulder by Mallard Lake, across Jeffers Street from Parkville UMC. The little northwest Illinois town was far enough away from Chicago's urban sprawl to offer a slower pace of living while still remaining within easy reach of airport connections and other specialties that were not locally available. This lakeside spot where Arthur and Irma sat and shared their thoughts had always been a favorite for them, but its significance became permanent after Arthur proposed there. They had met during the investigation of the death of the pastor Arthur had replaced several years earlier. At the time, Irma served as County Medical Examiner, and she worked with Arthur to resolve several unusual aspects of the case. She had since resigned from her CME post but continued to work with Arthur as he applied his past NASA engineering background in combination with his more recent ministerial training to investigate crimes stemming from events occurring in and around the church.

"Arthur, I remember Kristina Karga as a quiet but outwardly pleasant individual who never revealed much about herself during casual conversations. I saw her as an energetic individual who deliberately stayed in the background and never volunteered for anything. If she kept up a daily journal, it probably served as her emotional safety valve. She didn't share her feelings or show her reactions to anyone around her. What do you know about her history?"

"Kristina appeared in our midst a little more than six months ago. She never joined the church, but attended regularly. For her first few weeks here she lived at Sylvia's Bed and Breakfast. Then she found a small apartment off of Main Street, behind the Ford dealer. I have absolutely no objective justification for saying this, but I had the gut feeling that she was running away from something."

Irma removed a small spiral-bound notebook from her purse and wrote a few notes as Arthur spoke. "Did she have a job here?"

"She worked somewhere, but I don't think it was in Parkville. I can't recall ever seeing her during the week."

"How did she die?"

"Last Saturday, around noon, I received a call from Dr. Bernard Miggles at Parkville Care Center. He said that Kristina had been admitted that morning with a fever, complaining of a sore throat plus pain in her right leg. They had not yet developed a specific diagnosis, but she had experienced alternating periods of clarity and hallucinations with anxiety. During one of her alert intervals she asked for me, so he requested that I get there right away. By the time I reached the hospital, Kristina had lapsed into a coma. She lost brain function within an hour after that, and her heart failed ten minutes later."

"Her final transition went quickly. What did the autopsy show?"

"There wasn't one. She had listed her brother Ted as next of kin when she completed the hospital papers. We don't know of any other relatives. Ted refused to have an autopsy performed. There was no evidence of a crime, so Dr. Miggles didn't insist on one."

"I wonder why he made that decision. I would expect that he'd want to learn all he could about her death. I'll bet that you're going to tell me her body was cremated."

"Her brother planned to have her cremated, but I don't know for sure that it happened. Ted disappeared after he ran out of church, so we can't ask him until he resurfaces somewhere. When he does, we can try to convince him to take the autopsy route."

"Does he carry a cell phone? Most people do nowadays."

"I do have an answer for that one. He told me that he doesn't like them. He said that he needs to get away from everything and be unreachable so that he can think."

"He looked more like a doer than a thinker to me, but that comment says I'm wrong about him."

Irma climbed off the boulder and started pacing as she considered what Arthur's summary of Kristina's illness and death. "Let's visit Bernie Miggles this afternoon. He may have enough blood and tissue samples for a preliminary analysis. We may yet be able to have an autopsy after we locate Ted and reason with him, but it's more important to examine the hospital samples before they're contaminated or discarded."

"You referred to him as Bernie. Is he a friend of yours?"

"Let's just say that Bernie and I have a history from a long time ago. I also know that he tries to catch up with his overdue work on Sunday afternoons."

CHAPTER 3 – TED

He felt isolated. Ted hadn't realized that his rejection of God would cause him such psychological torment. He felt the way he had after Dad had crashed his small plane killing both himself and Mom. When he realized he was on his own after that trauma he had, at least for a while, turned to religion for comfort and support. Now that Kristina was gone and he had rejected religion, he faced the future without any remaining support system. He felt like an astronaut on an unknown planet. He was embarking on a totally new phase of his life.

After he left the church he'd pointed his car in a generally northern direction and driven slowly, not on the highways, but exclusively on narrow secondary roads that were unfamiliar to him. He needed time to think, and driving on deserted back roads helped. If someone had asked his destination, he would have said nowhere; it fit his mood. He might have been driving in circles on those winding back roads, but he didn't care. He pulled off the pavement at an out-of-business gas station to have a snack from his food stash in the trunk.

He had lived like a Nomad for a month since his someone had firebombed his Chicago apartment. A week later two teenage thugs attacked him on the street. Ted had escaped serious injury, but he knew that someone was pursuing him and would not abandon the chase. Since that time he had remained alert and kept moving. He planned to disappear in rural Wisconsin for a while, at least until there was a job opening for him. For now he would read his science fiction novel and await the shroud of darkness. Kristina had been his only safe human connection, and now she was gone. Life was too fragile to plan anything. God could reclaim it at any time. There he was, thinking about God again. He'd burned that bridge and could only rely on himself.

Several new chapters into outer space explorations, as the sun was setting, Ted closed his book, restarted his car, and drove onto an unpaved side road. Then he turned off that narrow way and parked behind some trees and bushes. He wanted to be sure that no headlights would reveal reflections from his car while he slept. Tomorrow he would plan his next move.

CHAPTER 4 – SAMPLES

When Irma and Arthur arrived at Dr. Miggles' office at Parkville Care Center, they found him disposing of a pile of crumbs remaining from a stale vending machine bran muffin. Arthur began to evaluate the doctor as a competitor for Irma's affections as they approached each other.

"Hello, Pastor Blake, welcome to my sanctuary. It's so good to see you again, Irma. Just let me clean up my mess. If this were a fully staffed hospital, I'd have time for actual meals. The way it's set up here, I have to grab packaged snacks between scheduled duties and visits. I did manage to set aside a block of time for you two so that we can try to resolve this Karga case."

Irma said, "It's good to see you too, Bernie. I hope you've followed my suggestions for keeping lab samples taken from your patients."

"Absolutely, Irma, I store samples properly and keep good documentation. You taught me well, and I'm hoping to use these techniques as a basis for petitioning the Care Center Board to give me an improved laboratory. By the way, I hear that you two are engaged now. Congratulations to both of you."

Arthur nodded and gave Bernie's extended hand a cursory shake. He wanted to learn more about the past relationship between Irma and Bernie before he got too chummy with the doctor.

Irma sensed Arthur's tension. "Can we adjourn to the laboratory so that I can see what patient samples we have available to analyze?"

"I have quite a few. I think you'll be proud of me." Bernie led them out of the office and down a long corridor to a corner room with a keypad entry lock.

"I'm glad to see that you're limiting access, Bernie. Hopefully, that minimizes contamination."

"I require everyone to put on lab coveralls and shoe covers to minimize dust from external sources. Select your proper sizes from this cabinet."

The three of them suited up and gathered at a stainless steel lab bench in the center of the laboratory. Dr. Miggles retrieved a patient history summary on the screen of his computer. "Irma, you can see that the inventory for Kristina Karga shows that I retained properly stored samples of blood, a DNA swab from inside her cheek, a tissue sample from her right leg where she complained of pain, and a posthumous needle biopsy sample of brain tissue. Her brother refused a full autopsy, but I was able to sample the brain tissue without disturbing the outward appearance of the body."

"You didn't do the needle biopsy while she was still alive?"

"I had scheduled a living tissue biopsy, but she died before it could be performed. She went very quickly. At least I obtained a posthumous sample for follow-up work."

"Well, hopefully that will give us our diagnosis. I think we should perform a PCR polymerase chain reaction assay on the brain tissue sample. Are you set up for PCR here? If not, I can get it done through a private lab."

"Irma, I wish I could say that we had the capability here, but you know that we're limited. I'd appreciate your taking care of it, if you don't mind."

"That's fine, Bernie. It shouldn't take more than a couple of days. I'll get it to the lab first thing tomorrow morning."

Irma and Bernie prepared the sample for hand-carrying to the outside lab. As they worked together preparing it, Arthur noticed their smiles and obvious familiarity. Even though he knew that their past relationship preceded his meeting Irma, he felt an odd sense of relief when he and Irma left the hospital with the packaged sample.

As they approached Arthur's car, he said, "You two looked very familiar with each other while you prepared this specimen. How serious was your past relationship?"

"I appreciate that little tinge of jealousy in your question. It confirms your feelings for me. As to Bernie, we went together for a while a long time ago, but I never could have married him."

"Why not?"

"Irma Miggles sounds too much like worm that wiggles."

CHAPTER 5 – WALLY SANBORN

Wally Sanborn, Arthur's best friend at Parkville UMC, had been a career Army man as well as a Peace Corps volunteer when he was younger. He used this background well in shepherding the youth on mission trips to a wide variety of places. His past experiences also served as valuable resources for Arthur and his ABC Consultants associates, Renee Andrews and Irma Custis, during the course of investigations. Arthur and Wally especially treasured their frequent brainstorming exchanges over mugs of coffee in Arthur's office.

Early Monday morning Wally announced his presence at the office as Arthur completed signing a church conference report form. "Hi, we need a session right now."

"That sounds ominous, Wally. Grab your mug, take some coffee from my pot, and sit down. I'll shove my papers aside and add some hot liquid to my mug too...

"OK, I'm all set. What's happening?"

"That performance by Ted Karga yesterday left a lot of church members upset. He ran out after shouting his defiance of God, and as soon as I returned from following him to the parking lot, people started coming to me with their worries. Whether it makes sense or not, they feel that this church is now jinxed, and that we should expect a lightning bolt or two to strike us in the very near future. Many feel that they're in the middle of an Old Testament saga and that we haven't been faithful enough to please God."

"But we have been faithful. Ted Karga is the only rebel among us, and he attended our church only once."

"Some are arguing that something must have been wrong with Kristina to cause God to take her so quickly and that Ted's rampage was only an aftereffect. They say that the inability of the doctors to determine what killed her proves that it was divine vengeance for something."

"We're working on the medical cause of Kristina's death, and I expect that we'll understand it within the next few days."

"That will help, but your flock wants something from you."

"What do they want?"

"There's a groundswell of sentiment, and for all I know a circulating petition, that you should hold a liturgical service to re-sanctify the church. They no longer consider this a holy place."

"Ouch! That smacks of superstition. I'm not sure the District Superintendant or the Bishop would go along with that one. I could get in trouble for holding that kind of service on my own. It would be like acknowledging the presence of the devil in our church."

"Well, if you don't want to lose a lot of members, you'll have to do something. What do you want me to tell people, or do you want to make a personal proclamation to them?"

"This sounds like a perfect problem to kick upstairs. Tell people that I am planning to get input from Angela King, our District Superintendant, and from Bishop Chandler on this matter. That should at least buy us some time. Maybe my superiors have had experience with circumstances like this before."

"That should sound reasonable to them. Bring on the heavy hitters."

"Something like that...After Ted ran out, did you catch up with him?"

"I stopped him just as he was backing out of his parking space. He said something about going on a crusade without God to support him."

CHAPTER 6 – ANALYSIS

Irma and Arthur sat with Dr. Bernard Miggles in his office when Bobby Andrews, the Parkville Police Chief entered.

Irma waved to him. "Come on in, Bobby. We're just about to look at the lab results." Turning to the others, she said, "I invited Bobby to join us just in case we turn up anything criminal or requiring his assistance with public health matters."

Bobby shook hands with Dr. Miggles and Arthur; then he sat down and opened the notebook he used for legal matters.

Bernie spoke while Irma removed the lab documents from their envelope. "I'm glad you're here, Bobby, because I have additional information that may require your attention. After we sent the deceased's samples to the outside lab, I went back and made a more detailed examination of her corpse. In keeping with the wishes of her brother, I did not do anything intrusive or perform an autopsy, but I looked for externally available information."

Bobby leaned forward. "Did you find anything suspicious?"

Bernie laid six photographs onto the table so that everyone could see them. "Let's say that I found some interesting and unexpected physical indications. Kristina had a poorly healed wound on her right calf muscle, which continued to be painful for her even though it was at least seven months old. I also found some scarring on her forearms of similar age, and some significantly older laceration scars on her back. Because of the age of these scars, they would not have caused her death, but they indicate that Kristina Karga had been assaulted and tortured more than

18

once. Death may have been due to natural causes, but something criminal happened to her in the past."

Irma looked up from the documents she was studying. "Hold those scars for a minute, Bernie. I'd like to focus on that poorly healed wound on her leg. The PCR test results indicate that she died from a rabies virus infection. She was probably bitten by a rabid animal or bat on that leg. That bite either caused the leg wound, or it transferred the virus into an existing wound leading to the infection that retarded the wound's healing. That infection also caused the pain that she continued to feel to the end of her life. Rabies in humans is symptom-free for a long period, two months to a year, but once the symptoms occur, it is incurable."

Bernie said, "This would be the first human death from rabies in Illinois for a long time. I knew we have been detecting an increasing number of rabid bats each year, so it was only a matter of time until someone would succumb. A man died in Missouri from rabies a couple of years ago, and a young girl died in Michigan last year. The pity is that if the patient seeks medical treatment right after a bite, it is always curable."

Arthur pointed at the photograph of the leg wound. "Let's suppose that she had a pre-existing wound on her leg when the bite occurred. She may not have even detected a bite if it occurred while she slept."

Irma took a closer look at the picture. "I know that bats have such small teeth that they have been known to get into a bedroom and bite someone overnight without it being noticed. They tend to kill the bat and discard it, when they should trap it without damaging its head and take it to Animal Control."

Bobby picked up a different photograph. "Bernie, you said that these scars on her forearms occurred at about the same time as the original wound on her leg, but that the scars on her back were older, is that correct?"

"Yes, it is."

"OK, then let me give you a cop's analysis of her history. Those scars on her forearms resulted from knife slashes as she fended off an attacker. The assailant probably gashed her leg during the same attack. The older scars on her back came from a whipping. I saw things like that when I was an Army M.P. in Kosovo. Kristina Karga suffered through some very intense experiences."

Arthur said, "You never would have known it from seeing her as a docile background participant in our church. What do you think, Irma?"

"You were right as usual, Arthur. When I asked you about her earlier, you said that you had the gut feeling that she was running away from something or someone."

"We'd better make an effort to discover her pursuer."

CHAPTER 7 – BOBBY ANDREWS

Bobby entered the Parkville Police Station and walked up to Sergeant Al Gomez at the front desk. "Hi, Al, it looks as though there's some suspicious background to the death of Kristina Karga, but it's not a police matter. We get a pass on this one."

"Don't be too sure of that, Bobby. While you were out, I took a call from a farmer who found an abandoned car on his property. He said that it had sat there for several days before he checked it and discovered the driver inside with his throat cut. I ran the plate number he gave me. It's registered to Kristina Karga. Kristina's brother must have been using her car. The murder scene is barely inside the rural part of Parkville, but it's our case. Do you want to come along?"

"After seeing what happened to Kristina, I have to find out who hates this family so much. Take some coveralls; this could be messy. Tell Gene Murphy to come along and to bring his crime scene kit. We'll see how much he learned at that last seminar. In the meantime, I'll call Renee and tell her that it will be a while before I get home."

"I'll call the Fire Department and ask for their ambulance crew to meet us there."

"Good - and ask Hank Robbins to visit Dr. Miggles at Parkville Care Center. Hank should take fingerprints from Kristina's corpse. Maybe they'll tell us more about her background."

CHAPTER 8 – PLANNING

Arthur and Irma sat on the pink-flowered couch in Irma's apartment, trying to think of their future rather than Kristina's death from rabies. The apartment served as headquarters for their ABC Consultants investigation business as well as Irma's residence.

"Arthur, what would your church people think if I moved into the parsonage with you?"

"Let's say that they'd be a lot less offended if I moved in here with you, but some wouldn't be happy with any cohabitation prior to a wedding."

"That's an interesting subject. When would you like to schedule it?"

"Oh, you are good. You manipulated me and this conversation to your priority topic. Is manipulation what I should expect after said wedding?"

"Of course not, we don't have to talk about the wedding right now. It's simply something we should have in the back of our minds as we talk about other things. Think of the money I could save if we lived together. It's a practical consideration."

"Well, if you're interested in saving money, Irma, you can have ABC Consultants pay the rent on this apartment. You can live here rent-free."

Arthur knew enough to duck so that the pillow missed his head and hit the bookcase behind him. "Hey, you're dangerous!"

"If you keep sidestepping discussions about our wedding, you'll find out how truly dangerous I am."

"OK, I'll get more serious about it, but if you want a wedding you'll have to agree that this couch with the big pink flowers has to go."

"I like this couch."

"More than you like me?"

"That's blackmail. What if I agreed to put it in the finished basement?"

"We don't even have a house, let alone a finished basement. Anyway, we have more immediate planning to do. Renee is about to have her baby, and she told us that she wants to drop out of ABC Consultants once the baby comes. She wants to stick to being Bobby's wife and mom to little Hoozitz."

"Hoozitz?"

"That's my shorthand for whatever they name him or her. Don't forget, they abstained from determining the baby's gender in advance."

"That was wonderfully old-fashioned of them."

"Yes it was, but do you have a candidate to replace Renee after the big event?"

"If I come up with a good replacement, can we discuss the wedding?"

"You do have a one-track mind. The replacement has to be approved by me first."

"That's not a problem. I suggest Jeremy Hadley."

"Jeremy still has a long time to go in his studies at University of Wisconsin, Platteville. He's in the right department, Criminal Justice, but he's not available."

"He already contacted me to see if he could work with us over the summer, and he says they have a co-op plan where he gets credit if he takes time out to work for an organization in the criminal justice field. He could go to school when we don't have a case, and he would be able to arrange for a leave to work with us when cases are active."

"That almost sounds workable."

"Come on, Arthur, either tell me you approve of Jeremy as our new associate, or tell me that you would like to take a chance on losing his mother, Shirley, as your church secretary."

"As I said, you know how to manipulate me. Of course, Jeremy would be a good addition."

"Do you want to continue talking about the wedding before or after dinner?"

CHAPTER 9 – CRIME SCENE

They outlined a large area around Ted's car with yellow crime scene tape before allowing emergency vehicles into the field. The gravel on the narrow rural lane would not reveal tire tracks, so they included an additional area within the yellow tape boundary in case a second car had parked in the field. Then they allowed the fire and police vehicles into the remainder of the field through a new narrow opening they cut through the roadside brush.

Al Gomez took a statement from the farmer while Bobby Andrews and Detective Gene Murphy approached the car, trying to avoid any bare ground where footprints might be detected. Al would photograph the soles of the farmer's boots for comparison with any footprints they found.

Gene and Bobby donned coveralls and gloves. Then they photographed the entire crime scene from several angles and distances, zooming in on a bloody mark on the front passenger door handle. They spotted a tire tread imprint in some bare ground near the bushes, and they took pictures of that from several angles after first indicating its position with a numbered yellow plastic tent marker. They also found and similarly marked and photographed a nearby boot print. Gene and Bobby checked the car body for any obvious fingerprints, but they found none. Then Bobby approached the car, gaining entry through the right rear door, so as not to disturb the blood on the handle of the front door. Gene stood outside to take notes on Chief Andrews' observations.

Bobby stared at Ted's body over the back of the front seat. "It looks as though he was sleeping with the driver's seatback partially reclined, when his

25

assailant entered through the right front door. This guy must have been a pro to get into a locked car without waking the occupant. Ted woke up and tried to defend himself, but he couldn't maneuver due to the bucket seats and the raised center console between them. His first reaction was to fend off his attacker with his forearms, and his reward for that was a set of cuts on his arms that resemble his sister's wounds from a knife attack some months ago. Once the attacker slashed Ted's neck, blood spattered all over the place, including the windows, dashboard, and the hand or glove that left a bloody print on the door handle. I'll bet you'll find a trail of bloodspots leading back to the spot where we found that tire imprint, Gene."

"I see a blood trail, Bobby, but there's more than just a few drops. I think Ted managed to wound the killer before he died. Can you see any kind of a weapon in the car?"

"I'll have to back out and open the driver's door to check." Bobby eased his way out and crossed in front of the car so as not to trample on anything between the back of the car and the place where they had found the tire imprint. Then he opened the driver's door, being careful to avoid touching or moving the body. He used his flashlight to search the floor beneath the steering wheel and the space under the front seat. He extracted something from beneath the seat, holding it gently between two gloved fingers before dropping it into an evidence bag he retrieved from his pocket. "You're right, Gene. Ted prepared for an attack, but he didn't rouse himself quickly enough to survive. I found a Walther .22LR handgun under the seat. The recoil must have bounced it down there after he fired it. My guess is that he shot just as the knife reached his throat. The attacker would have been leaning forward to reach Ted, so he probably took a shot to the chest or stomach. If it had been a larger caliber gun, we'd have two bodies here. Put out a bulletin to watch for anyone seeking treatment for a gunshot wound. Hopefully, the lab people will be able to test some of this dried blood and get the killer's DNA."

"I'll go back to the car and get the bulletin going, Bobby, but you should take a closer look over here. That tread print we spotted isn't from a car; it's too thin. I think our assailant was riding a motorcycle, and it's one with fairly narrow tires. The tread might be unique enough to trace the brand, if not the model."

"Good thinking, Gene; let's see if we can make a cast of it." Bobby walked over and studied the ground very carefully, illuminating it with his flashlight from several angles. "I think we have a less distinct impression of the second tire here. Hold it; the two tires on this cycle have different treads. One is a replacement, so the combination of the two may be unique. We have a killer who may have been wounded, riding an unusual motorcycle. Get the best pictures you can, and we'll circulate it to other police departments in Illinois, Wisconsin, and Iowa."

The Fire Department paramedics completed their documentation and loaded the body into their ambulance. A flatbed tow truck pulled into the field and awaited Bobby's authorization to take the car back to the police garage for closer examination. Things were going well, but the killer had left this site several days ago. Pursuit would be difficult unless he had walked into a hospital looking for emergency treatment.

CHAPTER 10 – DAMAGE CONTROL

Arthur grabbed his briefcase, opened the car door, and climbed out. He had taken only a few steps toward the church door when he saw Wally Sanborn running toward him with a very serious look on his face. "What is it, Wally? What's happened?"

"I can hardly believe it, but Ted Karga has been murdered. He died within one day of declaring that he would no longer believe in God! A farmer found the body today and called the police."

"That's terrible! Do they have a suspect or a motive?"

"Not yet, Arthur; it's too early in the investigation. My worry right now is that our church members, who were shocked by Ted's disowning God, will be shattered by his dying within one day of making that declaration. They'll assume that he was struck down by God because of what he said."

"Do you believe that he was struck down by God?"

"Of course not; I think God has more important concerns and wouldn't be so thin-skinned as to react to a single outlandish statement by a frustrated person. I'm worried that many of our people will feel they should stop coming to church."

"On the contrary, Wally, anyone who really thinks Ted died because he disavowed God should definitely want to worship with us. Their panic logic suggests that God listens to every word we say here."

"I still think it's a nasty situation, and I can't believe the coincidence of his immediate death."

"Now you're starting to be logical, Wally. I don't believe it was a coincidence either. From what you've told me, it sounds as though Ted was murdered by someone who attended our church service last Sunday."

"That's an interesting perspective on what happened. It makes sense."

"You followed Ted out of the church and were there when he drove away. Did you see anyone else drive away shortly afterward? Revisit the scene in your memory."

"Let's see, there were a few people who came out of the church behind me, but I assumed they wanted to be there in case I needed assistance in getting Ted to calm down."

"Did those people just stand around? Did some go back inside while some drove away?"

"For the most part, they went back inside after Ted left. I only remember two driving away. One was Mr. Hastings in his old brown Buick, and the other one was a youngish guy on a motorcycle."

"Can you describe that person?"

"All I remember is a figure in black wearing a motorcycle helmet. I didn't notice him before he put on the helmet."

"We'd better head over to the police station and share your information with Bobby."

CHAPTER 11 – RENEE

As Arthur and Wally arrived at the Parkville Police Station, they saw an unmarked police car with activated flashers rounding a corner two blocks away. They scrambled into the building and confronted Al Gomez at the front desk. Arthur said, "Al, what's happening? We saw Bobby rushing away in his car with the flashers going. Does he have a lead on the killer?"

"Right now the killer isn't his main concern. Irma called from Parkville Care Center. Renee is in labor. Irma and Renee had gone shopping together when the pains started. Irma took her to the hospital. It looks as though Renee's going to have her baby a month and a half early. She hadn't felt anything unusual when Bobby left home this morning, but things are subject to change without notice during the final months of pregnancy. At least she made it to the hospital before the baby came."

"Wally, I'd better put on my pastor's hat and get over to the Care Center. Give Al your information about the suspect while I'm gone. I'm sure you can hitch a ride back to the church with him afterward."

Al nodded, and Arthur ran out the door.

Irma met Arthur in the Parkville Care Center lobby. She gave him a quick hug and suggested that they get right up to the maternity waiting room to stand by for Bobby and Renee. As they waited for the elevator Arthur said, "How did you know I was on my way over, or did you sense it with your ESP?"

"It wasn't that difficult. I figured you ought to be here for moral and prayer support, so I made a few calls. My third try reached Al Gomez, and he said you were following Bobby's trail over here."

"How's Renee doing?"

"Right now she's pretty scared. The doctors have assured her that the baby is far enough developed for a safe birth, but she's worried. It turns out that her mother told her that she lost a premature baby before Renee was born, and she's afraid that history might be repeating itself."

"Why did Momma tell her that? That's not the smartest thing to say to your pregnant daughter."

"Relax, Preacher; Renee remembered that story from several years ago. She wasn't even married when Momma and she discussed how tough life had been decades ago, growing up on the South Side of Chicago. Renee remembers almost everything she hears or reads. That's one of her greatest contributions to our work at ABC Consultants."

They stepped out of the elevator on the maternity floor and signed in at the security desk. At the nurses' station they learned that Renee was in the delivery room. Booby was in there too, surgically gowned and appropriately nervous. There was nothing for Arthur and Irma to do but wait.

They sat on a couch that must have supported the weight of countless people anticipating additions to their families. The manufacturer could never have expected his furniture to endure such loading for so long, and the couch displayed its extreme wear despite valiant attempts by the housekeeping staff to keep it looking fresh. Shabby though it was, Arthur and Irma found it symbolically comforting as they wondered what it would be like to have children of their own.

Irma broke their meditative trance after a period that felt longer than it really was. "Did you hear about Ted Karga's murder?"

"Wally alerted me as soon as I arrived at church this morning. We talked about it in the parking lot and then headed for the police station to exchange more information with Bobby, but he had already departed for the hospital."

"You said you wanted to exchange information. What did you have to give him?"

"I theorized that Ted's death was not a coincidence, but rather the result of his killer's having been at our Sunday service. I asked Wally whether that person might have followed Ted when he rushed out of the church. When I prodded Wally to remember everything he saw in the parking lot on Sunday, he remembered someone on a motorcycle leaving at about the same time Ted did."

"Have you talked with Bobby about the crime scene?"

"No, I told you that Bobby left the police station before I arrived."

"Well, I did talk with him while they were preparing the delivery room, and he said that they found tracks of a motorcycle near the car where Ted was murdered. They're looking for a killer on a motorcycle, and it sounds as though Wally saw him on Sunday."

"That's why I left Wally with Al Gomez. I didn't know anything about the crime scene, but I thought the motorcyclist was important, and I wanted Wally to leave a statement with every detail that he remembered. Al is good at conducting interrogations. I'm sure Wally will remember quite a few details about that scene."

"I'm sure he will too, and I think you're right about the killer having been at church with us. Ted's dying so soon after his outburst against God was too much to swallow as a coincidence. Thanks to your thinking I can look at this as a case for us to investigate instead of a bizarre act of God. What do we do now, Arthur?"

"We sit here and wait for the baby to be born. A life is taken, and a short while later a new life comes into the world. There's something special and balanced in that. We'll get going on the investigation and get this guy, but first things first; there will be a new baby to welcome and bless."

"I think we're about to receive some news. A very large figure in surgical scrubs just came through that door, and he looks a lot like Bobby."

As Bobby advanced, they could tell from the size of his smile that things had gone well. They stood as he approached, and received a group hug from him. "Wow! I'm actually a father now. I didn't realize that I would feel so different. It's something special!"

Irma said, "What about Renee, Bobby? Did she come through in good shape?"

"I didn't want to jinx things earlier by talking about my feelings, but I was worried that she'd have extra problems because she's always been thin. Everything went well except for the baby's early delivery. Renee will be fine after some rest and pain pills."

Arthur said, "Excuse our curiosity, Daddy, but are you going to get around to telling us about the baby?"

"One beautiful little girl has joined us. Her name is Thelma Lou Andrews, and she weighs four pounds three ounces. She's small because she's premature, but she's bigger than a lot of preemies. As soon as she adds a little more weight, they'll let us take her home."

Irma gave Bobby a congratulatory kiss. "That's very good news. One thing is starting to bother me though. Why haven't we seen Momma? I can't believe she would stay away from the birth of her first grandchild. Is she here somewhere, or is she sick?"

"The answer to both of those questions is yes. Momma is here in the hospital, but she's here as a patient. She developed a case of bronchitis. They expect the antibiotics they're giving her will make her as good as new, but she won't be able to see Renee or the baby for a while. She'll appreciate a visit from you two, but I have to stay away so that I don't carry any germs back and forth between her and the maternity ward."

"Your pastor will stop in on Momma for a visit and prayers, and after getting sanitized, he'll do the same with you and Renee as soon as the doctors say that she's ready for visitors. Once you resume your professional duties, we can talk about Ted Karga's murder. We're pretty sure that Wally Sanborn saw the killer, and he's been working on a description and other details with Al Gomez at the station."

Bobby's happy daddy smile widened even more.

CHAPTER 12 – PENNY AND JOE GONZALEZ

Pastor Arthur Blake and Irma Custis had worked together to solve several unusual mysteries, combining their logical and technical talents with the police background of Renee Andrews in an investigative venture that Irma had christened ABC Consultants. Arthur usually took the lead in this enterprise, calling upon his background as a NASA engineer before he had entered the ministry, along with the human relations insights gained as a United Methodist pastor. Irma served as the administrator of ABC as well as contributing forensic and medical expertise gained through her earlier training and career as a medical examiner. Renee concentrated on handling the data gathering and analysis aspects of each case, drawing upon skills learned during diligent police work prior to her marrying Bobby, her former boss at the Parkville Police Department.

The main customer for ABC Consultants was a small clandestine federal agency guided by the married team of Penny and Joe Gonzalez. Arthur and Irma had met Penny and Joe during the course of an earlier investigation of Arthur's predecessor as pastor of Parkville UMC, and they had found that they worked well together. Penny and Joe's agency did not appear on any published government organization chart, and it possessed no official name beyond the cover identity shown on its outer office door, *Trading Trends Newsletter*, an actual publication having a very limited distribution. Their agency served the government well because it could tackle a wide variety of assignments without attracting any scrutiny by the press or by others engaging in political witch hunts.

During the course of working on cases together, Arthur had suggested that with all their investigative traveling, Penny and Joe could move from the Washington, DC area to any part of the country they liked and still be efficient at their work. This casual suggestion had developed into Penny's passion, and at the conclusion of a recent case she had convinced Joe that they should move. The surprise in this project had been Penny's decision to live near Arthur and Irma, somewhere in or near Parkville. Joe and Penny did not reveal this plan to their friends, but began house-hunting, via the internet plus a few surreptitious visits to Parkville and other nearby towns. After narrowing their choices to three houses, they had decided to conceal their pending move until the last minute.

The best part of their house-hunting project was that during the course of it, their caseload remained light so that they were able to give this effort their full attention. Each of the top three home candidates would require some renovations, for which they had already developed plans. They needed only to make their final selection.

CHAPTER 13 – BACKGROUND CHECKS

Bobby sat at his laptop computer preparing his standard spreadsheets to chart progress on current cases. He felt that solving the murder of Ted Karga would be relatively straightforward. A witness had seen a motorcyclist following Ted from the church on Sunday. They possessed blood evidence from the car as well as fingerprints taken from the corpses of both Ted and his sister Kristina, who had died from a rabies infection. Kristina's untimely death was due to natural causes, but the scars on her body convinced Bobby to prepare an extra investigation spreadsheet for her as well. The two deaths might be unconnected, but he expected that the results of the fingerprint and DNA checks would reveal a picture of the contributing factors in both cases. Bobby hoped for a simple solution that would let him focus on time at home with Renee and soon with little Thelma Lou after she grew herself out of the hospital.

The sudden appearance of Irma Custis in his doorway interrupted Bobby's musings.

"Hi, Irma, you startled me. I was considering possible scenarios for what led up to the deaths of Kristina and Ted Karga. You're welcome to contribute your views on their deaths, but first I'll let you tell me the purpose of your visit."

"You're smart to include Kristina's death in your investigations. I have a feeling that Ted was murdered because of something in Kristina's history. My medical examiner background also makes me awfully curious about how she contracted rabies. With regard to why I stopped in, I wanted some personal advice from you. Do you have a few minutes to talk?"

"Please sit, and let's chat. I've never been much of an emotions and feelings guy because of the tough neighborhoods where I was raised, but I've been morphing into that kind of person since I became a father. Maybe it's time for me to try talking more about personal things. What are your issues?"

"Arthur and I have been having discussions, almost but not quite arguments, about our differing outlooks on life. I like to be very organized and plan out my days and weeks as much as possible. Arthur says he feels uncomfortable about long term planning. He says he takes each hour and day as it comes, and reacts to each threat or opportunity as seems appropriate to him. He feels that he's emphasizing his faith in God by following whatever path appears before him. I can't do that. Even though I know from experience that I'll have to adjust my expectations based on unforeseen circumstances, I need to have that planning framework to let me think beyond my immediate requirements.

"Am I asking too much of him to want to plan ahead? Is this the kind of difference in outlooks that could or should ruin a relationship? I'm more confused than I've been in a long time, and I need someone to respond to my bewilderment. I don't even know whether I should look at this as a male versus female conflict. Every time I discuss it with Arthur, he either changes the subject or gets a bit hostile."

"From where I sit, I can say that I'm pretty sure this isn't a gender difference. It's far more a matter of background. As a scientist, you want to be methodical and organized. You set up laboratory procedures so that you will always take the same approach under similar circumstances. You mentioned that Arthur relates his enthusiasm for taking each challenge as it comes to his faith in a God who might throw any kind of pitch at him. I think it also relates to his background as a NASA engineer. Those folks like us to think that they calculate and plan every aspect of a space mission so well that nothing can go wrong. Arthur wasn't part of the planning side there. He was the kind of engineer who was charged with reacting instantly to real world situations in which things didn't quite match the theories and calculations. At NASA, he was part of the team that had to overcome unexpected problems in all kinds of missions. As the Boy Scouts say, he had to be prepared for anything. Because of that background he keeps surprising us by coming up with creative insights during an investigation. I can't get inside your head, but I'll bet his creative thinking is something that makes him attractive to you. You have to take him the way he is. If you changed him to think your way, he wouldn't be as special."

"Wow, I guess I came to the right place. Who would have thought that a rough and tough cop would be such a good psychologist? You're right, of course. If I managed to get him to make long term plans all the time, he might lose the spontaneity that gives him his edge over others. If I stopped planning and lived only for the moment, I might lose my clinical effectiveness and objective outlook. We need each other just the way we are, and we're going to have to learn to appreciate our differences rather than reject them. Thanks, Bobby." Irma leaned over and gave him a kiss on his cheek.

Bobby's dark complexion showed a slight blush as Sergeant Al Gomez arrived with a folder full of papers during Irma's kiss. "Al, that was just a thank you gesture between friends, nothing more."

"That's alright, Bobby, I've learned to keep my lips sealed, regardless of the type of kiss it was. Anyway, this folder contains the information on Ted and

Kristina that the lab obtained by tracing their fingerprints."

"Thanks, Al, and it was only a thank you kiss."

As he turned his back and left the room, Al said, "Whatever you say, boss."

Irma laughed at Bobby's discomfort. "Don't worry; I won't try to take you away from Renee. You'll be proving your fidelity to her with midnight feedings and diaper changes.

"On a more serious note, let's look at the background information they got from the corpse fingerprints you sent for analysis."

Bobby opened the file folder and separated the papers it contained into piles for Kristina and Ted. "Let's look at the information for Ted first…His file shows one arrest for being involved in a fight outside a bar in Chicago, but the charge was dismissed because the arresting officer failed to show up on the court date. Ted applied for the Police Academy in Milwaukee three months ago. His application received preliminary approval, but they put him on their active waiting list because they didn't have enough openings. He sounds like a straight-shooter who's suffered a few hard knocks along the way. I don't see anything here about his having been in the military, but I saw an anchor tattoo on his arm that suggests a Navy background. Of course, he could have worked on some kind of freighter or other merchant ship."

"He looked muscular enough to have handled cargo or some other heavy-duty work. Is there anything unusual in Kristina's papers?"

Bobby examined the papers for a minute before saying anything. Then he stood up and scratched his head. "I had a feeling that Kristina's history would be important. She was definitely hiding from someone or something."

"What makes you say that?"

"She attended Parkville UMC for six months or more, but she was actually a Catholic nun."

"She was a nun hiding in a Protestant church? That's pretty smart. Who would think of looking for her there?"

"She had served for several years as a missionary sister in Guatemala. That information plus the scars on her forearms and back say that someone felt threatened by her and wanted her dead. This case is getting a lot more complex."

CHAPTER 14 – CHURCH MEETING

Arthur contacted the District Superintendent, Angela King, to tell her about the misgivings and grumblings of various church members resulting from Ted Karga's church rant and subsequent murder. Angela had a history of conflicts with Blake about his suitability to be pastor of the Parkville church, but his ongoing achievements there plus increased attendance figures had led to a recent undeclared truce between them. When Arthur approached her with the current congregational unhappiness, she grasped the potential for losing members. At the same time she felt flattered that Arthur knew she was the right person to restore stability to a church immobilized by fears and distress.

At Angela's direction, Arthur had scheduled an all-church meeting for this evening, and families were gathering in and around the church following the dinner hour. A few with small children in tow were standing in the lower level parking lot finishing ice cream cones that had been the bribe for entire families to attend.

Everyone drifted into the sanctuary, ushers having been stationed at the doors to collect residual ice cream cone fragments and supply moist handwipes. Arthur stepped up to the pulpit and adjusted the microphone arm.

"Thank you all for coming to our meeting. We are honored to have our District Superintendent, Angela King, joining us. For many of you, this will be your first opportunity to greet her. Accordingly, she has agreed to stay at the conclusion of the meeting to answer any questions you may have on any church-related matter. I arranged for this assembly because I have received some expressions of misgiving from some of you, concerning statements made by Ted Karga, Kristina's brother, during our recent church service and his unfortunate death the next day. I want to assure you that Ted's death was not a mysterious intervention by God. The case is still under investigation by the authorities, but the most likely conclusion is that Ted died at the hand of someone who followed him when he left the church and the parking lot."

Ed Jensen, the Chair of the Church Council, stood up. "Arthur, are you telling us that his killer attended our church service that day?"

"That's probably a correct statement, Ed."

"Then some of us may have talked with him or shaken his hand."

"That's possible, but we don't know that this person was here for the whole service. It may have been someone who slipped in near the end of the service and then followed Ted when he left."

Sue Willoughby stood and waved at Arthur. "Excuse me, Arthur, but we came here because some folks felt that Ted's declared rejection of God was the cause of his subsequent death. Now you're suggesting that a killer may have attended church with us. That scares me more than speculation about God's vengeance. Are we safe here or not?"

"Of course you're safe in our church and in Parkville as a whole. We are not in any way suggesting that we were visited by someone who is out to attack people at random. It is still early in the investigation, but the authorities think that this stranger had pursued Ted for some time. He would not be a danger to anyone else, and we think that he fled the Parkville area based on evidence at the crime scene that I am not permitted to divulge. The police have assured me that Parkville is just as safe now as it was last month or last year. This was not an act of God, but of a man who had a specific target and who is no longer anywhere near here. If we are to act responsibly, we should all go about our routines with the same attitudes that we held prior to Ted's visit. There is no remaining threat."

A man wearing a Chicago White Sox shirt stood up. He had attended one or two past services, but he was unknown to most of those in attendance. "My wife and I have been looking at houses in the area. We want to move away from the crime that surrounds us in Chicago. Can you guarantee that we would be safe here?"

"You would be very welcome here, and safe too, but let me allow Superintendent King to address your concerns. She oversees churches in many villages and towns, not just Parkville."

Arthur walked away from the pulpit, and Angela took his place. "Thank you, Pastor Blake, for inviting me today. As Arthur indicated, I supervise pastors and churches within a large portion of Northern Illinois. I don't think that in our modern society I can guarantee complete safety to anyone, anywhere. However, I can look at the crime and safety statistics of various cities and towns, and I can certify that Parkville is a very safe place to live. Not only are there very few crimes, but also we have an excellent record of resolutions of those few incidents that do occur, in part because of Pastor Blake's close relationships with the Parkville Police Department and other investigative agencies."

This comment drew a smattering of applause from several people in the congregation. It also drew an expression of surprise to Arthur's face. Angela King had never complimented him before.

Angela continued. "I have to empathize with those of you who expressed shock, that Ted Karga, in his frustration over his sister's youthful death, turned his back on God in a very public way. This was an expression of his human frailty and insecurity, and not a reflection on this church in any way. If Ted had not made a sudden emotional exit from the church, Pastor Blake and others would have worked with him to make his grief process more bearable and to assure him that we are loved by God even when human events appear to be conspiring against us."

Arthur began to wonder whether the District Superintendent was feeling well. That was the second compliment she had bestowed upon him. This was the same Angela King who had said he wasn't adequate at his job and had wanted him to become a college chaplain instead of a pastor. He caught a smile aimed at him as she continued. "I know that many of you were alarmed when Ted Karga died so soon after he spoke out against God. All deaths are disturbing, and this one was particularly so, but it was not due to an act of God. I have conferred with the Parkville Police, and I have learned that Ted's death was due to a very aggressive assailant who attacked him while he slept. Pastor Blake has already explained that the evidence suggests the perpetrator followed Ted from this church. I can assure you that if God wanted to end someone's life during sleep, he would not need to use a human attacker as his instrument. This was a criminal act aimed exclusively at Ted, and it should not affect the relationships of the rest of us with our church. In case any of you would like individual counseling or discussion time, I have arranged with Pastor Blake for a private office in which I will be available for the next two hours."

Arthur ended the special meeting by leading the hymn, *This Is a Day of New Beginnings*, and then gave a brief benediction prayer.

After the meeting, Arthur led Superintendent King to the office that she would use for private counseling and then turned to leave and mingle with the congregants. As he moved away, he felt a hand touch his shoulder. He pivoted toward the touch and right into an emotional hug from Angela King.

CHAPTER 15 – SUPPOSITIONS

Irma put her breakfast dishes in the sink and started the coffeepot. Arthur would be over shortly to compare notes for organizing a full-fledged investigation of the deaths of Kristina and Ted Karga. This would be an ABC Consultants project, but Renee Andrews had ruled herself out due to her duties as a new mother. Because they had yet to get Jeremy Hadley involved, Arthur and Irma would initiate this case by themselves.

Irma and Arthur had ruled out living together prior to their wedding. They had based that decision on the complications it would have introduced into Arthur's career as a pastor. Irma had subsequently realized that this agreement benefited her also. She knew too many women who lived with a man and then married him, only to feel cheated because the wedding brought them no transition to a different lifestyle. She had waited a long time for marriage, and she wanted every aspect of it to feel new and special.

Arthur's rhythmic knock announced his arrival; she responded that the door was unlocked. He entered carrying a box from Hadley's Bakery.

"I picked up a few almond crescent Danish pastries from the bakery. They're great, and we can pretend they represent Jeremy being in the meeting if you want."

Irma gave him a long kiss. "I don't want Jeremy to be represented. I want this to be a meeting where the two of us work together alone."

"You're in a good mood this morning."

"Let's say that I consulted my other spiritual advisor and that now my outlook is completely compatible with yours."

"That's worth celebrating over coffee and pastry. Are you going to divulge the identity of this other spiritual advisor?"

"No way, Mister...A girl has to have some secrets. Grab your coffee so that you'll be ready to absorb new information I have for you regarding this case. How did your church meeting go?"

"Everything went pretty well. I think we convinced people that they aren't about to be struck down by God because of what Ted Karga did or said. Your suggestion of the ice cream cones worked well to induce whole families to attend the gathering, but I had to be very careful in choosing my words when I spoke about Ted's death. There were plenty of young children present."

"I'm sure you didn't scare them. Think of all the times you exposed them to worse occurrences from the Old Testament."

"That's actually one of my pet peeves, how people of all ages go into a trance when we read the scriptures and hardly remember any of it."

"Take a gulp of your coffee so that you'll remember what I'm going to tell you. I stopped by the Police Station, and I saw the reports that resulted from the fingerprint analysis for Kristina and Ted."

"I take it from your demeanor that you have some interesting results to share. You're practically panting like a puppy who wants to play."

"I'm not sure I'll go along with that puppy comparison, but I do have information that may change the scope of the case."

"What did you find out about Kristina?"

"Don't do that to me! How do you know the information isn't about Ted?"

"I'm sure you have something about Ted too, but he's pretty transparent. He was a muscular hothead whose temper sometimes got him into trouble. Ted was a good guy all torn up about his sister's death and feeling guilty that he hadn't been able to protect her from her problems. Am I close?"

"Not too bad, but I'll save the details for later. Yes, the more interesting report covered Kristina's background, and I'll bet you won't say you saw this one coming."

"OK, I'll bite. What did they find?"

"Kristina was a Catholic nun, hiding in your United Methodist church from person or persons unknown."

"You're right; I wouldn't have guessed that one, although given that information, I'd have to say that her personality fit with her being a nun. She may have been more aggressive than most nuns, but that could have been because of past skirmishes she had fought."

"You get some secondary points for that observation. She had been a missionary in Guatemala, and encountered some problems down there. She came back to the United States shortly before she appeared in your congregation. I don't know whether she randomly selected a Protestant church hiding place or if she had somehow learned of your investigative prowess and achievements."

"Whatever prowess there is, we share; but I'll grant that I get the church connection aspect of it. If she did have that information, she never used it. Kristina never consulted me on any problems. She participated in church events, but hardly spoke with me at all."

"She may have been sizing you up for confidentiality in future discussions that never materialized because of her death. She also may have been afraid to break her cover and reveal her identity."

"What did you find out about Ted?"

"You were on the money as far as figuring that he had a short temper and got into fights. Bobby found a record for Ted Karga showing that he was arrested once for a fight outside a Chicago bar, but he got out of that without a conviction. It turns out that he was on the waiting list for a job as a cop in Milwaukee."

"That's interesting. When he stormed out of the church he sounded like a cop playing the vigilante who wanted to go after anyone who had given his sister problems."

"That may have been what got him killed, Arthur. If his attacker was one of those who had harmed Kristina, and he heard Ted talking like that in the church, he may have felt threatened."

"That's a definite possibility. There is something else that may be a threat to me. I'd better stay alert."

"What do you mean?"

"I don't want to worry you, but Ted asked anyone who found Kristina's journals or information about their whereabouts to bring the information or journals to me. Those journals may contain information that jeopardizes the bad guys, whoever they are. If so, they might come after me if they think I have the journals or know where they are."

"Let's hope that doesn't happen."

CHAPTER 16 – NEWCOMERS

Arthur left Irma's apartment for the church. When he arrived, he stopped at the office to check with his secretary, Shirley Hadley, for messages and potential emergencies. He found Shirley writing a long memo addressed to him.

"Isn't that the way it always works out, I've finished about three quarters of this message, and in you walk. I won't bother with the rest of it. We have a potential new member who moved into town this week, and she would like Pastor Blake to stop in for a visit. It sounds as though she wants to interview you to see whether you're acceptable."

"We can always use new members. I'll have to make sure my hair is combed and my shoes are polished before I go. Where is she located?"

"She's at 410 South Bemis Avenue, just north of West Colden Street. Her name is Mrs. Washington. I didn't get her first name because she was talking very rapidly, and Bill Martin was hammering on something down the hall. You know he's always making repairs while I'm on the phone."

"That's fine, Shirley; I'll get the rest of the information when I'm over there. Will she be in all day?"

"I did get that much. You can go any time. She had an early appointment scheduled with the telephone company, but they should have finished by now."

"Good enough - I'll head over there right away, before I get involved in something major. Allow a couple of hours for this visit on my schedule; I'll check in with you if I'm back earlier."

51

Arthur took one of the church brochures with the UMC cross and flame logo superimposed on a photograph of the newer section of the Parkville church building. He added a member information form and a copy of the church calendar. Arthur always liked to leave goodies when he made a first contact visit. He would add his business card during the course of the conversation.

Ten minutes later he parked in the driveway of a white stucco house with a black shingled roof and matching black shutters framing the windows. Along the curb a series of short white wooden posts connected by white chains served to keep people from crossing the grass, while also adding a decorative touch to the property. He climbed the three stairs to the porch and rang the bell. In response he heard someone shout, "Just a minute!" from a distant room, probably the kitchen. Arthur visualized a woman resembling Julia Childs wiping flour from her hands onto her apron before running to the front door.

The door opened slowly. "Hello, Arthur, welcome to our cozy domicile." The woman smiled at Arthur's double-take in response to her unexpected appearance.

"Penny Gonzalez, what are you doing here? Are you visiting someone?"

"That's a negative, Arthur. Joe and I took your suggestion seriously, and we decided that living here in a home of our own was a big improvement on our Washington apartment. You once told us that with all of our travel on case investigations, we could live anywhere. We finally agreed, although I had to twist Joe's arm a bit, and we selected a spot where we would know a few of the neighbors. What do you think of the house?"

"I like the color and the tradition in its styling. You're going to feel as though you have roots here...You do know how to pull off a surprise. So Joe and Penny Gonzalez are Mr. and Mrs. Washington. How long have you been planning this move? Anyway, friends or not, you're going to have to endure my church membership recruiting speech."

Penny opened the door wider. "Come on in, Arthur. Joe's in the basement working on something. His favorite part of the move was the opportunity to get into redesigning an old house to match our tastes. You pretty much have to take what you get in an apartment, especially when you're on the road most of the time. We've hit a slow stretch as far as major cases, so we'll be able to spend some time working on the house."

Arthur followed Penny to a brown couch in the front room to the left of the entrance. The walls and ceiling had rough-hewn exposed wooden beam accents. As they stood in front of the couch, he said, "You might want to hold that leisure time thought for a while...Irma, Bobby, and I are working on a case that could lead to your involvement. It's too early to reach any conclusions, but I suspect it will interest you. Speaking of Bobby, he recently became a daddy for the first time. His little girl is still in the hospital, but she's almost big enough to go home."

"How's Renee? Did she come through it without any problems?"

"She's fine, and anxious to take her baby home. The doctors should be doing the final pre-release assessments of the baby's health this week."

Penny walked into the hallway and opened a door beneath the ascending staircase. "Joe, come on upstairs. Arthur's here to recruit us for church, and he's properly surprised by our move."

Joe thumped up the wooden staircase and emerged from the door carrying a rectangular sheet metal assembly with large hooks extending from it on all sides. "Hi, Arthur, welcome to our humble home. I'm having fun learning to design and build things."

"What is that creation?"

"I'm making a structure for hanging pots and pans over the island counter in the kitchen, just like in the restaurant kitchens."

"Joe, you're an excellent investigator, but you're not an engineer. Your design won't support those pots and pans. It's too flimsy. I suggest that you either buy a restaurant quality pot rack, or you let me work with you on a more robust design as a housewarming gift to you."

"I admit that this one is a little marginal for strength. I accept your offer; we'll work on it together."

Penny reappeared carrying a tray with a pitcher of lemonade and glasses. She lowered it down onto the coffee table. "Drink up, you two. Joe, Arthur said they're working on a case that we might want to review."

"Your little local cases always seem to have wider implications, Arthur. That's another reason for our move. You keep us coming here anyway."

Arthur summarized the events that had started with Ted Karga's emotional outburst in his church. He added the medical test results on Kristina plus the fingerprint studies and the background information resulting from them. Then he asked them for their reactions.

Joe said, "You don't have quite enough to justify our involvement, but the nun's work in Guatemala could lead to something significant, and the stealth of Ted's assassin suggests a professional killer who wouldn't be involved if something big wasn't at stake. What do you think, Penny?"

"I'm intrigued by rabies having been the cause of Kristina's death. Did she get infected in Guatemala or after she returned to the Midwest? What's your guess, Arthur?"

"Actually, I'm most concerned about Kristina's missing journals. I see Ted as having been killed to eliminate a possible threat to some kind of organization. I think he was a target of opportunity. The killer was in our church that day because of Kristina's death notice. Kristina was the center of interest. Anyone who knew much about her past activities would be in danger."

Penny exchanged glances with Joe. "You just bought yourself a security detail. Ted put you in danger as soon as he requested that any information about Kristina's journals be sent to you. We're going to have to study her past activities to get some idea about where she may have hidden them and what they might contain."

"Thanks, you two. Irma will appreciate the backup. Speaking of Irma, we'll have to think of a sneaky way to surprise her about your move."

CHAPTER 17 – THELMA LOU

The fledgling parents sat across the Parkville Care Center conference table from several members of the medical staff. Thelma Lou had grown to the magic weight of five pounds, triggering this assessment meeting in preparation for her release. Renee and Booby were both excited by the prospect of taking their baby home, but they suspected that the number of medical personnel at this meeting implied something unusual.

Dr. Marie Pallardi spoke for the staff. "Thelma Lou is a beautiful baby, and we have watched her continue to gain weight until she is now ready to go home. However, due to her premature birth, her central nervous system has not developed well enough for reliable breathing control. We call this condition Apnea of Prematurity or AOP. This is a condition where the baby occasionally stops breathing, and we have to help her restart the process either by massage or by giving her a few breaths of oxygen by squeezing a handheld bag to fill her lungs. At first our nurses had to monitor her very closely, but she is showing signs of improving. We feel that she can go home today, but we will have to supply you with a home apnea monitor and an oxygen pumping device. Following this meeting, the nurses will train you in the use of this equipment."

Bobby said, "Is this a long term condition? Will she have trouble breathing all her life?"

"You don't have to worry about that. This is usually something temporary that should disappear as she continues to mature. We expect that the apnea condition will stop after approximately ten weeks from birth, but it may take a little longer than that. At first you'll probably find yourselves feeling tense and watching the baby constantly, but you'll soon learn to predict the frequency of her episodes. The procedure for helping her restart her breathing after a monitor alert will become routine after a few days."

"Is this something that one person can handle, or do we need to have two trained people available all the time?"

"A single person will be able to handle it without any problem. The important thing to remember is that this is a matter of the natural development of the central nervous system, and the condition will go away by itself as the baby gets a little older. We will give you training before you take her home, and you will be able to train any other responsible adult to handle the procedure if you are not available."

Renee had been nervously scratching her left forearm without realizing it. "Are you sure the apnea will go away, Doctor?"

"It is rarely a permanent condition, and I'm sure that you would rather take care of Thelma Lou at home than to have her in a care facility until the apnea disappears. You won't have any trouble assisting her breathing when she needs it."

Bobby silently said a prayer of thanks. He realized that the problem with his new baby could have been a lot worse. He also knew that he would have to find a way to spend more time at home for a while, even though he had a murder and a strange rabies death on his platter.

CHAPTER 18 – JEREMY HADLEY

Summer vacation had finally arrived at University of Wisconsin, Platteville, and for Jeremy Hadley it meant a new stage in his career development and perhaps some excitement too. His mother had relayed the news that Pastor Blake and Irma Custis had agreed to have him become part of ABC Consultants during summer vacation and for the fall semester under the UW Platteville Co-op Plan. He knew that he would have to agree to have his performance re-evaluated after that period, both as a means of gauging his performance and as a fairness device in case Renee Andrews decided that she wanted to return to work rather than remaining a full-time mother. Whatever happened would be fine with Jeremy, so long as he had his shot at working with Pastor Blake and adding ABC Consultants to his resume for Criminal Justice work.

He had viewed Pastor Blake as a role model since the new minister had arrived at Parkville UMC. At first he had wanted to emulate Arthur's background working for NASA on the space program, but when strange events led to criminal investigations within Parkville and the church community, Jeremy had realized that he was more interested in the way Pastor Blake analyzed problems and discerned the details of crimes, even when others preferred to consider them accidents. Jeremy had pursued his interest in investigative work, first through a part-time job at the Parkville Police Department, and later by applying to UW Platteville's Criminal Justice Department, with the assistance of Pastor Blake and UWP Political Science Professor Edward Middlemiss.

Tomorrow he would have his first meeting with Arthur Blake and Irma Custis as his initiation into the consulting group. He had learned from his mother that once again the congregation had been traumatized by recent events. He would join the team working to explain them.

CHAPTER 19 – IRMA

Maybe Arthur had finally put priority on their relationship and the prospect of their pending marriage. She hoped so. Their courtship had been like going fishing. She'd had some nibbles on the bait and a few good bites, but she had not yet managed to land the big one even though he got closer and closer. Today Arthur had told her he wanted to have her come along on some of his pastoral calls. He had said that it would be good training for becoming a pastor's wife. Perhaps he was learning to plan ahead after all. She had dressed to make a good impression while still keeping her attire simple - a dark green jacket with black slacks and a multicolor blouse, and her sandy hair back in a pony tail. She didn't want to be too dressy for informal small town lifestyles.

Arthur knocked at her apartment door with his familiar rhythm. She silently counted to seven before opening it. "Hi, Arthur, I'm ready for visiting potential members. Is the outfit OK?"

"You look fine as always – elegantly simple."

"How many calls will we be making?"

"If your schedule isn't too tight, I'd like to visit three families, although one won't be a new member call. Ed Jensen, leader of the Church Council may still be bothered about Ted Karga's visit to our church and his subsequent death. We'll stop in on him first. After Ed's we'll make new member stops. Then we'll be free to go out to eat or do anything else you want."

"Sounds good to me; I'll opt for food plus a discussion of how we want to involve Jeremy in ABC Consulting assignments. Renee says that she and Bobby are taking Thelma Lou home from the hospital today. They're asking that friends hold off on visiting them for a couple of days. She says that they have to take some special precautions with the baby, and they want to work out their routines before dealing with company."

"That sounds like a good approach. Let's start our odyssey."

Arthur had a distant stare as he drove, and Irma understood that he was working through some thoughts, probably concerning the new case. She gave him a few minutes to navigate his puzzle, and then she intruded on his thinking. "Which aspect of recent events are you analyzing? I can tell that something is bothering you."

"I've been trying to look at things from Kristina's point of view. She had to have known for a long time that she was in serious danger, and yet she managed to attend our church for months, appearing calm and carefree. It may have been due to her faith and her training as a nun. Whatever the basis for her demeanor, I gain more respect for her as I learn more about her."

"Those wounds on her body weren't trivial. She had been whipped on her back and attacked with a knife. My guess is that the whipping was a warning at some point and that she suffered the defensive knife wounds later when her enemies decided to finish her off."

"I agree with you up to that point. She was a fairly slight individual. I wonder whether she fought off her knife-wielding attackers by herself or whether someone came to her aid."

"Good thinking, Arthur; she may have had an ally who would know what happened to her. Of course, that person might be in Guatemala rather than anywhere near here. Still, that's a good starting point for examining her history."

"Speaking of starting points, Ed Jensen lives in that brown split-level house on the right. We've arrived at our first stop."

They parked in the driveway next to Ed's boat trailer. Ed loved fishing, and he kept his aluminum skiff with its outboard motor ready for use on short notice. Arthur patted the boat as he walked by it, remembering the many fishing outings he had taken with his father and his 'Uncle' Albert. He wondered if Irma liked fishing. There were still so many things that he and Irma didn't know about each other. He climbed the two steps to the low porch and rang the bell.

Ed Jensen opened the door promptly and held a finger to his lips to ask for quiet. "Hi, Arthur; hi, Irma; let's talk out here on the porch. Martha hasn't been feeling well this week, and she's sleeping." He set up two folding chairs across from the cushioned glider seat.

Arthur said, "We won't keep you away from Martha for long, Ed. We're calling on a few folks, and I just wanted to be sure that you're not still troubled by recent events involving the church."

"No, Arthur, you've handled everything well. It's just been a little difficult for some of us to face the fact that we were in church with a murderer that day when Ted Karga spoke about his sister. Many of us thought that we could get all the way through life without having to get that close to evil and crime, but I guess we didn't quite make it. Nothing we can do about it now."

Irma thought back to the time when the Parkville UMC congregation had worshipped for months without knowing they had a decaying body in the church attic; but she said nothing, given Ed's frame of mind. He was more concerned about a live murderer passing through their church than he would be about a corpse in their attic. The fact that the attic problem had occurred three years earlier probably helped to distance it from his mind.

She leaned forward and rested her hand on his arm. "I hope Martha feels well soon. Would it be all right if a few of us sent over prepared meals for you so that she won't have to worry about planning menus and cooking?"

"That would be great, Irma. I've been handling the food this week, but I'm sure she'd enjoy a little deviation from hamburgers and salad every evening. You two have refreshed my day with your visit. Don't worry, Arthur; we're all getting back to normal. I don't know whether most folks treated those events as threats or excitement, but they sure shook us out of our boredom...Excuse my choice of words, Arthur, I didn't mean to imply that your sermons are boring."

"No offense taken, Ed, real events always have more impact than sermons. We've enjoyed this visit, but we should be moving on to our next stop. Give our best wishes to Martha."

As they drove away, Irma sat contentedly. "You handled that well. I'm seeing aspects of your ministry that are new to me. As Paul said in the Bible, you have to be all things to all men, and women too."

"It's not difficult. You have to have a feeling for people's attitudes and situations and then adopt their points of view when you talk with them. To show you how easy it is, I'll let you take the lead at our next stop. We're touching base with Mrs. Washington who may join our church but wants to know a little more about it first."

The parked in the driveway of a white stucco house with black shutters and walked up to the door. Irma wanted to show Arthur she could handle a visit to a potential new member. She rehearsed her opening line in her head and rang the bell. A man answered the door.

"Good morning, we're from Parkville United...Joe Gonzalez, is that you? What are you doing here? Is this some kind of undercover sting?"

She heard a laugh behind her and turned to see that Arthur was enjoying her flustered reaction.

Joe said, "Come on in, you two. Irma, we couldn't resist surprising you a bit. Believe it or not, this is our new home. Penny's being domestic in the kitchen, but she'll be out in a minute."

Irma punched Arthur in his right shoulder.

"Ouch! That's my pitching arm, and that's not the first time you've punched me. If you want to get a husband, you're supposed to show your love, not your boxing ability."

"You set me up for this. You made me think that I was getting training for being the Pastor's wife, when it was all aimed at surprising me at the Gonzalez house."

Penny entered the room with a platter of cookies. "What's all this commotion? Irma, don't blow our cover; it's Mr. and Mrs. Washington."

Irma looked shocked. "Do you mean that you're on a case, and I've stuck my foot in my mouth again?"

That got everyone laughing, and Irma realized she'd been fooled again. This time she punched Arthur's left shoulder.

"Hey, why hit me? Penny fed you that straight line."

"Well, I'm certainly not going to hit her! Welcome, Penny; welcome Joe. This will make it even more convenient for us to work together; but hopefully, we'll be able to have some fun too. It looks like a unique and special house. Penny, please give me a tour to get me away from these guys. They keep picking on me."

The women left, and Joe removed a sheet of paper from his pocket. "After your last visit, I did some checking on a nun named Kristina Karga working as a missionary in Guatemala. My sources tell me that she was a Maryknoll Sister working in a Catholic orphanage, a *hogar*, in Jacaltenango in northwest Guatemala, not far from the border with Mexico's Chiapas state. The Maryknoll Sisters also run the Jacaltenango Hospital and have other ministries there. Kristina was there for about four years before she suddenly left and appeared in your congregation."

"That must have been right after someone cut up her arms and her leg, trying to kill her."

"That's quite likely, Arthur, but she would have needed help to make her escape. Somebody was on her side. She wouldn't have been able to fight off determined attackers by herself."

"Irma and I also speculated that she had an ally. However she got away, she arranged to leave Guatemala shortly afterward. I'll bet she stopped communicating with the Maryknoll Sisters organization as soon as she returned to the United States. If she had stayed in touch with them, she would have been trackable by her enemies. She had to fade away."

"I think you're right, Arthur, and that tells me that she took the threats to her life very seriously. To be sure, though, I'll check with Maryknoll."

"Check very discretely. We don't want to let the bad guys know what we're doing or that a federal agency is involved."

"Roger that...Do you have any ideas about where we should look for Kristina's missing journals?"

"Not yet, but something's bothering me about those books that I can't quite pin down. I'll keep working on it."

Penny and Irma returned from their tour to find the men in the kitchen. Arthur was stretched out under the sink, looking at the pipes.

Penny said, "What's the matter, do we have a leak?"

"No, we're figuring out what it would take to install a garbage disposal in this old house."

Penny put her arm around Joe's shoulders. "See, Irma, I told you he was warming up to being a do-it-yourselfer, and he's a good manager too. He already has Arthur helping him to rehab the kitchen."

Arthur crawled out from under the sink. "And Joe's already helping us with our latest case."

CHAPTER 20 – INTERN TRAINING

Promptly at 9:00 AM the following morning, Arthur convened a gathering of the revised ABC Consultants team in his office. Jeremy looked excited and anxious to show that he could make a significant contribution. Irma looked amused. Arthur poured his coffee and sat down at the table. He stood back up again. "I'm sorry, Jeremy, I forgot to ask whether you would like some coffee or if I can get you anything else."

"Coffee would be fine, Pastor; I take it black, no sugar."

"It's Arthur during ABC and informal meetings. As I recall, you wanted to join NASA at one time, so here's coffee in a NASA mug. Irma, you look as though someone just told you a joke. Would you like to share it with us?"

"I might as well. Maybe I'm giddy this early in the morning, but I started to think that we've lost the *A* out of our ABC name with Renee Andrews on the sidelines. Then I decided that it still works out if we pronounce Jeremy's name with a Cockney accent: It's 'adley, Blake and Custis. The *H* at the beginning of his name disappears."

"Very good, but I hadn't realized that the ABC was so important to you. That would suggest that we shouldn't get married after all, because we'd lose the *C*."

"You won't get off that easily. I'll hire one of Bob Caspar's kids, Michelle or Kevin. They go to UW Platteville with Jeremy anyway."

"Before we worry about the youth movement taking over, let's introduce Jeremy to our new case."

Jeremy said, "Arthur, if we're talking about the deaths of Kristina Karga and her brother Ted, I've had most of the story from my mother. Why don't you continue, assuming I know all the details? I'll ask questions if you say something that doesn't jibe with my current information."

"Fair enough; welcome to our little group. We may not pursue a case following the procedures they teach you at school, but so far we've been effective.

"We've found that Kristina Karga, who worshipped with us for a number of months before she died, was actually a Catholic nun, and she was hiding in our United Methodist church from people who had tried to kill her. Apparently, the attempt on her life was made in Guatemala, where she had been working as a Maryknoll Sister in an orphanage in the town of Jacaltenango, near the border with Chiapas, Mexico."

Jeremy looked disappointed. "I guess I didn't know everything. I had heard that she died from a rabies infection. I assumed she had died from natural causes."

Irma said, "You're right, Jeremy, but we think the infection came from a rabid bat or other animal infecting an open wound in her leg. That wound would have resulted from the attack on her. Since she returned to the United States immediately after the attempt on her life, she could have received the rabid bite either in Guatemala or back here. What do you think, Arthur?"

"My guess is that after the attack she collapsed in some rural area nearby. Perhaps she spent the night there while she tried to regain her strength. That would be the most likely location for an animal or bat to bite her."

Irma said, "I'll go along with the likely site idea, but she would have had to get some treatment for her wounds first. Otherwise, she might have died from loss of blood."

Jeremy had been running his finger around the lip of his NASA coffee mug. He stopped and raised his hand to get attention. "From what I'm hearing, she must have had someone on her side to give her first aid, but that person didn't stick around afterward."

Arthur said, "Very good thinking, Jeremy, but you don't have to raise your hand. I discussed Kristina's attack with Joe Gonzalez, whom you met a while ago, and we agreed that she must have escaped death because somebody came to her aid. Finding that person might be essential to learning the whole story of Kristina and Ted."

Irma said, "I'll summarize our assumed profile of Ted and his outlook. He would have been very close to his sister when they were younger, but probably had been out of contact for several years prior to her death. That would be one of the reasons he was so upset; he felt guilty for having gone his own way without keeping in touch with her. Ted was athletic and probably a weightlifter. We do know that he had applied for a position with the Police Department in Milwaukee, and he was on the waiting list for a position at their Academy. Ted expected trouble, because when he went to sleep in his car he had a loaded handgun within easy reach. We don't know whether he too was running away from something, or if he was planning to track his sister's enemies, looking for vengeance. What else, Arthur?"

"Ted apparently had a temper problem. He had been in at least one bar fight but had not been convicted of anything. Based on his outburst at church, I would guess that he was looking for vengeance for his sister's death. If he was looking for revenge, where was he heading? He started out in a vaguely northwest direction, but he didn't get far enough away from here for me to extrapolate his destination."

Jeremy said, "He may have stayed nearby in order to cool his emotions before starting out on his quest."

Irma said, "That makes sense. Even Ted would not have gone after his sister's enemies without a plan and his wits in peak shape. I also think he would have wanted more information before committing himself to battle. What's your view, Arthur?"

"I agree with everything you've said. I'll add that since he wasn't headed for the airport to fly to Guatemala, he must have thought he had one or more targets for revenge in this country, and probably within easy driving distance."

CHAPTER 21 – PARENTHOOD

Renee, Bobby, and Momma had barely survived the ordeal of the last few days. Thelma Lou's home apnea monitor had been going off at random times during both the day and the night, causing all of the adults to be both sleep-deprived and very anxious about the baby's condition. The only good news was that the baby had responded well to simple massage as a means of restarting her breathing, so that they had rarely had to use the oxygen pumping device. They had all worked in shifts to keep one assigned person on call for assisting her at any given time. Renee and Bobby were thankful that Momma took a shift so that they had more time for sleeping than if only the two of them cared for Thelma Lou. After four hours of sleep, they sat at the kitchen table while Momma fed the baby.

"Renee, we've been doing this for four days now. Aren't we getting to the time when this preemie apnea is supposed to end?"

"Sorry, Bobby, all they could give us was statistical estimates. There's no way to predict how long it will last for a particular child."

"Didn't they say that it would end naturally and soon?"

"I think there was a *probably* in their statement. It's the one step at a time thing we're going through. She'll stop having the problem when she stops having the problem. In the meantime we have to be patient and do what we can to stay healthy and strong."

"I'm going to have to go back to work sometime, at least on a part time basis."

"I know that. Momma and I have already discussed it. Tomorrow you can plan on working

71

during the morning. We've arranged our shift schedule to cover that. If we manage well, you can add an hour each day. We'll be sure to let you know if we need you at home. Momma and I expect that we'll continue to get better at handling our little girl's needs, and hopefully her continued lung and nerve development will gradually make things easier. You go do what you have to do."

"I want to be here with you, and I'll feel guilty if I don't carry my share of the load, but I have a murder investigation to pursue, and people will get unhappy if they don't see the Chief on the job."

"You go to work. We'll get some assistance from Irma if necessary. Which is better help, a cop or a doctor?"

"The father is better, but I'm thankful for additional help. It's time to let our friends see our beautiful bundle of joy anyway. We're not just parents; we're proud parents, and it's time to show her to the world, or at least to those who will submit to thorough disinfection before they meet her."

CHAPTER 22 – VISITORS

On his first morning back at work, Bobby Andrews stopped in to see Arthur at the church, where they discussed what they had learned so far about Ted and Kristina. Arthur also informed Bobby that Joe and Penny Gonzalez had moved to Parkville.

After about an hour of relaxed conversation at the church, Bobby received a message from Sergeant Al Gomez that he was needed at headquarters. A reporter had arrived to inquire about the status of the investigation of Ted's murder, and Al had responded that he was not authorized to talk with the media. Bobby promised Arthur he would return after he finished with the interview. After he dispatched the reporter, he would also send an email request to the Milwaukee Police Department for a copy of Ted's Police Academy application file.

Irma had gone to the Andrews home to see the baby and assist with her monitoring, so Arthur would be uninterrupted at the church, especially since Shirley was downstairs on the lower level with Bill Martin, setting up modifications to the classrooms for additional work stations.

Arthur used his solitary time to do a computer search on the organization and missionary work of the Maryknoll Sisters. Then he researched the frequency of human deaths from rabies in the Midwest. The results of the latter search convinced him that Kristina must have been infected in Guatemala. Government health agencies had recorded only two previous Midwest deaths from rabies within the last ten years.

He heard a knock and looked up to find two men standing in his doorway. One was short and swarthy with shoulder length black hair, and the other was tall and thin with blond hair. Both wore hooded sweatshirts with blue jeans; the taller man's hoodie was black and the shorter man's was dark green. Arthur stood up from his desk chair to greet them.

"Good morning, can I help you?"

The taller one said, "Are you Pastor Blake?"

"Yes, I am. Do you need the services of a minister?"

"We're here about the journals of Kristina Karga."

"Do you know where they are? Her brother wanted to locate them."

"That's the wrong question, Pastor. We've been told you have them, and we need them in connection with a legal matter."

"I'm afraid you've been misinformed. I would like to locate them, but I have no idea where they are." Arthur did not like the aggressive looks of these two.

"You're lying, Pastor, and that's not a good thing to do." The taller man made a move toward Arthur around one end of the desk. Arthur backed off toward the other end, but saw the shorter man edging toward him.

"Those journals must be pretty important to you, but I assure you that I don't have them and have never seen them." They had him penned in, and he knew he would have trouble defeating both of them in a fight. Arthur depressed Shirley's intercom button so that their words would be heard in the office, even though he didn't think Shirley was there.

The shorter man said, "Let's see if we can improve your memory about the journals." He grabbed Arthur's left arm and twisted it while pushing Arthur's torso onto the desktop. His strength was that of a much larger man. Arthur's forehead hit the computer monitor, and he felt blood begin to ooze downward toward his nose. The taller man held Arthur's right arm tightly as they hoisted him to his feet.

Arthur grunted and said, "Whatever you do, I can't give you information I don't have. Who are you guys anyway?"

The tall one said, "Just call us bad news." He punched Arthur in the stomach twice.

Before he could land a third punch, someone taller and stronger pulled him backward by his shoulders. Then the tall visitor felt his right arm twisted behind his back while a strong left forearm pressed against his throat.

Recovering from the body blows, Arthur straightened up slowly. "Jeremy, you're a welcome sight. Thanks for the assistance." He turned his attention to the shorter man. "Now Mr. Tough Guy, let's see how well you do when it's one-on-one." Arthur aimed a fist at the swarthy man's face and connected with his cheek. He felt the cracking of a bone. He stepped back ready to swing again, but Arthur knew that the shorter man was stronger than he was, and he would only be able to control the fight for a short time.

Jeremy said, "I called Bobby. He's on the way."

"Correction - he has arrived!" Bobby's massive frame came through the doorway, and he grabbed the shorter man's arm halfway through its trajectory toward Arthur's chin. Bobby landed a punch of his own into the man's midsection, collapsing him onto the floor. "Are you all right, Arthur?"

"I'll live, thanks to both of you. That was a great cavalry charge. How did you manage it?"

Jeremy said, "I was sitting in Mom's office waiting for her to return when you pushed the intercom button so that I could hear everything. I called Bobby for backup and headed right over."

Bobby added, "I was getting ready to come back as planned anyway, so I added a little rush to my trip." He activated his radio and called for a car to pick up his two prisoners plus paramedics to treat Arthur and the shorter assailant.

Arthur said, "I'm OK; I don't need any treatment, Bobby."

"That's your adrenalin talking, Pastor. Your forehead is a mess, and your hand may have a fracture. Sit down and relax; rest your right hand on the desk until they arrive...Do you think one of these guys killed Ted?"

"I doubt it. They're strong-arm types. Ted's killer was stealthy and athletic."

CHAPTER 23 – REACTIONS

"You really benefited from the added security I provided." Joe Gonzalez shook his head as he sat on the parsonage couch looking at Arthur across the dining room table. The top of Arthur's head was wrapped in gauze bandages adorned with a bloody splotch looking like an emblem on his forehead. His right hand resided in a cast.

"You couldn't have provided constant security anyway. I lucked out, with Jeremy and Bobby responding to my call for help."

Irma walked in from the kitchen carrying a camera. She took three pictures of her patient from different angles. "I'll want to have evidence of your heroism for the future."

Arthur said, "I hope you realize that I'll tell everyone that you did this to me."

"That's what you get for dating a strong girl like me...Seriously, I'm grateful that you had the presence of mind to push that intercom button."

"I didn't think it would do much good at the time, but it was the only defense I had. Shirley was downstairs with Bill, and I didn't even know that Jeremy was in the building."

"Score one for my suggesting that we add a big, strong, young guy to our ABC team."

"Are you calling me old and weak?"

Penny Gonzalez came into the room from the kitchen carrying a tray full of appetizers. "Now, children, let's not bicker. Arthur, you did very well against overwhelming odds. However it happened, the cavalry arrived on the scene just in time, and I bet we'll learn a lot from your two assailants."

Joe shook his head. "I don't know about that, Penny. They're probably pretty low on the food chain of a big organization. Still, they may know more than they think they know. We'll have to analyze their statements and backgrounds very carefully. We don't have too many cases where the crooks come to us."

Irma said, "Don't look now, Arthur, but Joe and Penny just said they're getting involved in our case."

Arthur stood up and took an appetizer from the tray with his left hand. "So, you've conferred and decided that our case is not just a local matter. Where do you see the interstate implications and that big organization you mentioned?"

Joe nodded to Penny and she spoke. "Your two strong-arm characters are Marco Antonio Fernandez, illegally in this country from Guatemala and Gustav Savage from Chicago. Savage is the taller one of the two. Both have been arrested multiple times for assault and attempted murder. Fernandez was deported once, and he came right back within three months, thanks to his connections in the Zeta Mexican drug cartel. The Zetas and another cartel called Sinaloa have extended their operations into Guatemala due to the Mexican government starting to crack down on cartel violence."

Joe continued. "The Mexican government has been very pragmatic about their pressure on the drug lords. Its forces are aiming at the reduction of violence rather than the diminishing of drug traffic. They figure that if they don't put down violence, they'll lose their tourist trade and capital investment from abroad. The government has left it to U.S. agencies to try to reduce the drug traffic."

Arthur sat down again but had trouble finding a comfortable rest position for the cast on his hand. Irma patted him on his left shoulder. She asked, "How does the tall guy, Gus Savage, fit into this?"

Penny said, "We're not sure yet; he's either tied to a smaller illegal network within Guatemala, or he's just local muscle. We'll fill you in on those details as we learn more."

Arthur looked as though he had either found a good rest position, or he was concentrating too much to care about comfort. "OK, we've found evidence that Kristina served as a nun in Guatemala. We also know that the two toughs who came looking for her journals have ties to international crime organizations. What could she have had in her journals that would make such operations worried?"

Joe said, "That's the key question, and it's the reason for our being interested in your case."

CHAPTER 24 – OUTLOOKS

Momma was on call for monitoring the baby's needs and apnea episodes, so Renee and Bobby finally had time to take over the living room for a discussion of their new roles as parents.

Bobby put his arm around Renee as they sat on the couch. "Are you upset because Thelma Lou has this problem?"

"I'm certainly not happy about it, but I can cope."

"What if it turns out to be something she'll always have to handle? We're already past the average time for it to disappear."

"What are you getting at, Bobby?"

"I'm thinking about this case we're investigating, about how Ted Karga couldn't accept the death of his sister, so that he screamed out against God. If Thelma Lou's health remains fragile, how will you react?"

"Hey, husband, don't you for one minute think it would rattle me. I've lived in places where people had a lot worse things to worry about than that. We'll take things one step at a time, and we'll build a loving family. You have to have faith that we'll all thrive together. God provides, and if anything isn't perfect, we'll supply whatever else is needed. Agreed?"

"Absolutely, and I'm sure that between us we'll have the necessary resources, no matter what happens, but I wanted to hear it from your lips. I do have confidence in you, but I sometimes want to be sure that I'm not just projecting my feelings on you and saying they're yours."

"Usually mine are similar to yours. We've been a lot more compatible in our attitudes than I had any right to expect. I have to admit that I thought you'd be dominant and want me and Momma to follow your macho way all the time, but you've been one cuddly Teddy Bear to us."

"I'm a lot cuddlier to you than to Momma, but don't make this conversation public. I don't want my image spoiled. Police Chiefs are supposed to be rough and tough."

"I heard you were plenty rough and tough with those thugs in Arthur's office."

"They deserved it. My friend was about to be pummeled, and I couldn't allow that. Jeremy's alert came just in time for us to save Arthur from a bad beating. Those guys were pros."

"Have you learned anything from them?"

"Nothing yet from the interrogations, but their attack told us that Kristina's journals are very important. We'll have to locate them soon."

CHAPTER 25 – LEFT-HANDED THINKING

"Irma, would you please bring me some lemonade in a left-handed cup?"

While Arthur nursed his fight injuries, he had temporarily moved into Irma's apartment. He sat in a reclining chair, feeling weary due to prolonged inactivity, while she finished baking a batch of oatmeal cookies in the kitchen. He heard the clink and clunk of dishware and cabinet doors.

Irma entered carrying a cup and smiling. "OK, Mr. Smart Guy, enjoy your left-handed cup of lemonade. You must be bored stiff to start playing games like that."

Arthur stared at the cup. "Touché, I admit I was being goofy; but you actually had a left-handed mustache cup? Is it a residual from a former boyfriend?"

"Nope, it's my treasured remembrance of my left-handed mustached father. One year I spent a whole day shopping for it for his birthday. That was back before you could search and order online. He really appreciated my effort in finding it, and he used it for the rest of his life."

"That does make this special. I'll do my best to take care of it, if you'll let me use it until the cast is off my right hand."

"Why not use a regular cup turned around? They are reversable you know."

"Sure, but now that I've heard your story, I'd like to feel closer to your dad. Maybe I'll even grow a mustache."

"That's pleasantly sentimental of you, Arthur, but just use the cup. I don't think I'd like a mustache on you. What else can I get you?"

"How about giving me an opinion? I've been sitting here thinking about Ted Karga's death, and I wondered why they decided they had to get rid of him?"

"I'd guess that they saw him as a threat. The killer saw this big guy at church, ranting about his sister's death and looking as though he was out to avenge her when he ran out of the church."

"That's plausible, but I have to wonder why they wouldn't try to question him about the journals and his relationship to Kristina before they killed him."

"What if the murderer acted on instinct without consulting his bosses?"

"I could see that happening. Would he have been criticized or punished for it later?"

Irma walked to the front window and back while she thought about the crime organization's reaction to Ted's killing. Then she turned to Arthur and said, "I'd guess that they felt they had missed an opportunity to get more information. They tried to offset that mistake by having their strong-arm men visit you. The thugs' first job would have been to get the journals from you if you had them."

"And what would their second job have been?

"It would have been to kidnap you and take you back for questioning."

"That's my conclusion too. It appears that my rescue by Jeremy and Bobby did more than save me from a worse beating."

CHAPTER 26 – HOME PROJECTS

Penny walked in from their combination den and office to find Joe twisting the stair railing spindles. "What are you up to, Joe?"

"I'm seeing which spindles are loose and which are tight. I'll sneak a little glue into the sockets of the loose ones. That will keep everything solid, at least for a while. I have to tackle short projects first, because this case of Arthur's is going to steal a lot of my home project time. What news are you bringing?"

"Steve DuBois emailed from our office that the Maryknoll Sisters had been worried about Kristina and her health throughout the period when she was hiding. They had no idea where she was, but they knew enough about her problems in Guatemala that they tried to find her through the Catholic Church grapevine rather than alerting the police and possibly making her situation more perilous."

"Did Steve find out why she was in danger?

"He spoke with a Sister Rosemary Dawes. Sister Kristina told her that she had tried to help more children than her Catholic orphanage could house and assist. In the process of placing additional children in private orphanages, she became the victim of an illegal adoption gang."

Joe set aside his tools. He sat on the stairs listening intently. "In other words, they sold the children. What did she do after she realized what kind of places these were?"

"She couldn't ignore the missing children, so she acted like an undercover detective in order to document how the illegal adoptions worked."

"So that's what's in those missing journals. She may have recorded all the details of the operations, and that's why they were looking for her."

"That's also why they want to get rid of anyone who has seen the journals or might have access to them."

"We're going to have to do more to protect Arthur and his church people. It's bad enough that he was beaten, but they may think the journals are hidden in the church and invade the place."

"That's not a pretty picture. I doubt that it would come to that, Joe, but we have to treat it as a possibility. If a gang invaded a church like that, the public would demand an intensive search for the culprits, and savvy politicians would lead the charge."

"Anyway, we're starting to get a feeling for the contents of the missing journals. She may have even more explosive material in them. They've killed her brother, and the attack on Arthur suggests they're ready to kill again if necessary to get those notebooks. Steve is going to get back to me shortly, after he checks another interesting statement by the Maryknoll contact. It must be something intriguing, because he was very secretive about it."

CHAPTER 27 – MILWAUKEE

Sergeant Al Gomez walked into Bobby's office and interrupted Bobby's telephone conversation with Thelma Lou's doctor. "Chief, please come see me as soon as you're through with that call. We have a development."

Bobby knew that it had to be important. The signal was that Al had been formal and had called him Chief. He kept his voice calm as he completed the discussion with the so-called specialist. The doctor had demonstrated his lack of expertise by calling to tell him that they couldn't understand why Thelma Lou's Apnea of Prematurity had not yet disappeared, even though her lungs must have fully matured. Bobby made an appointment to bring the baby in for further tests and terminated the conversation. He rose and walked to Al's desk.

"What is it, Al?"

"We received Ted Karga's application file from the Milwaukee Police Academy, and per your instructions I shared a copy of it with Joe Gonzalez since his agency is getting involved."

"So?"

"Joe emailed back that his agency had been in touch with Maryknoll Sisters, the Catholic order that Kristina had served as a nun."

"I repeat: So?"

"So – the Maryknoll Sisters told them that according to their records, Sister Kristina Karga was an only child. She did not have a brother."

"But Ted indicated that Kristina was his sister on his Police Academy application?"

"Yes he did."

"He either lied, or the records at Maryknoll are incorrect."

"Are you a betting man? Odds are that he lied."

CHAPTER 28 – CHURCH PRECAUTIONS

Bill Martin, the Chair of the Trustees Committee, had joined Shirley Hadley, the church Secretary in cleaning up Arthur's office and repairing a side table that had collapsed during the fight with the two assailants. Shirley had also installed a new coffee maker to replace the one that had broken when it fell from the damaged table. They gave the room a final inspection, and turned to leave just as Arthur and Jeremy arrived.

Arthur looked approvingly into his workspace, thanked Shirley and Bill, and silently prayed for a return to normalcy as he entered the office and poured his coffee.

Jeremy remained with the others. "Mom, if you don't mind, I'll hang around the church for a while. It's superstition on my part, but my happening to be in your office when Arthur called for help by hitting the intercom button saved the day once. I'll feel better if I don't leave him completely alone right away."

Bill said, "Go right ahead if it makes you feel better, Jeremy. I'll come back in an hour or so and do some hanging around myself. We don't have to say anything to the pastor, but there's no need to leave him alone right away."

Shirley laughed. "We're all thinking along the same track. I was going to be sure that I didn't leave for home before he did today. We're all feeling a little jittery because of the invasion by those thugs, but it should pass in a day or two. I did take the precaution of pressing that famous intercom button, so we can go back to my office and share some pastry from Hadley's Bakery while still being prepared for another invasion." They all headed for the church office and left Arthur to his thoughts and paperwork.

Arthur hadn't heard the conversation in the hallway. He focused on his coffee after discovering that the new coffee maker produced significantly tastier brews than its predecessor. Leaning back in his chair, he savored his favorite beverage and concentrated on the new information he had received from Joe Gonzalez. *If Ted had not been Kristina's brother, where did he fit into the picture? He had definitely reacted to Kristina's death with raw emotions. His rejection and defiance of God had sounded genuine, and his murder belied any affiliation with the group that had sent strong-arm men to the church. Are there two groups anxious to get those journals? Alternately, Ted's killing could have been a personal matter rather than part of the search for those notebooks. There were too many possibilities and too few facts to use in sorting them.*

Arthur had lost track of time. His coffee mug was empty, and he didn't know how long he had been meditating on different aspects of Ted and his true identity. A loud knock on the doorpost and a familiar voice brought him back to the present.

"Are you all right, Arthur? I was in the area, and I thought I had better stop in to check." District Superintendent Angela King sounded genuinely concerned for his health as she lowered herself into his guest chair.

"Oh, hello, Angela, welcome to the scene of the crime. They've done a good job of restoring my office after the battle. Thank you for your concern."

"It's more than concern, Arthur. In the past I've been pretty hard on you, and I feel a little guilty about that. You've done a good job for Parkville UMC and managed to fit in some significant civic accomplishments too, sometimes suffering bodily harm during the process. I've come to apologize for some of my past comments and to declare that I have no more qualms about your qualifications and outlook."

In the church office, Shirley, Bill, and Jeremy listened intently to the conversation coming from the intercom. Irma looked in through the open door, and they waved her to an empty chair while munching pastry and continuing to listen.

Arthur said, "Why thank you, Angela, I appreciate your candor and your revised rating for my work here. As a token of friendship, will you join me in a cup of coffee? I have a new coffee maker, and it does a good job."

Shirley smiled in reaction to the overheard endorsement of her latest purchase.

Angela rose and approached the table. She poured coffee into the smallest mug three quarters full. "I'll take a little creamer in mine, but no sugar." She stirred the creamer into the liquid and sat back down. "I'd like to extend an offer of friendship to you too, Arthur. Please allow me to perform the ceremony when you and Irma get married."

In the church office, Irma's face bore a questioning expression. She leaned forward to listen intently as the others studied her reaction.

Arthur said, "That's a very kind offer, Angela; I'd like to discuss it with Irma if you don't mind."

"Why does it need discussion? Do you have reservations about my marrying you?"

"There's no problem. It's just that I haven't received a complete rundown of information on Irma's relatives, and I thought she had said something about there being a minister in the family. If so, I thought I should let her decide whether she wanted that relative to perform the ritual."

In the office, Irma stood up and walked out. Soon, the others heard a knock on Arthur's doorpost through the intercom.

"Hi, Arthur, I hope I'm not interrupting anything, but when you're done I'd like to talk with you about scheduling a visit to see the Andrews baby."

"Welcome, Irma; I think you know Angela King, our District Superintendent."

"Yes, of course I do, but mostly from a distance. We haven't had the opportunity to chat before. Hello, Angela."

"Hello to you, Irma. Arthur and I have been talking over coffee, and I told him that I'd feel honored to perform the ceremony at your wedding. Would that be acceptable to you?"

It was very quiet in the church office as three people concentrated on the intercom speaker.

"What a nice offer, Angela; are you sure you could work us into your busy schedule?"

"In the interest of better relationships, I'll modify my schedule to accommodate it. When is the big date?"

Arthur said, "We haven't actually set it yet." His look at Irma begged for help.

Irma said, "No, we haven't selected the exact date, but it will be in about three months."

Angela made a note on Arthur's telephone message pad and tore off the sheet. She stood and tucked it into a pocket of her purse. That's fine, Irma, I'll blank out several possible weekends around that time. You just let me know as soon as you finalize things." She shook Irma's hand, gave Arthur a brief hug, and left.

Arthur looked at Irma for about ten seconds before he said, "Will I have to wear a tuxedo?"

"You can wear anything you want, so long as you show up on time and give affirmative answers to the ceremonial questions."

CHAPTER 29 – INFANTS AND CHILDREN

"Hello, you two, welcome to nursery central." Renee accepted Irma's package decorated with ornate wrapping paper and three pink bows. Then she ushered Arthur and Irma into the living room. They stood for a moment, appreciating the sight of the massively muscular police chief cradling and bottle-feeding his tiny daughter.

Arthur said, "This scene is truly special, Bobby. I've had the feeling that you've wanted to display your soft side for a long time. You two are poster models for parenthood."

Renee patted Bobby on the shoulder as he continued to feed Thelma Lou. "After she finishes her bottle, you two can hold her and burp her. It's amazing how calming it is to embrace her and think about all that might lie in her future."

Irma stepped forward, but Arthur said, "I'll take the first shift if you don't mind. I have abundant experience from cradling babies during baptisms, and I always feel special when I hold them."

Renee and Irma exchanged smiles. Renee said, "This man of yours appears to be looking forward to children in his own future. Have you set a date for the wedding yet?"

Bobby reacted to his wife's question. "Be careful, Renee, you don't want to put pressure on these folks. They haven't firmed up their plans yet."

Arthur shifted his weight from his right foot to his left and edged forward. "It's not a problem, Bobby. Earlier today Irma announced our intentions, and I'm starting to get used to it. You can debate about when

93

to open the magic bottle, but once the jinni is out, it's out."

"Arthur, are you objecting to the time frame I suggested?"

"No, I said that it was a magic bottle, so the announcement also was magic. Three months from now it shall be. Can we keep the planning phase simple so that we can concentrate on our case too?"

Irma pouted. "That's what a girl likes to hear: Your wedding will be secondary to a murder investigation."

Renee said, "Cheer up, Irma; once you're married you get domestic bliss like we have. Don't forget, I had to schedule our wedding between cases also."

Arthur said, "She's only pretending to pout. Irma's actually taking a victory lap in celebration of the way she finessed my reluctance to set a date. Sometimes a man needs a woman to be aggressive."

"I'll remember that comment sometime when we're alone."

Bobby said, "You got him with that one, Irma. He's blushing. Arthur, is it hard to be holy and sexy at the same time?"

"Enough about me and Irma, people – we came to see and talk about Thelma Lou. Is her health improving, Bobby?"

"We're taking her in for some more tests because the local doctors don't understand why she hasn't outgrown the apnea. If they don't come up with an answer after the tests, we'll take her to a major hospital in Chicago. Somebody should be able to come up with a course of treatment that works."

Renee said, "Yes, Bobby's keeping us on track with a positive mindset. That's why he's so endearing to me."

Arthur said, "Who's blushing now?" They all looked at Bobby, who chuckled quietly.

Arthur continued, "Regardless of the medical situation, you two should give thanks. Thelma Lou is beautiful, and you'll keep her safe and love her.

"The latest input we received from Joe Gonzalez on our case indicates that Sister Kristina inadvertently exposed infants and small children in Guatemala to baby trafficking and the illegal adoption racket. Women down there temporarily surrendered their babies to orphanages because of economic problems, and the babies disappeared out of the country."

Renee said, "I'd never part with Thelma Lou, even temporarily, no matter how difficult it was to support her. How could a mother do that?"

Arthur said, "They have very little income, and in many cases they have six or more children. They start believing that an orphanage would be better for their baby, or the father refuses to support another child. Some of the youngsters that become objects of this trafficking are just snatched off of the street."

Bobby had finished feeding Thelma Lou. Despite Arthur's earlier request for first rights, he handed her off to Irma along with a towel to protect Irma from any burping mess. "Sister Kristina's journals must document the baby trafficking racket. That's why somebody powerful is after them."

Arthur put his arm around Irma as she held the baby. Renee took a quick picture of them, surprising him. Then he said, "The part that surprises me is that I used to think of an illegal adoption as being a nonviolent crime, at least in this country. I must be naïve. The organization looking for Kristina's journals has already murdered once and almost kidnapped me. They are definitely willing to get their hands dirty.

CHAPTER 30 – ALIAS

Five of the people sitting around the conference table at the Parkville Police Station had worked together on enough cases that they considered themselves both colleagues and old friends. The sixth and youngest, Jeremy Hadley, looked forward to the day when he would be accepted as an equal by the others. Habituated by his coursework at University of Wisconsin – Platteville, Jeremy placed an open notebook in front of him and diagramed the conference table indicating the meeting attendees and their seat locations. Bobby Andrews, as host, sat at the head of the table. Penny and Joe Gonzalez sat on the side to his left, while Arthur Blake and Irma Custis sat on the side to Bobby's right. Jeremy sat at the foot of the table.

Bobby said, "I want to thank you all for coming. I thought it would be a good idea to compare notes on the things that have been going on around here and their implications. Jeremy, you worked part-time for our police department for a while, and I want to welcome you back as part of the ABC group.

"The death of Ted Karga was the first violent murder in this town for quite a while, and we've taken it as our top priority, because we don't want our Parkville people to be afraid that we have a crazed murderer on the loose. I do apologize, because I've had to divide my personal attention between this case and my new baby daughter, but I'm getting more efficient at that routine now."

Irma said, "Bobby, Thelma Lou is a beautiful child, and you'll have to show her off to the rest of this group in the near future, not that you'd be shy about that."

"Thanks, Irma. Arthur, sometime when we can spare time from this case we'll have to schedule her baptism. Penny and Joe, it feels strange to welcome you back to our conference table as Parkville residents as well as federal agents, but you two are welcome additions to our town. Arthur, you were in on all the steps of this case from the beginning, so how about summarizing things?"

"I'm glad you referred to the progression of this case, Bobby, because it has seemed to be spinning outward from its initial events in several different directions. First, we had the emotional irate brother lamenting his sister's premature death and cursing God for allowing it to happen. Then we had his brutal murder, apparently by somebody who had been at that traumatic church service. The next step was our discovery that Ted's sister Kristina had been a Catholic nun hiding in our Protestant church and that she had died of a rabies infection that occurred following a violent assault on her sometime before she came to Parkville. Now, thanks to investigations by Penny and Joe's agency, we know that Ted Karga was not even Kristina's brother. Are we any closer to knowing who he really was?"

Bobby said, "I used my police databases to find out more about him, and he came up as Ted Karga, both because of his application to become a Milwaukee policeman, and because of a minor bar fight arrest from which he had been dismissed without charges. I don't know why that information would be incorrect, but if Sister Kristina did not have a brother, it must be."

Penny looked at Joe, and he nodded for her to respond. "You followed the procedures that normally would be reliable, Bobby, but this was an unusual case for which you didn't have sufficient resources. We checked some of the federal databases, and we

97

have an alternate and intriguing identification of our victim. We found him in the Peace Corps records. It turns out that your Ted Karga was actually Horace McCabe, otherwise known as Horse McCabe because of his physical strength. Joe has Horse's story."

Joe removed a file folder from an envelope and opened it. "Horse McCabe served as a Peace Corps volunteer in Guatemala working with citizens of the Mayan Indian town of Santiago Atitlan to help rebuild homes and other buildings that had been destroyed by the mudslides of Hurricane Stan in 2005. Rebuilding had been a slow process requiring extreme fitness and stamina, and Horse was well-suited to it. He had been stationed there for a bit more than a year when he was accused of raping a local Mayan girl who then ran away because of her feelings of shame. His accuser was a slippery middle-aged man who had been involved in drug dealing, and many wondered whether the accuser had been the actual rapist instead of Horse. Anyway, the Peace Corps wanted to avoid controversy, so they moved Horse to Jacaltenango in the northwest part of Guatemala and put him on probationary status. He had to stay out of trouble, or he would be sent home."

Irma said, "Jacaltenango was where Sister Kristina was a missionary. That must be where they first met."

Arthur pointed at Joe's file. "Does it say whether he stayed out of trouble after his transfer?"

"He did for a while, but about eight months ago he got into a fight with some local men. He was pretty badly beaten, but he won the fight and his opponents fled the scene in even worse shape. When Horse wouldn't talk about the battle with the police, they labeled him as a trouble-maker and told the Peace Corps he was no longer welcome in Guatemala. They sent him back home to Wisconsin and cut their ties with him. That's the last entry in the file."

Arthur said, "I'm beginning to understand what happened. When we looked at Kristina's body, we found an old knife wound on her leg that was the site of the rabies infection and scars from knife slashes on her forearms. We wondered how she could have escaped from her attackers without assistance. Horse must have been her rescuer. She ran away after the attack and collapsed in the thick forest where something bit her. Horse fought off those who tried to kill her, but wouldn't talk about it afterward."

Jeremy asked, "Why wouldn't he talk about it? He didn't do anything wrong. He saved Kristina's life. He also would have been the one who gave her first aid after the attack before she ran away."

Irma said, "I'll take that one. He wouldn't talk about it because there was more than friendship between him and Sister Kristina. You don't talk about such relationships in a Catholic country."

Arthur nodded. "That would explain the anguish he displayed in church after her death. I wondered why he would be so shaken if he hadn't been her brother. He had been her lover."

Jeremy turned the page of his notebook. He had been writing rapidly. "Was Kristina hiding in our church from the gang that had attacked her or from Horse?"

Arthur said, "We don't have enough information to answer that one, Jeremy, but it looks as though she and Horse remained separated after he was sent home. He may not have even known that she was back in the United States."

CHAPTER 31 – ARTHUR AND IRMA

They were enjoying an early evening walk around Mallard Lake after eating dinner at House of Ming. Arthur had been skipping flat stones off of the lake surface and had just had a particularly good throw despite the awkwardness of his cast, with six hops before the stone sank.

"Arthur, how do you really feel about my having set a time frame for our wedding without getting your agreement first?"

"I'm not quite sure. You may have done me a favor by getting me beyond my limbo status, but I would have been more comfortable if we had reached such an important decision together."

"Well I hinted and prodded enough times to try to get you to agree on the timing."

"I know you did, Irma; I guess I was hesitant because my first marriage failed, and I didn't want any chance of repeating that process. That breakup made me a lot less optimistic than I was earlier. I don't ever want to have a pessimistic outlook toward life."

"Are you assigning a significant probability to our marriage failing?"

"No, of course not; I just tend to live in the present rather than the future."

"Uh-oh; you're back to our argument over whether we should plan ahead or just let things happen. Well, without planning ahead, I opened my mouth and spewed out a schedule for our marriage. You should be pleased and let things happen."

"You make a good argument for what you did. Don't worry about it. As a matter of fact, this conversation may help with our current inquiry. I

100

realize that's not a very romantic thing to say, but we work well together even when we're talking about something totally different."

"Don't try to get out of trouble with flattery. How will this talk help the investigation?"

"I stated that you made a good argument for putting a timeframe on our wedding. That leads me to wonder about the brother performance. What was the motivation or argument for Horse McCabe to pretend to be Ted Karga, Kristina's brother? I can see at least two motives. First, if they really did have a romance, they may have planned to live together as sister and brother without ruining Kristina's standing as a nun. Of course, Kristina would have had guilt conflicts to resolve, and this motive disappeared when she died."

"What would the second motive be?"

"As her brother, he would be able to claim her worldly goods, including her journals."

"That gives him a less romantic and more opportunistic image."

"Yes, and it could also cast him as one of the villains despite his having saved her during the earlier attack. We need to learn more about the people who tried to kill Sister Kristina in Guatemala."

"And we need you to say that you're definitely happy with our wedding schedule."

"I'm definitely happy with our wedding schedule."

"Good...Then I'll give you a third possible motive for Horse to assume the role of Ted."

"What is it?"

"He may have wanted to have a new identity because of the rape charge against him in Guatemala."

CHAPTER 32 – STATE OF MIND

It had been a bad morning. The doctors had called to tell him that the results of their tests had been inconclusive. They still didn't have any idea when or whether Thelma Lou would outgrow her Apnea of Prematurity. Bobby hated to think of her having a precarious existence throughout her childhood. The telephone rang, and he answered it without looking at the Caller I.D. panel. "Parkville Police, Chief Andrews speaking…"

"Good morning, Bobby; it's Arthur. Are you feeling alright? You sound tired or blue."

"It's nothing either one of us can do anything about. I'm in no-man's-land because the doctors can't figure out how to eliminate Thelma Lou's apnea problem."

"She's in my prayers and on the congregation's prayer chain so that others are praying for her too."

"Thanks, Arthur; that will make our family feel less alone. Momma has been going through the folk medicine books, looking for traditional cures also. Anyway, you called me, so I should give you the opportunity to tell me why we're having this conversation."

"Something bothered me overnight, and I wanted to check it with you."

"Go ahead; I hope it's something useful. I need a positive development today."

"Do you still have Ted's car there?"

"Sure. We processed it for evidence and then locked it up in our garage in case we needed to look at it again."

"As I recall, Sergeant Gomez said that Ted had borrowed Kristina's car. That car may have a story to tell. I'd like to take a closer look at it."

"Arthur, I must have been glossing over things because of the baby. I can't believe I missed anything that obvious. We looked at the murder evidence, but didn't pay very much attention to the vehicle itself. Bring anyone you want, and we'll do it today. We'll get every possible bit of information from that car this time around. Let's meet in the police garage at two o'clock."

Bobby headed for the detectives' office. Even though he'd had plenty of experience with Arthur's breakthrough thinking, he always felt a little bit irritated when the amateurs showed the professionals how to improve their police work.

CHAPTER 33 – PENNY AND IRMA

During the course of the several cases they had worked on together, Penny Gonzalez and Irma Custis had become close friends, and each of them almost considered the other to be the sister she had never had. Now that Penny lived in Parkville, they could improve their relationship even more. Today they continued to bond while they painted Penny's dining room.

Irma had the tedious job of masking the trim and fixtures while Penny filled small holes and cracks in the walls. "Penny, my mother told me that you painted a room in a light color to make it seem larger and a dark color to make it feel smaller. You're using a darkish green for the walls with white trim; will the room appear smaller or larger than it is?"

"Don't ask someone who has had to settle for the universal white of a Washington apartment. I need to have a new look to convince myself that I'm in charge here. I've seen décor like this in magazines, so I want to have it for my own."

"Good for you, Penny! This is your time to be creative and independent."

"Are you looking forward to rehabbing the parsonage after you and Arthur marry, or will you leave it the way it is except for cleaning up after his bachelor habits?"

"Arthur's pretty neat actually. The problem will be that after a few more years he'll get assigned to a different church where we'll have another parsonage or a rent allowance, and then the cycle will repeat after another bunch of years. In the United Methodist Church pastors are lucky if they stay five to ten years in one place. Many move on after only a couple of years."

"You can't do that. We've moved here to be near you folks."

"We'd probably remain within easy driving distance after a move. Normally, they keep pastors within the district, which isn't too large. Anyway, my point is that we're not likely to own a house for a long time."

"If it will make you happier, you can paint and repair my house any time you want."

"Well thanks, Penny; will I get to choose the decorating schemes for rooms I work on?"

"Maybe I'll let you do the design for one room. Which one would you like for your project?"

"I'll take the nursery."

"You may not have a project for a long time. It took me a long time to convince Joe that we should move and have a home of our own. I had to promise that I wouldn't push for kids until we were well settled into it."

"Were you hoping to have your own children, or were you planning to adopt?"

"I'm too old to have my own, aren't I, Irma?"

"You might be able to handle it with fertility treatments, but not if you wait much longer."

"Then I'll plan on taking the adoption route. There's no way Joe's going to give up our active lifestyle and joint careers in the near future. I'm not even sure I'd feel comfortable about trying to beat the clock and go the natural way. I've seen too many statistics about increased problems as you grow older. Renee's thirty-nine years old, and she had a problem with Thelma Lou."

"I'll wager that Thelma Lou will be fine after a little more time passes. Her apnea should have cured itself already, but there are cases in the books of it taking a little longer to resolve itself. You're two years younger than Renee anyway."

"I won't be this age when we decide it's time for us to have children. I'll make the decision when Joe's ready. I don't want to push him on the subject...Your comment about apnea cases in the books tells me that you're getting a little bit nervous about the situation with the Andrews baby. You've been studying case histories for her condition."

"I'm not nervous about it. I'm following up on Bobby's feeling that the local doctors don't know what's going on with her. I may have specialized in pathology, but I can still work my way through the latest state of the art treatments for a specific disease or condition."

"Fair enough; do you come out of your studies feeling optimistic or pessimistic?"

"I'll be a qualified optimist on this one. The qualification is that there are only limited statistics available for this condition, and they do show that in a small number of cases the child never outgrows it."

CHAPTER 34 – AUTOPSY OF A CAR

While Penny and Irma painted, Bobby, Arthur, Joe, and Jeremy gathered in the police department garage to take a closer look at the car in which Ted (alias Horse) had been murdered. The police mechanic, Chet Quinto, would assist in case advanced automotive knowledge and skills were required.

Bobby called for quiet. "I want to apologize for my not catching the fact that this car was Kristina's and might give us more information about her. Al Gomez traced the plate when the farmer first found the car with the body in it. I went back and checked the entire registry file after Arthur suggested we examine this vehicle again. In that file I found something that will surprise you. I found an unprocessed change-of-name application. The updated version of the registration shows this car's registered owner to be Kristina K. McCabe."

They all exchanged surprised murmurs. Jeremy said, "So she married Horse McCabe. He saved her life, and she married him."

Joe said, "She may have married him, Jeremy, but she may have faked the name change to make it more difficult for people to find her. Horse was doing the same thing, presenting himself as Ted Karga. The evidence we've found up to this point suggests that Horse didn't know where she was. We think that they returned from Guatemala at different times, so when did they get together to marry?"

Arthur said, "A marriage would also say that she had given up any hopes of returning to the Maryknoll Sisters, either because she had lost her commitment or because she was afraid to revisit the role in which she had been targeted for murder. What do you think, Bobby?"

"I doubt that she was living in fear. Kristina appears to have been a very determined and resourceful person. A marriage would explain the emotional outburst by Horse, pretending to be Ted, at your church."

Arthur said, "I also told you earlier that we didn't see Kristina around Parkville during the week, but she was a regular on Sundays. I had assumed that this was due to the nature of her job, but perhaps she went to Milwaukee to be with Horse during the week."

Joe said, "That's all interesting and probably valuable speculation, but now let's do a thorough examination of Kristina's car. It may contain some valuable clues. Bobby, you organized this show. Assign us to our tasks."

"Thanks, Joe. Chet, you're the specialist, so you should look for clues in the engine compartment. I'll take the front seat and controls. Jeremy, you check the back seat. Joe, you and Arthur can look for hidden compartments in the doors, fenders, and trunk. Kristina was serving in a place where drug smugglers fix up cars for hiding drugs, and she may have picked up some of their tricks. I don't think we have to worry too much about keeping this car in perfect condition, but please be neat about anything you take apart so that we can document our work and possibly reassemble everything."

They all separated and started to work on their assigned areas, using tools and flashlights that Chet had provided. Arthur and Joe decided to work on opposite sides of the car, starting at the front and moving rearward. Joe took the left side, and Arthur took the right. Joe was the first to find something.

"I found a magnetic hidden key box under the left front fender. It has a car key and a crucifix in it."

Jeremy walked over to look at the items. "What's the difference between a crucifix and a cross?"

Arthur said, "A crucifix is primarily used in the Catholic Church, and it shows Christ on the cross during the crucifixion. Protestant churches normally use a plain cross that is a symbol of the crucifixion but not a representation of it. It looks as though Sister Kristina kept her crucifix hidden, but still with her wherever she drove. Bobby, check to see whether that key fits this car."

Bobby took the key from Joe and tried it in the ignition. "It fits, but I won't turn it all the way, with Chet working in the engine compartment."

Chet looked out from beneath the hood. "Thanks for that courtesy, Chief. I don't think the engine would start anyway. While it sat outside, this car had an infestation of squirrels under the hood. The cables are chewed up, and there's some shredded nesting material and peanut shells on top of the air filter. Credit the shells to Al Gomez. He throws peanuts out back for the birds and the squirrels. He must have pitched some peanuts with the shells still on them."

Joe said, "Squirrels didn't invade our cars in Washington. Now I realize that I am out in the country. Anyway, If Kristina hid a crucifix and a key in her car, she may have used it as a treasure chest for other hidden things. Let's get back to our autopsy of this beast."

Bobby unbolted the driver's seat and pulled it out of the car. He turned it over, but found nothing more interesting than two crumpled napkins lodged in the springs underneath it. Then he spotted a slit in the carpet and probed at it with a screwdriver. "I have something. There's an envelope under the carpet, and it must be significant because someone sealed it inside a plastic bag to keep moisture out." He carefully cut the bag with a pair of scissors, removed the envelope, and then gently lifted the flap. "It's a Certificate of Marriage between Kristina Louise Karga and Horace John McCabe. They were married four months ago in Madison, Wisconsin by the Dane County Clerk."

Arthur said, "I wonder if Horace, or Horse, had family up there. I imagine that the County Clerk personally performs only special marriages. That might be worth checking, but I'm not sure it would be important to the investigation. What do you think, Bobby?"

"I want to be as thorough as possible after missing the significance of this being Kristina's car, so we'll check it out. I agree that it may not be significant."

Jeremy said, "While you folks were gabbing about the carpet slit and the marriage certificate, I removed the back seat, and I found three Guatemalan coins and a cigar butt under it. If Kristina didn't have this car in Guatemala, then she had a man from there in the back seat. I doubt that Horse smoked cigars, given his physical fitness penchant, but I can't be sure."

Bobby said, "Jeremy, take a pair of tweezers from the tool cart, and put the coins in one evidence bag and the cigar butt in another. They may help us discover what Guatemalan man was in the back seat. Has anyone seen any modifications to the car outside of the slit in the carpet that might reveal a secret storage area?"

Arthur closed the right rear door firmly. "I've found nothing unusual. The doors show on the right side show no signs of tampering. Did you find anything unusual about the left side doors, Joe?"

"Nothing there; I'm moving on to the rear fender and the trunk."

Chet Quinto said, "Joe, the gas tank is on your side. Be sure to check under the fender beneath the gas filler pipe. That's a favorite spot for smugglers. They wrap or drape something around the filler pipe where it can't be seen underneath the fuel access door assembly."

"Thanks, Chet, I have it. No, there's nothing under there. Do we have to dismantle the gas tank?"

"Bobby said, "Let's leave that for last, and if we decide it's warranted, we'll do it outside and away from the building. That could be a safety issue, and I can't see someone like Kristina putting something in the gas tank that she hoped to retrieve later. You've been quiet, Arthur. Have you found anything interesting?"

"You might say that. I bent back the trunk liner on the right side, and on the fender wall underneath I found painted in red a cross with the Latin words *In hoc signo vinces* underneath it. For those of you who aren't up on church history and the Latin language, that phrase translates to *In this sign you will conquer.* It was the motto of the Knights Templar military order that dates back to the Crusades."

Jeremy approached Arthur for a closer look inside the trunk. "Why would she have painted that under the trunk liner? What does it mean?"

Arthur shrugged his shoulders. "It may mean that Kristina considered herself to be on a crusade to right the wrongs she had discovered. It may also have been a reminder to her that whether she functioned within the Maryknoll Sisters organization or entirely on her own, she should remain focused on the cross and maintain her religious dedication."

Joe joined Arthur and Jeremy at the open trunk. "Let's strip everything out of the trunk. It's the easiest place to hide something, and that painted motto says she treated the trunk area as significant."

The three of them completely removed the trunk liner, the cover for the tire storage compartment, the compact spare tire, plus the jack and tire iron. They set those items on the garage floor, and examined the interior steel walls for any additional painted messages. They saw none, and turned their attention to the articles they had put on the garage floor. Joe checked the reverse surface of the trunk liner and found nothing unusual. Arthur examined the jack assembly and the underside of the storage compartment lid. Jeremy picked up the compact spare tire and stood cradling it in his arms.

Arthur said, "What's up, Jeremy? Is there anything special about the tire?"

Jeremy inverted the tire to show the bottom sidewall. On it there had been painted a red cross similar to the one on the steel wall of the trunk. He said, "Behold: in this sign you will conquer."

Jeremy laid the spare tire on a workbench. Chet came over with a tire pressure gauge and a small pry bar. He pressed the protruding pin on the back of the gauge head against the valve stem pin to deflate the tire. Then he used the pry bar to separate the tire sidewall from the steel wheel rim. Chet repeated the process on the other side of the tire and then eased the tire completely free of the wheel.

Arthur said, "There's something in there."

Chet retrieved three cylindrical bundles from inside the spare tire. "There are three somethings actually." He handed them to Bobby who unwrapped, unrolled, and flattened them on the workbench.

"Good job, folks; each bundle is a plastic-wrapped notebook. We have three of Kristina's journals. Now we'll learn why they were so important to Ted, alias Horse, and to the people who killed him and attacked Kristina in Guatemala and Arthur in his church."

CHAPTER 35 – PRISONERS

Marco Fernandez and Gus Savage sat on their bunks across from each other in the Parkville Police jail cell. Parkville had a peaceful enough history that the police had managed quite well with only the single barred cubicle. Marco rose and began to pace as well as he could within the restricted area.

After a few minutes Gus said, "Marc, cool it, will you? There's not enough room for real exercise, and you make me nervous when you do that. We have to be patient until the lawyers get us out of here."

"You don't get it, Gus. There won't be any lawyers. We were supposed to scare that preacher into giving us the journals or take him along with us if he didn't come up with them. We blew it on both counts. We're worth nothing to the people who hired us."

"They'll have to help us out of here, or we'll tell the cops whatever they want to know."

"Sure you will. And how much do you know to tell them? We only know that a stranger picked us up at Lefke's Tavern and paid us five hundred dollars each to do this job, with another thousand each promised if we were successful. We'll never see that thousand, we don't know the stranger who hired us, and we don't even know what's in the journals we were after. We've got nothing to use as bargaining chips. They'll just let us rot here."

"We could at least tell them that the guy was someone who goes to Lefke's."

"That might have been the first time he ever went there. They probably had someone else pick us out, and we never even noticed him checking on us. Our client reminded me of some people I knew in

Guatemalan government circles. Everyone thinks that we work as a team with me as the muscle and you as the brains, but I know better. We work together because I need a front man who looks like an Anglo and can pass for an exec when dressed up."

"OK, you're the brains and the muscle. Now tell me how we're going to get out of here, smart guy."

"I'm still working on that one. We could offer to deliver phony journals to the guy who hired us so that the cops could follow him."

"That's not smart at all. First, too much time has passed for that guy to believe we got the journals. Second, we're safer in here than we would be if we pulled that trick. They'd know where to find us whenever they wanted to get rid of us."

"Do you have a better idea, Gus? Let's see how smart you are."

"I think we should stay right here and play dumb. Nobody knows we were going to kidnap the guy. All they have us for is throwing a few punches. We didn't even trespass, because the church is open to everyone. We didn't use a weapon, so it's a simple assault case. How much time can we get for that?"

"Are you sure you didn't go to law school or something? That's not bad, at least for you. My problem is that they already deported me once, and they'll probably do it again."

"So, you figured out how to get smuggled back into the States before. You can do it again. At least we won't end up with killers after us. I don't know about you, Marc, but I like living."

"Yeah, I do too. You're getting better at this thinking stuff, Gus. If they kick me out of the country again, you can join me in Guatemala. Tough guys can do pretty well there."

"We'll talk about the future later. For now, just relax and wait for them to bring dinner. The food's pretty good here."

CHAPTER 36 – JOURNALS

Joe and Arthur walked into the new *Casa Gonzalez* where they were met by two paint-spotted but beaming women. Penny and Irma had actually painted more walls than they had planned while the men had been off doing something or other.

Penny approached her husband with a big grin on her face. "Don't take this as a put-down, Joe, but by getting you guys out of the way, we did a fantastic amount of painting. Irma and I are feeling like pros. Did you two huddle over coffee as usual, or did you do something different and interesting while we worked?"

Joe kept a straight face as he exchanged glances with Arthur. "We're both happy that you achieved so much. It's probably a fair tradeoff of time. You did some great decorating. What I can see from here looks great. We weren't quite as productive. All we did was unearth Kristina's missing journals."

This time it was Penny who exchanged glances with Irma. "You did what? You guys have all the fun while we work."

Arthur laughed.

Irma glared at him. "What's so funny?"

"You two were telling us how much fun you had painting, and now it seems it was tiresome work while we were out having all the fun. You can't have it both ways."

Irma looked at Penny and shrugged her shoulders. "It was fun painting because we accomplished so much. Then you two walked in, and we discovered that you achieved even more than we did. That gave you the edge in the fun race."

Joe said, "There's no competition here. Today has been good for all of us. You knew in advance that you

116

would achieve some special results from your painting. We were only searching for evidence, and we got luckier than we could have anticipated. They're two different types of accomplishments, both of which are satisfying. Give us the tour of your painting exploits, and then we'll sit down and discuss the journals.

Twenty minutes later they sat around the kitchen table. Arthur retrieved the journals from a case he had brought with him. "We have to be very careful with these, both because they are delicate and because Joe had to fill out some special forms before Bobby would let us take them away. Joe had to officially declare federal jurisdiction so that we wouldn't be breaking the chain of custody for this evidence. We don't yet know how significant the journals are, but people have been willing to kill in order to get them or to keep others from getting them."

Penny said, "Start with telling us how you found them, and then we'll examine them together. I don't think that anyone in this town knows we represent a federal agency, but to be on the safe side, I've already swept the house for possible listening or video devices. It's safe for us to discuss the case here."

Arthur said, "Joe, if you don't mind, I'll take the lead on this one."

Joe nodded and leaned back, tilting his kitchen chair. Penny reached over and pushed the back of his chair until it was level again.

"Joe, I don't want you or that chair to get broken, so let's keep all four of its legs on the floor...Go ahead, Arthur, I just had to take care of my wayward boy before he got into trouble."

"OK, here's the scoop. It all started when I realized that the car in which Ted Karga, alias Horace 'Horse' McCabe, was murdered had Illinois license

117

plates instead of the Wisconsin plates that would match his residence. That led me to question Sergeant Al Gomez, and I found out that it was Kristina's car instead of Ted's. Even though Kristina had been coming to our church for months before she died, I had never noticed what kind of car she drove. Bobby checked the full registry file, and he found an application to change the name on her registration to Kristina K. McCabe."

Irma said, "That's scandalous! Our nun married Horse McCabe."

Arthur continued, "We weren't sure whether that was the case. Kristina might have been hiding behind the McCabe name in order to elude those who were searching for her. Anyway, we started to search the car for hidden items, and we soon found an envelope inside a sealed plastic bag beneath the driver's-side carpet. It contained a certificate of marriage. Kristina had indeed married Horse McCabe, but I have the feeling that she kept him in the dark on many issues."

Penny said, "What do you mean? You're making it sound as though Kristina operated on several levels at the same time."

"That's exactly it, Penny. She was a crusading undercover nun; she was hiding from those who were after her; and she was trying to help Horse regain his reputation after facing that rape charge and being kicked out of the Peace Corps. I assume she took the audacious step of marrying Horse because she loved him, but by doing so Kristina demonstrated her willingness to color outside the lines of her religious icon picture."

"I get you, Arthur, she retained her zeal and dedication, but she was a Mary Magdalene type of disciple. She was unconventional and misunderstood by many around her."

"That's it exactly, Penny. I see Kristina as a person who took action when she saw injustice of any kind. She was not content to preach to the choir of other nuns or sign petitions. She was out to change things for the better, regardless of whether she could do it within the rules and confines of her order."

Irma drummed her fingers on the table unconsciously. "She must have been very dedicated. She wanted no attention or glory for what she was trying to do."

Joe said, "I don't think she had the option at this stage of her efforts, Irma. She had already drawn enough attention for people to try to kill her. She couldn't seek attention and hide at the same time. Once a crusader has a big following, he or she can act in the open because an attack by the enemy creates a martyr and a cause for all of the dedicated followers. Kristina knew it would be too dangerous to attract attention yet, so she combined worshipping in a Protestant church with marrying Horse McCabe to become invisible to her enemies."

Irma became conscious of her finger-drumming and picked up a pen to avoid her nervous habit. "So, tell us more about the journals and where you found them."

Arthur said, "As you can see, there are three flexible notebooks. They had been rolled up individually and hidden inside the compact spare tire of Kristina's car. The dates of their entries cover the period from June of 2007 until November of 2009. Kristina returned to the United States from Guatemala in August of 2011, so we are not at all sure that these are all of her journals. She may have written more in Guatemala, and she may have continued to log her experiences after she repatriated. We can learn a lot from studying these notebooks, but they may not contain the whole story."

Joe said, "I flipped through the pages a little bit at the police garage, and my first impression was that Kristina wrote hastily and in many short segments. Her handwriting appeared agitated and rushed, as though she had been afraid someone would catch her doing her secretive documentation. My guess is that she recorded things that would get her in trouble if anyone discovered her writings."

Penny asked, "Is there anything unusual about the notebooks themselves, Joe?"

"They're a type that is readily available in Guatemala City, but rare in remote towns. Their most remarkable feature is the blood spattered on the last blank pages of the final volume."

Irma reached across the table to receive a notebook from Arthur. "I'll have the DNA of that blood checked against Kristina's records. Someone may have violently terminated her writing session."

CHAPTER 37 – EXCERPTS FROM JOURNAL NUMBER ONE

June 21, 2007 – Guatemala is such a beautiful country in which to serve. Eden must have been like this. Thank goodness most of the atrocities of the past death squad periods are behind us. Nuns and priests weren't immune from them. I know that I'll have to make my notes in these journals sound neutral in case anyone else ever reads them. It is always well to speak and write positively about this country and its government because there are unknown and unexpected eyes and ears everywhere. Still, the campesinos of Guatemala are family-centered farm workers who make the best they can of what little they have. I'm amazed at the loads they carry up the mountain roads and distressed by the many makeshift monuments along those roads where so many have been killed by out-of-control cars and trucks. It's an imperfect paradise...

July 17, 2007 – My back still hurts from those whippings two years ago. Sometimes I think stepfathers should have to be approved in advance by children. Rodrigo put on a good act until we discovered his true nature. I hope Mother is still coping. I don't think she's left him. Her letters are few and say so little. Still, Rodrigo gave me my intro to Spanish and the defiant courage to leave that nastiness and serve God. The priests down here don't think much of nuns. They're happy enough to have us handle the day-to-day mission work while they get the adoration and respect of the people. It will take a nun to teach such priests humility.

August 13, 2007 – I have been assigned in the highlands town of Jacaltenango to a local hogar which is an orphanage. There are so many young children and unwanted infants requiring care. We can only do so much for them. Some of them come from families that have grown in size beyond their means for raising children. Why do men have to show their macho nature by keeping their women pregnant? They would be so much more revered by showing their abilities to be good providers. Some of our poor children are all that remain of families that disappeared at the hands of the death squads. It's always about power and control. Why can't they submit to God's will and take only what he provides?

September 29, 2007 – I will have to do a better job of maintaining my journal. Some days I am too tired to write before going to sleep, and on other days I am so angry I might destroy the journal instead of writing in it. They tell me that we can care for no more than forty children here, but I see so many more that have to live on their own and subsist on scraps and handouts. At least Father McShane encourages people to share what little they have. He is a good man, but he wouldn't have any idea how to build a community organization to work together and save something toward a better future. The sisters don't want me to say too much about such things, either. They keep saying that if I pray longer and harder, God will provide. I'm sure that he will, but it won't be because we begged harder. God leads and we follow; we cannot manipulate him with our prayers.

October 10, 2007 – Today I traveled with Father McShane and two other sisters to Antigua. He wanted to show us the ruins of the old cathedral and tell us about the first Spanish settlers. It was good to get away for a while. In Antigua I met some Peace Corps people. They have some good ideas for helping the people, but they are too worried about what others will think of their projects and their people. Their government regulations pervade everything they do. Still, it is better to try within the framework of these restraints than not to try at all. Some of their people are very young and some look too old to be so active. I pray that they will have success in their efforts. I asked Father McShane why they didn't clean up the ruins and rebuild the cathedral a long time ago. He told me that some are trying to do that now, but that he felt that the cathedral ruins have become a holy shrine for pilgrims and that they should not be disturbed. I would have felt better if he had said that he had reached his opinion because engineers predicted that a rebuilt cathedral would tumble again in future earthquakes. The priests don't involve technology in their thinking. God gives us many resources to use for all the people.

November 3, 2007 – Jacaltenango is in the mountains near the Mexican border. Because of that, some of the sisters at the Maryknoll Hospital are Mexican, although most are Guatemalan. There are just a few of us from the U.S.A. Sister Patrice is quite a bit older and from somewhere in Texas. Sister Michelle is from Pittsburgh; she is just a little older than I am but very timid and a by-the-book type. Sister Monica is from Boston and will be returning to the States next week. As long as I do my work well, I don't have to worry about close oversight, and that suits me fine. I am properly devoted to our Lord, but I am not an organization person.

November 24, 2007 – Thanksgiving would have been a couple of days ago, but we didn't have enough Americans here to celebrate it. I thought about it, but I didn't miss it too much. I'll bet the Peace Corps people made a big event of it. Too bad we don't have any of them in town right now. People here have so little compared to what we have at home. Yet they manage to survive and give thanks, at least the religious ones

123

do. I'm learning that nearly everyone goes through the rituals of the church, but only a small percentage really believe and have faith. We will have to do a better job of teaching while also learning from the people. Many have their own versions of Catholicism that include native gods and idols in local shrines.

December 13, 2007 – This will be my first Christmas in a warm place. If only we could provide for all of the children who are in need. Many of the families cannot care for all of their children. Many youngsters live on the streets and survive only by the sharpness of their wits. We are so limited in the numbers for whom we can provide shelter and safety. In the New Year I will talk with families and other orphanages to see whether they can take in a few more of these street urchins. We are in the remote northwestern province of Huehuetenango. Other provinces have worse conditions for children than we do.

January 16, 2008 – Today I visited a private orphanage on the edge of town named Our Children Together. They welcomed me and appeared to be good people. They told me that they get their funding by appealing for donations on the internet. Their advantage seems to be that they have no specific religious affiliation and as a nonprofit organization they are supported by a wider range of donors. They are hoping to build additional homes and told me that they would be open to accepting some of the infants and children that would come to us if we had more capacity. This is a very exciting development. I will talk with them again and see whether their expansion really occurs before I say anything to the other sisters. Many people in Guatemala talk about great plans that never become reality. Maybe I should contact some additional private orphanages. I may find homes for some of the children. I have a new project. Thank you for showing it to me, God.

Thy Will Be Done

February 2, 2008 – It is actually happening. I spoke with several local mothers who cannot care for all of their children, and I told them I would see what I can do to help. Then I asked two of the private orphanages if they would take in some of these children for a few months until the start of the harvest season when the parents will have more money to support them. They both agreed, and I have placed four toddlers with them so far. In many cases a temporary placement is all the people with large families need. I will also try to make friends with some of the children who have no parents and live on the streets.

March 13, 2008 – I have spoken with some of the street children. They are beginning to trust me enough to talk with me. I think it will take a few more meetings with them before I dare raise the subject of their possibly living in an orphanage. I will tell them that they should consider it because the streets are so dangerous for them. In the meantime, five more mothers have asked for temporary placements, and one mother has brought me her six-month-old daughter for a permanent home in an orphanage. She said they will never be able to care for another child, and her husband had told her to find another home for this one. She asked whether the church might someday allow her to do something to keep from having more babies.

March 24, 2008 – I pray that I have not done something foolish or evil. I have finally gained the confidence of some of the street children. They told me about their lives and the tricks they have learned to obtain food and shelter. They even sell souvenirs made by Indian weavers and craftsmen to the tourists. Thank goodness Guatemala's weather is kind to them except for the rainy season. I have not yet learned how they handle that period. Anyway, I raised the subject of their living in an orphanage, and they laughed at me. They said that it is safer to live on the streets than to go to such a place. *Several of them said they had friends who had been kidnapped on the street and taken to orphanages. When I asked why such a thing would happen, they said that those places sell children to people in other countries. They felt that it would be better to be poor but have friends and relatives in Guatemala than to take a chance on being shipped away to a place that could be a lot worse. I will have to check on their stories. Our Catholic orphanage is safe for the children we house. Is it possible that some of the others are not?"*

March 26, 2008 – *I went to check on the children I placed in privately run homes. The one called Our Children Together would not let me in to see them. They said that their policy is to keep the children free of outside influences while in their care. They said that the only way I could see them would be for me to have their mothers apply to get them back. The home manager knows that the mothers can't take them back until their husbands put aside more money to support them, and I have no alternate sanctuaries for them that have been proven safe. At this point I do not know if the home is doing a good job of caring for the children or if they are even there. I will check at a different home tomorrow.*

March 27, 2008 – *I went this morning to the Huehue Heights Home for Children. At first they didn't want to let me in, but I told them that Father McShane had sent me to teach the children some prayers. Around here, people always respect the priests, so that gave me some leverage. Once they gathered the children together for me, I spotted only one of the four children I had placed there for temporary custody. After teaching the prayers I asked to see the other three. They said that they had been transferred to their other location, but they wouldn't give me an address for that place. Then they had two large men usher me out. It can only* mean that those children are gone forever. How will I face their parents?

April 4, 2008 – I have been studying old magazines and searching the internet too. I had not realized that I am serving God in the middle of a nest of snakes. I have learned that Guatemala is a center for illegal international adoptions. Some of these homes are probably selling young children to international traffickers for adoption elsewhere. The government here is trying to crack down on these crimes, but so far their new regulations have only slowed the process. I will have to learn more and do what I can to protect local children. I can only pray that those who have already been taken away will be treated well by their new families.

April 28, 2008 – While keeping up with my regular duties, I am continuing to study about illegal adoptions. I know that I am not yet ready to take any overt action. These are dangerous people, and I don't want them to focus on me as a problem. The more I know about these crimes, the better I will be able to gather evidence against them. I read today that one of every one hundred Guatemalan children is adopted by an American family. There were almost thirty thousand American adoptions between 1990 and 2007. Some of these adoptions were illegal, but I don't know how many. I will have to learn more.

May 16, 2008 – I've discovered a report that Guatemalan police broke up a child-trafficking ring in Antigua last August. They rescued forty-six children from a house there, some of whom had been kidnapped and some of whom had been forcefully taken away or purchased from their parents. Two lawyers at the house were arrested. Apparently, potential adopting parents from other countries would mingle with the tourists in Antigua and would visit these lawyers to negotiate the price for an adopted child. *The lawyers would handle all the paperwork, including fraudulent certifications that the child had been willingly placed for adoption by the parents. They have Indian women who work for them and claim to be the mothers. The Guatemalan government is planning to institute DNA testing to eliminate sham certifications by pretend mothers. The report even indicated that some children had been sold for organ harvesting and that in one Guatemalan village a mob had killed two women who had been accused of murdering and dismembering a young girl for her heart and kidneys. How can people do such things?*

CHAPTER 38 – LAWYERS

The collision between two weather fronts had generated swirling winds and choppy waves on Lake Michigan this morning. John Krimmens stared out his office window at the lake for what seemed to be a half hour, but was actually only five minutes. The waves gyrated hypnotically, transfixing him on the motion of the water and the hint of the Michigan shoreline in the far distance beyond this inland sea. Staring at the horizon, he contemplated the actual and psychological distances between his glassed-in Chicago office and the Guatemalan rural towns where contacts arranged terms for the subjects of the agency's business transactions. He pivoted away from the vista and approached his partner's desk.

"Miriam, I know our business would be considered controversial in some quarters, but I really believe that over the years we handed those kids a better life than they could have ever expected down there. It's not some form of slavery; we gave those kids a free ticket to prosperity."

"Are you still chewing on that old bone, John? You're lucky you're only performing your song and dance for me. We've been over this same ground many times. We're lawyers, and we negotiate contracts between prospective parties to transactional agreements. We happen to work with principals in Guatemala. We're independent business people, and so are they. Whatever type of transaction we handle, we are fair and open with all parties. They don't tell us how to run our business, and we don't intrude on their procedures. Everything is done at arm's length, and we negotiate fair prices for our services. There is nothing for you to fret about."

"I want to see things the way you do, Miriam, but during the course of arranging past adoptions, I kept worrying about the feelings of the birth parents."

"I'm sure they were bothered for a while, but the ones with big families probably couldn't have afforded to raise those kids anyway. The teenage girls should have waited before having kids, so we gave them a second chance to straighten out their lives."

"What about the kids who were taken from the streets?"

"I doubt that there were any cases like that; it's just a myth. Even if street kids had been snatched, they would have headed to a much better life than they could have achieved on their own."

"But..."

"Drop it, John. We helped kids have better lives...period. And don't ever let our clients hear you talk like this. You have a rewarding career; you don't want to lose it. Anyway, our patrons are phasing in a new business enterprise that should ease your qualms."

John returned to his window, and Miriam Gilbus continued her review of requests from potential customers for their services. Most of the inquiries had few or nonexistent details, but some were trying to match conceptual ideals. In most cases, customers wanted only quick and private transactions. Law firms like Miriam's guided potential parents to family expansion through unconventional arrangements. Last week she had filed thirteen minimal requirement requests, and the office in Guatemala had already found seven promising opportunities. Their agency collected the bulk of their agreed fees as soon as they initiated the process; only a minor portion remained for the final completion of the adoption. It would be a future of prosperity for both of them if only John's misgivings didn't anger their associates.

CHAPTER 39 – EXCERPTS FROM JOURNAL NUMBER TWO

June 9, 2008 – Today I read about the theft of yet another child. The brazenness of these abductors saddens me.. This time it was a mother going to Guatemala City on a bus with her daughter. They had to change buses for the final leg of their journey, and while they were waiting for the second bus, a woman befriended them and offered to buy the mother a soda. She went into a store and came out with two sodas, but the one she offered as a gift made the mother dizzy, and she collapsed. When she awoke, her daughter and the woman who bought the drinks were gone. How can I be a servant of Christ and have to preach that you should trust no one? The women are just as bad as the men in this trafficking of babies and children.

July 21, 2008 – The street children have become my friends. Their leaders are Rosita Valdez and Ricardo Cisneros. They know that I want to help, and they have begun to tell me their personal stories along with tales that they have heard about the criminal networks. They may exaggerate to some extent, but most of it rings true because it agrees with what I have learned by reading and by talking with the priests. I have gained the confidence of several of the priests through Father McShane, and although they are forbidden to cite specifics and reveal names, they have told me enough about what they hear in counseling sessions to let me understand some of the tricks used by these criminals. The children told me one story that almost exactly matches one that I had heard from a priest. They said that a girl in the town who is seventeen years old had a baby girl at the Jacaltenango Hospital. Upon discharge, as she was waiting for a taxi across the road from the hospital, a van pulled up. Two people jumped out of the van. One grabbed the baby while the other pushed her into some bushes. By the time she had picked herself up, the van and the baby were so far away that she had no hope of reading the license plate.

August 6, 2008 – Ricardo Cisneros has told me about a local lawyer and Notary who works with some of the homes for children. Ricardo says that this man, Carlos Benitez, is supposed to create the legal papers for legitimate adoptions. They say that he has bragged to others that his paperwork for many not-so-legal adoptions has made him a wealthy man. When he first arrived in town he was as poorly dressed as the street children, but now he has a fancy Mercedes car and better suits than most government officials. I will try to learn more about him.

September 23, 2008 – I called on Senor Carlos Benitez to ask for a donation for our orphanage. He made a generous contribution and asked whether we placed children in international adoptions. I could see that he was almost salivating at the idea of processing adoptions for the Catholic home for children. I held him off with a declaration that all such arrangements and paperwork are handled by the Maryknoll Sisters order internally. I almost felt as though I was holding off a guy as he tried to pick me up in a bar. I'm sure that he'll come back and use some other approach to seek business from us.

October 1, 2008 – I was right. Carlos Benitez came up to me on the street today and asked me to have coffee with him. I agreed and was suitably proper as I sat drinking coffee while he talked. I knew that he would have some kind of proposition to discuss. After about ten minutes of inconsequential chatter, he built up enough courage to suggest that he would have additional periodic contributions to make to our orphanage if I would just add a note of blessing to the paperwork for the adoptions he arranged. Since I knew that many of those adoptions were illegal placements of stolen children, I declined, but I gave the reason that only a priest would be authorized to do such a thing. I didn't want to reveal that I knew anything was wrong with his activities. He told me that he understood my position and that he would pursue the matter with a priest. I think that will be the end of it with Carlos. I expect that I will have to contact someone else to find evidence against these organizations.

November 10, 2008 – When I left the orphanage at the end of the day, I found Carlos Benitez and a man who looked and sounded Mexican waiting outside. Carlos introduced the other man as Miguel, but he didn't volunteer a last name. Miguel said that he was the owner of several small private orphanages. He wanted to know if he could have a copy of the procedures manual that we use to train the staff in our Catholic orphanage. He said that he wanted to do a better job of training his employees. I said that I didn't see a problem with that, and I promised to bring a copy to Carlos tomorrow. As soon as I left them, I informed my supervisor, Sister Marie, of my action and asked whether it would be approved. She said that she saw no problem with my giving Miguel the training manual. I didn't tell her about my suspicions as to the nature of his facilities. I need evidence before I say anything to anyone.

November 11, 2008 – I met Carlos at the coffee shop and gave him the personnel training manual that Miguel had requested. Carlos expressed his thanks and asked whether I would do one more favor for him. He wanted me to meet with one of the adopting couples to answer any questions they might have about

Guatemalan children and their backgrounds. I agreed because I wanted to keep this communication channel open, even though I knew that I would have to be very careful not to cross the line into an illegal assistance position.

December 3, 2008 – Carlos Benitez asked me to come to his office across from the market square at three o'clock in the afternoon. When I arrived he introduced me to an American couple, Joshua and Isabelle Weadle. Carlos told me that the Weadles had come to Jacaltenango to complete their adoption arrangements and take their new daughter Juanita home to the United States. The Weadles explained that Juanita, who was three years old, would be renamed Jane when she joined their family. As this was just anglicizing her name, I concurred that it would be a practical step for them. They asked me whether I thought it would be important to have the girl continue to speak Spanish while she learned English, and I suggested that if they wanted her to have a well-rounded education, they should continue with the Spanish because children are most adaptable to language skills during their early years. I had to admit that I was impressed with these people who appeared to be both religious, even if not Catholic, and well-educated. They even told me that they planned to tell their new daughter that she was adopted as part of her bilingual training. I answered a few more questions for them, and then they thanked me and I left. I came away from this meeting wondering whether it might be true that Juanita, or Jane, would have a much better life under this illegal adoption arrangement. I felt disturbed and confused when I returned to my room and said my evening prayers.

December 8, 2008 – Carlos again asked me to visit his office and talk with some adopting parents. I could hardly refuse, given the positive aspects of my first such experience. When I arrived I met George and Mable Benton, who were quite different from the Weadles. They were adopting an eight year old boy, Pablo, and they didn't ask for suggestions for helping him with his transition to American life or talk about their plans for raising him as a member of their family. From a quick glance at their paperwork I learned that they were from New York City. They did ask about the ways that Guatemalan parents disciplined their children and whether I thought that children from rural families would be able to cope with the fast pace of city life. They said that Pablo would be their first adopted child but that they planned to adopt another boy and several girls. I asked if they had other children of their own, and they said their only son had died the year before. I expressed my sympathy and left. Again, I felt disturbed following this interview, but this time I was bothered because I could see nothing but fear and danger in the futures of any children this couple adopted. I also wondered whether my earlier experience with the pleasant Weadle couple had been a setup to sucker me into cooperating with Carlos.

January 14, 2009 – I have met with three more couples in Carlos' office, and most of them have left me with the impression that they would not be good parents, perhaps even that they planned to use their adopted children rather than nurture them. I am compiling a table listing each couple along with their new child's name and their home city. I hope to check on the well-being of the children when I return to the States. Perhaps there will be a way to help them return to their birth families in Guatemala if things do not turn out well.

CHAPTER 40 – REFERRAL

Thelma Lou's condition had not improved, and the doctors at Parkville Care Center had not shown sufficient understanding of Apnea of Prematurity to satisfy the tensions and impatience of her parents. Renee and Bobby Andrews contacted the American Academy of Pediatrics and obtained a referral to a Chicago specialist named Henry Kerski. By telephone on Monday morning, Dr. Kerski asked them to obtain copies of Thelma Lou's medical records from the doctors at Parkville Care Center and then bring the records and the baby to his office in two days.

Renee and Bobby had sensed optimism in Dr. Kerski's voice, and they felt relieved that he had specified that he would examine and treat Thelma Lou in his office rather than in a hospital. Renee packed and rearranged their schedules for the trip, while Bobby visited Dr. Marie Pallardi at Parkville Care Center to apply for copies of Thelma Lou's records. After signing all of the authorization forms he felt refreshed as he returned to the police station.

He stopped to check with Al Gomez before going to his office. "Greetings, Al, I want to let you know that I'll be out of town on Wednesday. We're taking Thelma Lou to see a specialist. He sounds as though he's handled a bunch of similar cases, so we hope we'll get the baby's problem behind us. Do you have any problems or emergencies for me?"

"Not much – Chet Quinto has reassembled Kristina's car, and he even thinks he can get it running again, as soon as you authorize him to replace the wiring those squirrels chewed up. Jeremy Hadley was in to ask whether we had obtained any significant information from those thugs who attacked Arthur. I told him that they hadn't said much during the first quiz session but that you were going to give them a second round of interrogation."

"I almost forgot about that one. I'll give it a couple of hours this afternoon. I have to clear the decks for Wednesday. Have any lawyers shown up to represent them?"

"Nope, my guess is that their bosses want nothing to do with them now that they've been caught. That also says that the people who run their organization don't think these guys have anything worthwhile to tell us."

"That's quite likely, but maybe they know more than they think they do. I'll give it a try a little later. Right now I have to finish some paperwork. I let Joe Gonzalez take the lead on this show by certifying it as a federal investigation. That gives us less field work but more documentation."

CHAPTER 41 – EXCERPTS FROM JOURNAL NUMBER THREE

March 23, 2009 – I talked with my street children friends again today. Twelve year old Rosita Valdez and eleven year old Ricardo Cisneros have convinced me that they can cope very well with the dangers and hardships of street life. These independent and resourceful children are proud of their mixed race Guatemalan heritage. They are as comfortable among the Quiche Indians of Mayan descent as they are with the more citified Spanish people or even English speakers. They learned their English by bargaining with tourists for the souvenirs and woven goods they sell. People of Mayan ancestry are natural negotiators. Their voices erupted with excitement as they told me that we now have some Peace Corps volunteers in town. Three volunteers who had been working in Santiago Atitlan have been transferred to Jacaltenango to teach well-digging and the construction of water filters to the Quiche Indians. I look forward to meeting them.

March 26, 2009 – Today Rosita introduced me to the newcomers. Horace McCabe, Joanna Perkins, and William Finch work with the Peace Corps. McCabe likes to be called Horse because he is strong and because he doesn't like his given name. They are staying on a farm at the western end of town. Even though I have lived here long enough to call this my home, I have to admit that it feels good to have some more American acquaintances. They had been working in Santiago Atitlan clearing what's left of the mudslides from that big hurricane a while ago and rebuilding damaged houses. They didn't volunteer details about why they had been transferred here, but I'll find out as we become closer friends. Joanna and William said that they had never known a nun before, so we're facing something new on both sides.

April 6, 2009 – Carlos Benitez seems to think that I work for him now. He has three sets of adoptive parents lined up for me to meet this week. If I weren't so determined to find out more about the people who steal infants and children, I'd turn my back on him. I don't fear him, but some of those he works with, like Miguel, are definitely dangerous. I wonder whether Miguel is pushing Carlos to keep me involved, or if Carlos is acting on his own. Carlos tries to be friends, even when we aren't talking about adoptive parents. He told me about a trail he uses for hiking at the rim of the city's mesa. I may try that route soon. Looking at the mountains will be more relaxing than looking at crowded neighborhoods and dodging loose chickens while I walk. As I sat having coffee with the Peace Corps people, I heard Joanna tell William that there would be no problem if Horse spent some time with me. Something else to wonder about – what did she mean by that?

April 13, 2009 – I have learned more about the three volunteers. Joanna and William are both about twenty-six years old, much younger than I am. Horse is thirty-three years old, almost my age. The funny thing is that the two younger ones act as though they're supervising Horse. He must have done something that put him into some kind of probationary status. He's the friendliest of the three, so I'll try to learn more about his background.

April 27, 2009 – Carlos Benitez acts like a poker player. He keeps as much information hidden as possible. Yesterday I saw him talking to a government man I had seen earlier at our hospital. When I was in Carlos' office today I mentioned seeing their meeting, and he said that he was just giving directions to a stranger. This man is involved in more than one shady operation. Nevertheless, he has been true to his word and has made a steady stream of donations to our orphanage and our other charities. Perhaps he is trying to buy his way into heaven.

May 4, 2009 – Per Carlos' suggestion, I hike along the edge of the bluff most mornings. Today I was surprised to meet Horse waiting for me about a mile down the trail. He must have studied my routines. Horse said that he had been looking for an opportunity to talk with me without his keepers around. He knew that I had wondered about the arrangement, and he wanted me to see the circumstances from his point of view. He told me that in Santiago Atitlan where he had been working on rebuilding damaged homes and teaching building techniques to the Indians, he had been accused of raping a local girl who had run away from home because of the shame resulting from the assault. He swore on a pocket Bible that he had not attacked her. He said that the man who had accused him may have been the rapist and that the accusation was a way for him to shift the blame to a stranger. With the girl gone, there had been no way for him to clear his name, and he had accepted this reassignment with other volunteers monitoring him, as an alternate to being kicked out of the Corps and sent home. I like Horse, and I believe his story. I told him that he could join me on my walks whenever he wanted.

May 15, 2009 – My supervisor, Sister Marie, told me that she appreciates the donations that the order has been receiving from Carlos Benitez. She indicated that I should continue to assist him so long as I was not asked to do anything that violated my vows. I didn't tell her about my suspicions because I will have to continue to appear naïve if I want to gather any useful evidence against these people.

May 22, 2009 – Horse and I have become friends. I can talk to him about things I cannot share with the other Sisters. He said that he knew about children being stolen even when he first trained in Antigua before I came to Guatemala. He said that he had to be careful about getting involved now because of his probationary status and because the Peace Corps did not want to accuse host countries of tolerating crime and corruption. It makes me angry to realize how many governments and large institutions look the other way when it comes to crimes against children. It is likely that a lot of powerful people are being paid to remain silent.

June 10, 2009 – Something terrible has happened. On my walk yesterday between the rainstorms in the early evening, I heard a cry for help and spotted a man lying about a hundred feet down the mountain from my trail at the edge of the mesa. I climbed down to the man and found that it was Carlos Benitez. He had been shot. He told me that one of his reasons for befriending me had been to make me his insurance policy – that was the term he used. He said that he knew he was dying but that he wanted me to help him get vengeance against Miguel and his other associates. Carlos had me remove three little computer flash drives from his pocket. He said they contained details about the people who steal children. He cautioned me to hide them well and to show them to no one until I returned to the United States. At first I was afraid of the danger I would face if I accepted the drives, but I had pledged to God to do what I could to save the children. I took the data devices and said prayers for Carlos as his breaths became weaker. I wished that I was a priest who could give him the last rites sacrament, but my prayers will have to suffice. After he died, I left his body for the police to find and covered any of my tracks that I saw as I climbed back up to the bluff and the trail. The next rainstorm would wash out any remaining signs of my presence. I also knew that I would have to change my walking habits to avoid any future connection with that place. I will not share what Carlos said or the existence of the computer drives with anyone. It would be too dangerous.

June 16, 2009 – The death of Carlos has been described in the newspaper. His body was found three days after his death by someone walking a dog. The dog barked while walking on the trail and tried to take its owner down the mountainside. Sometimes animals are smarter than people. I plan to restrict myself to work at the orphanage so as not to involve any of my friends and contacts outside the order. People will assume that I am upset because someone murdered my friend Carlos. I will have to remain discrete for at least two months before I take any kind of unusual action that might draw attention. As far as the world is concerned, Carlos Benitez is dead, and his secrets died with him.

August 5, 2009 – I have started to take walks more frequently. There has been a lull in the rains. I have again expanded my world to include the street children, Rosita and Ricardo, and occasionally Horse. I will not tell him about my charge from Carlos. It would be too dangerous. Horse told me that he has dug more than seventy-five wells and has taught many other people to do the same. There is plenty of water during the rainy season from mid-May to mid-October, but for the rest of the year the country people need wells. Otherwise, they have to carry containers of water from distant lakes and rivers. I am proud of all Horse has done. He is a good and dedicated man.

September 3, 2009 – I met Horse during a walk this morning. He joined me for about half a mile. Then the rains started up again and we had to take shelter in a cave we found. It was one of the most pleasant *sojourns I have had. I know that I will have to leave this place soon. Change is coming.*

October 23, 2009 – I reread my journals this morning, and I now realize that I will soon have to stop recording my thoughts. If anyone reads my journals I could be in danger. I will start to think about a good hiding place for them. I need a place where neither the other sisters nor outsiders will be able to find them.

November 7, 2009 – That Mexican, Miguel, is back in town, and he must be suspicious of me. I've noticed two of his men taking turns following me whenever I leave the orphanage and other church facilities. Like so many farmers and other Guatemalan men, they carry machetes that could cut people to pieces. Sometimes I get nervous when I see machete carriers all around me. At one point this afternoon I decided to try to slip away from Miguel's men and visit Horse. I managed to take a series of quick turns in the town and then get on a bus without their seeing me. Imagine my disappointment after all that effort when Horse wasn't even home. Then on the way back I walked through some thick bushes and scratched my hand badly. I have made a mess of this page with my blood. At least I proved to myself that I can elude followers when it is necessary.

CHAPTER 42 – APPRECIATION

They had been taking turns reading her journals aloud. Irma had recited the final few segments.

"Wow, I have to say that I'm impressed by Kristina's courage. She learned more about those child-trafficking organizations than most of the professional investigators."

Joe said, "She got close to them because they didn't think that she was a threat. They thought they were using her, and it turned out that she was using them."

Penny restacked the journals in sequence. "What do you think of that Carlos Benitez? He couldn't use Kristina as an insurance policy in the sense of avoiding his death, but he made sure that his death would carry a big price tag for his murderers."

Joe said, "He had those flash drives in his pocket when he was shot, so he had probably hoped to meet Kristina on that trail and give them to her. Now all we have to do is locate them. I had thought these journals would be our big prize, but it appears that they're only the first step on our quest. Arthur, you've been quiet. What do you think about our information from the journals?"

"I think that she was smart to stop writing when she realized the potential danger from her written words. I also realize that because she took that step, we won't be able to find out anything about events between November of 2009 and August of 2011 when she returned to this country. That's a long time."

Irma drew a graph grid on a pad of paper. "Let's take the forensics approach. Look at what we do know rather than what we're missing. We have a series of events during the period covered by the journals, and we know that a group of people tried to kill Kristina shortly before she returned home. Maybe we can find information from other sources to help us connect the dots."

Joe said, "I can tell you that during that time gap the government of Guatemala was trying to clamp down on the trafficking of babies and children. As Kristina indicated in her journals, they instituted a law that required DNA matching between the birth mother and the child she put up for adoption. This was aimed at curtailing the use of paid impostor mothers to sign papers for stolen children and infants."

Penny said, "In addition, several European countries took the major step of banning all adoptions of Guatemalan children. The effect was a big reduction in the business of both legal and illegal adoption agencies. There were quite a few U.S. adoption agencies that shut down during that period for lack of available children."

Irma noted these items on her pad of paper. "I'll also add that the world economy was in bad shape, and that also would have caused fewer adoptions. It was not atypical for an illegal adoption to cost one hundred thousand dollars by the time all the agencies and governments were paid their fees."

Arthur nodded his affirmation. "What we're all saying is that business diminished for these child traffickers, so that they were hurting and unhappy. All it would have taken for them to send thugs to kill Kristina would have been a tiny suspicion that she had colluded with Carlos to hurt their enterprise. I'm sure her continuing relationships with the street children and with the Peace Corps workers could have caused trouble also."

Penny said, "What if they had done something to rescue children already in the system or to fight off some kidnappers? If the traffickers saw Kristina as the ringleader of efforts to thwart their acquisition of children, they would have reacted with violence."

Arthur said, "Any way you look at it, the attack on Kristina came at a time when the bad guys were frustrated enough to lash out at any target. The surprising thing is that they were willing to kill a nun, given the huge influence and power of the Catholic Church there."

Joe said, "That may have been true once, but don't forget the assassination of Archbishop Oscar Romero of San Salvador in 1980. The Catholic Church has to compete for power in Central America with other religious denominations, political movements, criminal organizations, corrupt politicians, and the military. The Church no longer has the final authority over people's lives."

Irma wrote a few additional notes. "Whatever triggered the attempted murder of Kristina, it probably occurred in the early evening on a road that passes through some woods, probably outside of town. My guess is that she was on her way to visit Horse when she was attacked."

Penny said, "You do a good Sherlock Holmes imitation. How did you get all that?"

"It's a combination of forensics and studying Arthur's techniques. The attack occurred in the early evening on a wooded road because she must have collapsed afterward in the dark woods, and that's when something bit her in the leg wound, causing the rabies infection that later killed her. It wouldn't have happened in the town because the mountaintop land there is too valuable and well-traveled for thickly wooded areas, especially when they exist on all the mountainsides outside Jacaltenango. Finally, Kristina had written in her journal that Horse lived on a farm outside the town which is likely to have been her destination. She would have been far from the Maryknoll Sisters compound."

Arthur added, "That all makes good sense, especially if, as we suspect, Horse rescued her from her attackers. Everything we've learned so far suggests that he was that person, because he left Guatemala shortly before she did. My guess is that the fight violated his probationary rules, and he was asked to leave. I have two remaining questions. Did Kristina and Horse coordinate their departures and plan to reunite after returning to the United States, and where would Kristina have hidden the flash drives with the evidence against the traffickers?"

CHAPTER 43 – SECOND TRY

Bobby sat across the interrogation table from Gus Savage. He would interview Marco Fernandez separately so that the two of them couldn't coordinate a concocted story. Gus looked relaxed, but Bobby wasn't sure what that body language implied.

"Gus, we talked briefly when we first arrested you at the church, but now we're going to discuss your situation in more detail. This conversation is being videotaped so that we'll have an accurate recording of both your actions and your statements during this session. Anything you say may be used against you in a court of law. Now, we caught you in the act of beating Pastor Blake, and we have his statements about what you were after, so would you like to explain why you went to Parkville United Methodist Church?"

"Chief, we don't have to go through all this. I admit that I was at the church and that I hit Pastor Blake. It wasn't trespassing or anything because the church is open to all; it was simple assault. I'm sorry if I hurt him."

"And who paid you to visit the church and Pastor Blake?"

"It was some guy who came into my favorite bar. I never saw him before or since. We were to get a second payment later."

"How were you supposed to get paid?"

"I was to leave anything I obtained from Blake in an envelope at the bar, and he or an associate would trade my payment for the envelope."

"What if you didn't get anything from Blake? Did that mean you wouldn't get paid?"

"We hadn't thought things through that far. We assumed we'd get something."

"I notice you included your friend Marco in answering that question. Before that you spoke only about yourself. Were you in charge, or was Marco?"

"Of course I was in charge. Marc was along for muscle."

"So, beating the pastor was part of your plan. It didn't just happen."

"We wouldn't have touched him if he had given us what we wanted."

"Why didn't he do that?"

"He said he didn't have what we wanted and didn't know where it was."

"Didn't you believe him?"

"Our contact said the pastor would have it."

"What did your contact look like?"

"He was a big white guy with slicked back dark hair."

"What kind of car did he drive?"

"Some kind of European sports car. It was red and real low to the ground. When he first showed up I said to Marc that I bet he had trouble getting in and out of it."

"Then it was a hardtop, not a convertible?"

"It was a hardtop."

"How long have you known Marco?"

"We met a couple of months ago, and we've hung out together on a regular basis."

"One more question...Did the guy who hired you wear a suit?"

"No, he wore a no-sleeve t-shirt so that everyone would see his tattoos. He had them up and down both arms."

"Do you remember what any of them looked like?"

"That's an extra question, but he had an American flag on his right shoulder and a Mexican flag on his left shoulder. He also had a dragon on each arm muscle and Harley-Davidson stuff on both lower arms. The one on his left arm had a blond girl on a Harley with her hair flowing in the wind. It was real art."

"OK, Gus, that's all I need from you right now." Bobby pushed a button, and a policeman entered to take Gus away. Bobby asked him to bring in Marco from the holding room after he returned Gus to the cell. He smiled as Gus left the interrogation room.

A few minutes later the same officer returned with Marco Fernandez. Bobby offered him either bottled water or coffee. He took the bottled water.

"Marco, what's your version of why you went to the Parkville UMC Church?"

"What do you mean by my version?"

"I've already spoken with Gus, and I want to see whether you both have the same stories."

"I don't know what Gus told you, Chief, but I don't tell stories. I tell the truth."

"Well, what's the truth?"

"We went to that church because the guy who hired us said they had something that was his."

"What kind of something?"

"A set of notebooks - he called them journals."

"So why did you attack the pastor?"

"He said he didn't have the journals and wouldn't give them to us."

"Did it ever occur to you that he might not have them or that he didn't know where they were?"

"I'm no dummy. We didn't believe him, and we were testing his statements by applying a little pressure. That's all."

"Your pressure is going to get you a stiff jail sentence, especially with your record. Tell me about the guy who hired you."

"There's not much to tell. Gus and I were in a bar, both out of work, when this amigo came in and offered us a job."

"When you say amigo, you're indicating that he is Latino?"

"He is, but he's one of those guys who pretend they've been here forever, like he's ashamed of his roots."

"Is he Mexican, Guatemalan, or what?"

"He's pretty good at acting Anglo, but he's Mexican. Those guys don't have the polish of Guatemalans."

"Describe him for me."

"He wore a t-shirt and carried himself like he was big and tough, but I'll bet I could take him in a fight. He had longish dark hair combed back and some tattoos."

"What kind of tattoos?"

"I didn't notice, except for one of a blond girl with hair blowing behind her. The guy who did her body was a real artist."

"Do you have a steady girl or a wife?"

"I was married once, but I left. There were too many women out there to stick with only one."

"Did the guy who hired you come alone, or was someone else with him?"

"There was a dame in his car. From what I could see, she wasn't anything to brag about."

"What kind of car did he drive?"

"A red one; it was some kind of showy sports car – too low for my taste. I'd rather have a truck."

"Do you know anything about him? Had you ever seen him before?"

"He didn't think I knew him, but I saw him once showing off with two flashy broads at a White Sox game. He had them in box seats down front. I saw him talking to Pedro Garcia. That's another reason for me to guess he's Mexican, because he hangs with Pedro. Anyway, they talked for a few minutes and then Pedro went back up to his own cheap seat. A little later I bought him a hot dog and a beer and asked him a few questions. Then he left the park early, like he was going someplace on orders from the show-off."

"Tell me about Garcia. Where do you know him from?"

"He's some kind of glorified errand boy. I talked with him in a bar once or twice, and he bragged that he gets to visit fancy lawyers in the Loop. He said that he likes mingling with rich people downtown but that he's still more comfortable in the suburbs. I think he told me that he lived in Aurora, but works somewhere else."

"I see you have a pretty good memory. How did you meet Gus Savage?"

"We saw each other a few times in bars, and then a while ago, I had a job where I needed an extra person. We've hung out together since then."

"So is Gus your assistant, or are you his?"

"Gus likes to think he's in charge, but he's too slow to get anywhere without my guidance. He hasn't had enough hard knocks in his life to survive a tough situation. He does make a good impression on people when I need a front man."

"I have one final question for you. Do you think you could pick the guy who hired you from a set of mug shots?"

"I can do better than that, Chief; I can tell you he calls himself John Samson. Pedro spilled that info when I was talking with him at the baseball game. I don't know his real name."

CHAPTER 44 – IRMA AND ARTHUR

Having returned to Irma's apartment after the journal-reading session, Arthur listened to his cell phone messages while Irma prepared some cut vegetables and dip for a snack.

Arthur completed the message check and then sprawled on the couch. "I'm in good shape. There were no emergency calls or angry criticisms." He watched Irma working on the nibbles. From the expression on her face and her apparent lack of concentration, he realized that something was bothering her.

"Irma, would you like to sit and talk for a while? You can finish that later. I have a feeling that something in that session with the journals triggered some disturbing thoughts for you."

She wiped her hands and joined him on the couch. "It's nothing rational. I remembered daydreaming a year or two ago about what life would be like for us after we were married. Part of that vision included me on a shopping trip at a mall with two children of elementary school age. The boy looked as though he came from some kind of a Middle Eastern background, and the girl looked oriental. I thought at the time that it was my way of realizing that by the time we got married, we would have to take the adoption route for children. Now I see that I might have been thinking about the possibility of international adoptions."

"It's intriguing that so long ago, you were pretty sure we would get married. As far as the adoptions, what would be the difference whether the children were of domestic or international origin?"

153

"The difference is that if things developed in keeping with my daydream, we would be potential candidates for illegal international adoptions."

"Most international adoptions aren't illegal and work out well. The illegal ones go to people who aren't willing to take all the time and adhere to all of the formal procedures that are normally required. We both have morals and patience so it's not likely that we would take the illegal route. Look at how much time has passed since your daydream, and we're still not married. That's patience."

It was worth the impact of the pillow on his head to see that she was smiling again.

"You love to throw things at me."

"And you love to tease me with comments that raise doubts as to whether we'll ever get married."

"I'm giving you opportunities to change your mind."

"And I'm not going to let you off the hook. Get used to it Pastor; you're spoken for, and you'll have to spend time thinking about our future together."

Arthur sat silently with a blank expression.

"What's the matter, Holy Man; did I say something that bothered you?

"No, you asked me to think, so I'm thinking."

"What do you see in your thoughts?"

"At that mall scene, I'm off getting ice cream. I bought four cones: strawberry for you, pistachio for the boy, butter pecan for the girl and banana for me."

"What else do you see?"

"I forgot to get napkins."

The second pillow hit Arthur before he could duck. It was followed closely by Irma hugging him tightly.

CHAPTER 45 – PUZZLE PIECES

The Parkville Police Department conference room had filled once again in response to last minute invitations from Chief Bobby Andrews. As the guests arrived Bobby greeted them with a big smile. He obviously expected to enjoy this meeting, which would involve the usual investigators: Arthur, Irma, Jeremy, Penny, and Joe – plus another old friend.

Bobby opened the meeting. "Thanks for coming on short notice. It's time for us to compare notes and see whether we can sketch out a diagram of the criminal activities and conspiracies that have brought us to this point. We need to figure out who our adversaries are and where we need to go to pursue them. I've invited Wally Sanborn to join us because he served in the Peace Corps and might be able to help us understand Horse McCabe better. Penny, you and Joe have given this case federal jurisdiction, but I have new information from our two local thugs who attacked Arthur. I think the meshing of their statements with the journal contents will give us our first overall picture of the foes we face."

Wally Sanborn waved to the others and chuckled. "Bobby is showing that I'm not the only person in this room with a military background. That opening summary was as good as any I've heard from a general. I predict that you'll soon say that the purpose of this meeting is to agree on the correct strategy and tactics for this campaign."

Bobby said, "Affirmative, Colonel."

Arthur rose to get coffee from the pot and spoke as he returned. "Thanks for inviting us, Bobby. I think you're taking a good approach. We've been studying the journals in order to get a better idea of what happened in Guatemala. That plus the Parkville crime scene evidence and forensics from the bodies will tell us more about Kristina and Horse. The interrogation evidence will give us some leads to the local end of the child-trafficking operation. We need to understand how the various parts work together in order to track the murderer and shut down the operation. What do you think, Penny? Can we have an interagency partnership going forward?"

"We always do, in one form or another. I doubt that the U.S. part of their operation is based in Parkville, but it's somewhere not too far from here. I think we should start by letting Bobby present what he has learned from his prisoners."

Bobby had been chewing on a toothpick while the others spoke. He set it aside and walked over to the whiteboard. With a black marker he wrote the names: Marco Fernandez and Gus Savage.

"These are our two prisoners. Gus is the tall one, and Marco is the stocky muscular one. The most interesting thing about them is that each thinks he is the smarter one of the duo. I've used that fact to let each compete to give me more information than the other. Gus is much better on descriptions and details, but Marco knows more about the people who are behind them."

Joe said, "So they do know the person who hired them and the organization behind him."

Bobby shook his head. "No, they don't really have that information, but between them they gave me enough details of his description, characteristics, and associates for us to work it out. The man who hired them calls himself John Samson. I've done some police database research and determined that his real name is Juan Samosa. He's a Mexican national who has been here legally for about seven years. He became a citizen four months ago. He's been involved in some shady operations, but hasn't been arrested for anything. Samson's a biker with a Harley and he also drives a red Ferrari 458. He likes speed on the road and surrounds himself with women. He's big on tattoos, and likes to show off his body art, including Mexican and American flags plus Harley-Davidson symbols and motorcycles.

Joe said, "We know some biker groups are involved in drug distribution, but do we extrapolate from this individual to suggest they're involved in baby and child-trafficking too?"

Penny shook her head. "Negative, Joe. We've been bitten before by jumping to conclusions without enough evidence. We don't even know how deeply involved this one individual is. Bobby, do you know where this guy hangs out and who his associates are?"

"I have only one known associate except for our two strong-arm men. That would be Pedro Garcia. He runs errands for John Samson and lives in Aurora. Marco gave me the impression that Pedro is expected to be on call at any time. He also said that Pedro told him he sometimes goes to fancy lawyers' offices in Chicago."

Irma said, "That would certainly fit with illegal adoptions. They would take care of the paperwork and meet with the clients to give the transactions an aura of legitimacy."

Joe agreed. "I think our next step should be to talk with Mr. Garcia. The problem is that it will be difficult to pull him in for an interview without tipping off John Samson and his buddies that we're investigating them."

Wally Sanborn cleared his throat. "I think it would be premature to make official contact with Pedro Garcia. I have two alternate suggestions. We could either make a deal with Marco Fernandez and let him contact his friend Pedro with one of us along to control the situation, or I could make the contact along with a couple of my Mexican background Army friends."

Arthur said, "If Marco were to cooperate and go with Joe Gonzalez to talk with Pedro while we held Gus Savage in jail, I might be persuaded to drop the charges against my assailants if they got some useful information out of Pedro."

Penny said, "We can't put those two back on the street until we find the murderers and baby stealers. They'd tell everyone about the investigation."

Arthur said, "Don't worry about that, Penny. I didn't say when I would drop the charges. I'm sure Bobby can hold them for a while. The machinery of the legal system meshes slowly. There are many perfectly legal reasons to delay bringing them to trial, and I won't mention the possible dropping of charges until the last minute. Anyway, Marco will know that his chance to go free depends on his getting something useful out of Pedro. It also depends on whether Joe Gonzalez can pass as Marco's illegal immigrant friend."

CHAPTER 46 – CONTACTS

At the conclusion of the conference, they decided that Joe Gonzalez, assuming the role of Jose Lopez, would accompany the prisoner, Marco Fernandez, to meet the gang's messenger. Penny Gonzalez would pretend to be the younger wife of Wally Sanborn, and as soon as they learned the identities of the lawyers the messenger visited, they would contact them to ask about adopting a child through their system. In the meantime, Arthur and Irma would contact the Guatemalan Consulate-General in Chicago, posing as a couple wishing to adopt a child, in order to learn whether any official would refer them to a faster, less traditional, procedure for adoptions. Joe had suggested this last approach to see whether a government official might be feeding customers to the traffickers. Jeremy's responsibility would be to stay at the church, where he would be on guard against another visit from people seeking Kristina's journals, while being the central contact for information coming in from the three field teams. As soon as Bobby returned from his scheduled visit to the apnea specialist, he and Sergeant Al Gomez would remain on call at the Police Station in case Jeremy needed assistance.

It all represented a multi-pronged effort to engage the American end of the child-trafficking pipeline. Hopefully they would have at least some success.

CHAPTER 47 – A NEW APPROACH

Renee and Bobby entered Dr. Kerski's office sharing a blend of optimism and trepidation. They knew that Kerski's promised new technique might be their last hope for keeping Thelma Lou's apnea from being a handicap to her normal growth schedule. They sat down in the waiting room after checking in with the receptionist. Why was it that so many waiting rooms tended to have uncomfortable furniture with shiny steel tubing structural frames? Renee wondered whether the furniture had ever been new, or if it had been passed from one doctor to another over the course of many years. After exactly thirteen minutes a nurse appeared through an inconspicuous door Renee hadn't noticed. He ushered them into a tiny examination room at the end of a serpentine hallway. Six minutes later the door to the small cubicle opened, and the unexpectedly youthful Dr. Kerski bounded into their lives. He reminded Renee of the baby's Tigger stuffed animal toy, but with black-rimmed round-lens glasses.

"Hello, I'm Bob Kerski. I hope I didn't keep you waiting too long. This must be Thelma Lou. She is indeed a beautiful baby." He extended both arms, and Renee gently transferred her daughter to him.

He continued. "She looks well-developed, and I'm sure she'll progress well once we get rid of her Apnea of Prematurity. You two must be giving her very good care at home."

Renee said, "I like your positive outlook, Doctor, but some of our local medical people didn't have much success with their efforts."

"That's understandable Mrs. Andrews. May I call you Renee? Good, I like to keep things informal. They

160

probably restricted their therapies to traditional techniques, both because they are conservative and because they have not seen very many of these cases."

Bobby said, "Doctor, when we spoke on the phone, I took you to be quite a bit older than your appearance suggests, and yet you're implying that you've handled large numbers of infants with Thelma Lou's problem. How did you squeeze all of that experience into a relatively short medical career?"

"I understand your skepticism, Bobby. The fact is that I took part in a five year study of such infants from 1999 to 2004. It was what we call a double-blind study where neither the medical personnel nor the parents of the infants knew which babies were being given the medication that was under study and which ones were being given a placebo, which means a harmless substitute."

"Was this study successful?"

"It was, Renee. We were pleased with the initial results, and we continued to follow-up on the condition of the children in this study until they were five years old."

Bobby asked, "What was the nature of the medication, and what were the adverse side effects?"

"You did say that you're a police officer, and your line of questioning confirms that. I'm not going to hide anything from you. Without getting technical as to precisely how we did it, we confirmed that repeated administrations of caffeine can be valuable to the treatment of Apnea of Prematurity. We continued to study the subjects until they were five years old in order to determine whether they developed a greater-than-usual number of other abnormal conditions after having had the initial therapy for the apnea. We also wanted to determine whether the apnea would reappear with the passage of time. The results showed that there was not a significant difference in death or disability during the first five years between the two groups of children."

Renee said, "Pardon me, but what are you saying about death and disability?"

Bobby put his arm around his wife to show his support as they stood facing the doctor.

"I didn't mean to upset you. Sometimes I speak in clinical terms when I should phrase things more carefully for non-medical people. All I meant to indicate is that there always will be some probability of other conditions developing beyond the initial apnea, simply because the child was born prematurely and had a low birth weight. There is absolutely no suggestion that anything will happen. It's just cautious doctor-talk."

Bobby asked, "Is this caffeine treatment considered experimental? How safe is it?"

"We're past the experimental stage. No less a medical authority than *The New York Times* in their Health Guide section lists the administration of a caffeine preparation to babies like yours as a standard treatment."

Renee said, "If you're optimistic, Doctor, so are we. You can't blame us for being nervous and tense about our baby's health."

"Your comments and actions simply confirm that you're good parents. I'll have some minor paperwork for you, and then we'll get you set up for the therapy."

CHAPTER 48 – AMIGOS

Marco Fernandez knew he had an important decision to make. Chief Andrews had promised him better treatment in the courts if he cooperated with the investigation of John Samson and his associates. Marco would have to pretend that he was friends with an investigator known as Jose Lopez and help Lopez make some contacts. It would be easy enough to do, and he didn't owe anything to Samson that would push him to rat out this Lopez guy. The Chief had said that if Marco failed to cooperate they would add extra charges involving conspiracy against him and Gus Savage. Marco really did like Gus, despite their arguments, so he decided to play this one straight.

Jose Lopez turned out to be someone he could relate to. He was a little older than Marco had expected, but he spoke well in both English and Spanish. Lopez was an educated guy, but Marco suspected that he would act more like a peasant when they met up with Pedro Garcia.

They started the effort over a cup of coffee in a local breakfast place. Lopez returned Marco's cell phone and suggested that he use it to call some mutual friends asking for Pedro's phone number. Marco had no luck on his first four calls, but by the time they were on their second round of coffee refills, he had found a girl who had once dated Pedro and had his number. She said she would trade it for a date with him, and Marco agreed. He took down the number, but told Estella that their evening together would have to wait for a month or so. In this Marco was telling the truth as he saw it, but Estella's shouts over the telephone emphasized the fact that she didn't believe him. Marco protested that they would indeed get together, and then clicked off the line.

Lopez looked amused. "Judging from that shrieking I could have heard across the room, that lady really wants you."

"She's not bad to look at, and sometimes she's funny, but she's been bouncing from one guy to another looking for someone to marry her. That makes guys nervous. I guess her mother's telling her that if she gets any older she won't land a husband."

"Once things are straightened out will you spend time with her?"

"Sure, I'll give it a shot, but I'm not sure how long I could take her trying to force the situation. If she'd just relax and cool it, she could be a good friend. Anyway, we both know it will be a while before I see her, so maybe she'll have calmed down by then."

"Now that you have the number, give Pedro Garcia a call, and tell him that you'll buy him a couple of beers if he'll give a friend some advice."

"What's your story in case he asks, not that I think he's smart enough to think that far ahead?"

"Tell him that I'm recently arrived without papers and that I'm looking to work for a group that has room for someone who follows orders and wants to stay away from government people."

"A huge number of people fit that description. What is there about you that would make him interested?"

"I'm good in either Spanish or English, and I know how to tune engines for best performance."

"That will attract Samson's attention, but do you really have that skill?"

"I'm a little rusty at it, but when I was younger I worked in the pit crew of a racing team. It'll come back to me."

"If that's the case, you do have a chance of getting accepted by Samson. Whether you get any further is another question, but you said I've done my job as soon as I get you some time with Pedro – right?"

"You get some good comments in your case file as soon as I get that first meeting. Then you'll have to sit in jail like Gus for a while, but you'll be on your way to easier treatment."

"How does Gus fit in?"

"It's a package deal. Gus gets the same points that you get, and I'll even be sure to let him know that you helped him."

"That being the case, I'm calling Pedro right now. It's time for Gus to realize that he needs to follow my lead if he wants to come out of this smelling like a rose."

CHAPTER 49 – CONSULATE

Irma was obviously enjoying the new wedding band alongside her engagement ring. She fingered Arthur's matching ring as she held hands with him and walked across the Michigan Avenue Bridge in Chicago. "I know we're not over the marital threshold yet, but adding these rings makes me feel awfully close to it."

"Just remember, we're on an investigative assignment, and these are props to make our contacts believe we're married. Don't overact."

"Who has to act? I've wanted to feel this way for a long time. When we get there, I'll even be the dutiful wife and let you do most of the talking."

They entered the Michigan Avenue office building and took the elevator up to the Guatemalan Consulate-General. A receptionist with long dark hair greeted them.

"Welcome to you both. Are you looking for information about Guatemala?"

Arthur approached her desk trying to look as friendly and relaxed as possible. "We wanted to inquire about the procedures for adopting a child from Guatemala."

The woman sensed their sincerity. "I'm afraid that you're about four years too late. In the past there were thousands of adoptions of Guatemalan children by Americans, but there were also many documented cases of children having been stolen from their parents or kidnapped into the illegal adoption pipeline. Because of this, our government is not allowing any more international adoptions. You will have to look for American children or children from another country. The United Nations is trying to close off all international adoptions, but I personally don't think that is the best solution." She saw shock and disappointment on the faces of her visitors.

Irma said, "You're saying that nobody in another country can adopt a Guatemalan child now?"

"That's correct. Our government has instituted so many controls and tests over the process that it is impossible. Women who want to give up children for adoption have to be DNA tested to prove they are the birth mothers. All paperwork at every stage of the process has to match precisely, or it is rejected. There are even about nine hundred cases that were in process before these controls were instituted, at least four years ago, that have not yet been allowed by the authorities. For the foreseeable future this will not change, although some preliminary low-level discussions have taken place with your State Department. I don't expect much to come from those meetings. They will not succeed in changing our governments resolve to prevent the continuation of past adoption abuses."

Arthur grasped Irma's hand and squeezed it so that she would know to follow his lead. He thanked the receptionist and added a few words about planning a vacation in Guatemala soon. Then he picked up a few brochures from the display rack, and they headed for the exit.

When they were back on the sidewalk, he turned to Irma. "We've been on the wrong track, and we wouldn't have realized it for a while if we hadn't come here."

"What do you mean?"

"The people behind this aren't involved in large-scale child-trafficking. They couldn't get away with it any more, at least not with Guatemalan kids."

"But what about the missing children mentioned in the journals?"

"I'm sure there are still a few illegal adoptions, or maybe the children have been taken for another purpose. Without the camouflage of thousands of legal adoptions to cover their activities, these people would be easy to spot if they trafficked in large numbers of children. Creating believable paperwork when the adoption doors are closed would also be a big problem for them. There has to be something else going on." Arthur looked both energized and puzzled.

"We'd better see what Joe found out from his expedition with that prisoner, Marco. I hope that guy turned out to be trustworthy."

"I think he'll follow the script, Irma, because it's in his own self-interest. Anyway, Joe assigned a federal agent to follow them, as a security measure."

"Arthur, do you mind if I wear my prop wedding ring until we get back to Parkville? It does feel special."

"Feel free, but the permanent one will be a lot better quality."

"Now that's a very positive statement about wedding plans, and you made it without my prodding or hinting."

"I'll go along with your wedding plans while we try to figure out the plans of this international outfit. They're up to something that's not obvious."

CHAPTER 50 – JOSE LOPEZ

In his guise as Jose Lopez, Joe Gonzalez had added a pronounced limp by wearing special shoes that effectively made his right leg longer than his left. The resulting appearance of lameness looked natural and consistent. Together with Marco Fernandez he had driven to Aurora where they would meet with Pedro Garcia at the Mesquite Tavern and Grill. The tavern neighborhood was new to both Jose and Marco, so they ended up taking several incorrect turns before they found the place. At two o'clock in the afternoon the bar would be private enough for talking, the lunch crowd having departed, and laborers still occupied at their worksites. Jose pulled the nondescript borrowed car into the small parking lot and scanned the surrounding buildings for any obvious threats. Having detected none, he gestured to Marco to lead the way inside.

Jose blinked his eyelids rapidly multiple times to help his eyes adapt from the outside brightness to the minimal lighting within the black-walled tavern. It was always easier to keep places dark rather than clean. The musty odor reminded him of a sewer tunnel he'd once been forced to explore while searching for a kidnapped child. He saw Marco wave to a slight man with close-cropped black hair, owl-like round glasses, and a mustache. The haircut shouted military background. Jose added that information to his mental notes as he trailed behind Marco toward the booth. Following a brief introduction and curt handshake, he slid down into the seat next to Marco.

Pedro Garcia was the first to speak. "So you're working for Samson now too. I heard you weren't

169

successful on your first assignment. How do you think he'll react to that?"

Marco said, "It had crossed my mind, but I don't really care. I'm not Samson's boy like you are. I'm independent. If it means I don't get my second half of the payment, it won't bother me. I can always scare some illegal Mexican into paying me protection money."

"Hey, let's not talk with chips on our shoulders. We each have our own ways of getting income. I'm fine with that. You called for this meeting, and here I am. What do you need? Is it something to do with Lopez, here?"

Marco nodded to Jose Lopez, indicating that he should speak for himself.

Jose said, "I need a little favor. I have skills that lots of people need, but Marco said you can connect me with someone who won't care that I don't have papers."

Marco nodded to Pedro in confirmation of his friends words.

Pedro said, "I have connections, and many of them are not too particular, but what are your skills? It will cost you something for an introduction. The more you can pay, the better the opportunity I get for you. Why should someone hire you?"

Jose said, "I fix things. I can do everything from making old lawn mowers work to tuning engines on race cars. I worked on cars in La Carrera Panamericana for the past three years. I had to keep them going through two thousand miles of roads from hell. Just figuring out what spare parts would be needed was something that made me special. A lot of cars with fancy mechanic teams couldn't do what I did, because I knew the country and I knew what parts would break. You can be a great mechanic, but if you don't have any parts, you're worthless."

Marco could see that Pedro was impressed. For that matter, Jose had surprised the hell out of him. He knew they wouldn't have given him an undercover partner who was clueless, but if Jose really had these skills he was valuable. If Pedro couldn't connect him with racing people, he could. Anyway, Jose wanted an intro to particular people. Still...

"Well, Pedro, did I bring you a guy with potential or not? Do you think you'll have something for Jose?"

"It's a possibility. What do you know about motorcycles?"

Jose said, "What don't I know about them? You give me something with an engine on it, and I'll make it do tricks for you."

"Sounds good, but for that kind of contact I'll need five hundred dollars up front. When can you get me the money?"

"I'd give it to you today, but I don't think you want to be seen with that much cash in a dive like this. We'll meet you two blocks down the street after we leave here. I feel better carrying cash with Marco riding shotgun than I would if I had to come with it alone. Beside, he's my witness in case you can't keep your end of the deal."

Pedro said, "Don't worry, I know several people who might want to pay for your skills. If you play your cards right, they might even compete for you. Write your cell phone number on the back of this card, and then we'll take that two-block ride. My wife's been after me to buy her some new clothes."

CHAPTER 51 – CALL-BACK

Back at home later that afternoon, Joe Gonzalez was in the midst of regaling Penny with his story of having been Jose Lopez at the tavern when his undercover-use cell phone rang. He glanced at the screen and held up a cautioning hand to request silence as he answered it.

"Jose Lopez here."

"Greetings, Jose; this is John Samson calling. Pedro Garcia told me that you're a pretty good engine technician. Is that right?"

"I can keep a beat-up car running like new, and I can make a new car run like next year's model. What do you need done?"

"I need someone to take care of a couple of sports cars from time to time plus some motorcycles that get beat up on back roads. Would you be interested?"

"Sure, I'm looking for work. The only problem is that I need something that's a steady diet. I could look at your cars and bikes as a sideline when you need someone, but I have to find something that I can live on and that will keep me busy."

"That's a good attitude, Jose. I didn't give you the whole picture. I'm looking for someone who can keep the engines tuned and who can make some custom equipment for me. It would be a full time job, or as many hours as you felt would be enough. I know you need something steady. It's the kind of job that could grow as we got to know you."

"You don't know me at all right now. Either you're desperate for someone, or Pedro gave me a glowing recommendation. Where would I be working, and what would this job pay?"

"You'd have to go different places now and then, but your primary worksites would be in Rochelle and Wheeling."

"I know where Rochelle is, but is Wheeling in Illinois too?"

"Wheeling's closer to Lake Michigan, more convenient to the Chicago area. We use Rochelle for inland business."

"Who's the 'we' you mentioned, and what's the business?"

"Look, Jose, we'll get to know each other more as time passes. Do you want the job or not?"

"You haven't told me how much it pays."

"I'll give you two thousand dollars to cover the first month. Then we'll see what you can do and how much you're worth to us. Don't worry, I'm pretty generous to people who produce for me. Just ask Pedro Garcia. He's very happy with his pay."

"Fine, John, count me in, at least for a while. Where and when do I go to work?"

"Meet me at nine o'clock tomorrow morning in the Rochelle McDonald's, and I'll fill you in on things. I'll be driving a red Ferrari 458. Have you worked on a car like that?"

"I haven't, but I can."

"Good enough; I'll see you in the morning. Bring your tools so that I can see what you have." Samson disconnected.

Joe repocketed his phone and turned to Penny. "It's one of those good news and bad news things."

"What do you mean?"

"The good news is that I've made the connection. The bad news is that I need to get some well-used mechanic's tools in a hurry and that I may be undercover on this case for a lot more of my time than I expected."

"Just be careful. Can you handle the engine work you'll be facing?"

"I should be OK. Those years before we met when I worked at the stock car races should finally pay off." Joe got up and prepared to leave.

Penny said, "I can see your getting antsy. Where are you off to?"

"I'm going to see if I can schedule some time with Chet Quinto at the Police Garage for a refresher engine course. I'll also inform him that the government is about to buy him a new set of mechanic's tools in exchange for his old set. I hope he doesn't have any police decals on them."

CHAPTER 52 – BRAINSTORMING

After having received phone calls from Arthur, a new group assembled for discussions in his church office. Of those he had called, only Chief Bobby Andrews had declined. Joining Arthur around the conference table were Irma, Penny Gonzalez, Jeremy Hadley, and Wally Sanborn. Joining them by speakerphone were Steve DuBois from Penny and Joe's agency and Professor Edward Middlemiss from the Political Science Department at the University of Wisconsin at Platteville. After those assembled in the office had claimed their coffees and other drinks and goodies from the side table, Arthur initiated the session.

"Thank you all for attending on relatively short notice, especially our remote colleagues, Steve and Edward. May I assume that the speakerphone is working properly?"

"This is Steve, and I hear you loud and clear."

"Edward here...I can hear everything as well."

Arthur said, "Good. This is essentially a new gathering of the brainstorming team that worked so well on an earlier case. We've added Jeremy Hadley and Penny Gonzalez for some fresh viewpoints. Bobby Andrews had a prior commitment, and Joe Gonzalez is on assignment. Everyone in this group has been involved in our present case to some extent except for Edward. Jeremy, did you brief your Professor?"

"I did, Pastor, and I hope his Political Science specialty will help us determine what the criminals are doing."

Arthur said, "Thanks, Jeremy. Here's the problem. Following the death of Kristina Karga and the murder of her supposed brother Ted, who turned out to actually have been Horace 'Horse' McCabe, we found the hiding place for Kristina's journals from her years spent as a Maryknoll Sister in Guatemala. These journals had been sought by Horse when he appeared as Ted in our church. They had also been the target of an attack on me in this office by a pair of thugs hired by a criminal group. Both of these attempts to get the journals indicated that they were valuable because of information they contained. We reviewed the contents of the three notebooks, and we concluded that we were dealing with an international illegal adoption ring operating in Guatemala and the United States. To follow up on this theory, Irma and I posed as a couple wanting to adopt a child, and we contacted the Guatemalan Consulate to learn the legal adoption procedures and also to see whether they would hand us off to an outside group that could shortcut the process illegally."

Irma said, "It felt very natural, playing the couple looking to adopt. We'll have to do it again sometime." She winked at Arthur, who reddened slightly.

Penny said, "For the benefit of those joining us by telephone, Pastor Blake just blushed."

Arthur continued without admitting his discomfort. "The important point is that we learned at the Consulate that adoptions from Guatemala have been completely shut down by rules implemented following earlier illegal adoption and child-trafficking scandals. Any illegal trafficking continuing from Guatemala would have to be very limited. That tells me that this criminal outfit has to be involved in something else, and it would have to be something significant for them to have murdered Horse and attacked me at the church in the course of their search for the journals."

"Arthur?" The voice came from the speaker.

"Yes, Edward."

"I don't think you can definitely link those two crimes as you did in your last statement. The thugs who roughed you up wanted the journals, but we have no evidence to prove that Horse was murdered by someone who wanted them. He may have been murdered for another reason, or even by someone not affiliated with this criminal group."

"You're right, Edward; we were taking the easy way out by linking the two events. We'll have to keep that possibility of independent events and perpetrators in mind as we proceed. That comment is proof of the value of this brainstorming process. We get fresh ways of thinking. Who else wants to contribute something? Penny, did you see anything else of value to criminals in those journals as we read them?"

"The obvious answer to that is the three computer flash drives that Carlos Benitez gave to Kristina as he was dying from gunshot wounds. However, if Kristina stayed true to her words in the journal and didn't tell anyone that she had them, these people might have been after her for something else that they expected to be in those notebooks. That might have been information about the other nuns, or the priests, or about their projects. They could also have been after her for documenting the names and locations of people involved in illegal adoptions."

Irma asked, "Why would Horse have been after the journals, Penny? As far as we know, he wasn't part of anything criminal."

"That's a little harder to figure out. He came to the church pretending to be Kristina's nonexistent brother. During the course of his address to the congregation he said that he hadn't known where she was or what happened to her. That part may have been true. Perhaps Kristina didn't trust Horse, even though she married him. She may have even married

177

him just to confuse her pursuers or to turn him into a family man rather than the accused rapist he had been before. It's also possible that she didn't want to give him any information that would have endangered him. However you look at their relationship, I don't think he knew about the flash drives. My guess is that he realized that Kristina had been keeping her background and activities hidden from him, and he saw the finding of those journals as his last chance to learn her secrets."

Arthur asked, "Why was Horse murdered? Was it because he declared that he was looking for the journals? Edward, your professorial logic suggested that the two crimes might not be connected. Would you like to speculate as to why Horse was murdered?"

"Gladly, Arthur...I'll start by suggesting that the two crimes might be connected but not driven by the same motivation. I think it would be pushing the coincidence button to say that separate aggressors chose the same time to murder Horse and attack Arthur without any connection. It does seem reasonable to me to consider the possibility that the thugs who came after Arthur for the journals did so because of information the murderer, who was at church when Horse spoke, passed to their employers. That would imply a connection, but Horse may have been killed because of something in the past between him and the murderer, that had nothing to do with the journals."

Wally said, "I follow your logic Edward, and it makes sense to me. Why was the murderer at church that morning, and why did he leave when Horse left rather than staying for the rest of the service?"

Irma nodded her head and wrote something on her yellow pad. "It's not often that you get academics and military men to agree, but I like your logic. If the murderer had been after the journals, wouldn't he have stayed until the end of the service? Somebody in the congregation might have volunteered a clue regarding their location during the remainder of the service after Horse left. I think the murderer followed Horse from the church because he had followed him to the church in the first place. The murderer was looking for Horse, not the journals, but he may have told those who wanted the journals that Horse had asked that they be given to Pastor Blake."

Steve DuBois' voice came out of the speaker. "Maybe the killer was after Horse for something that happened in Guatemala. That would give us the clue that he had also been there."

Edward said, "Watch that logic again Steve, the killer could have been someone from here who was mad because of something Horse did in Guatemala."

Steve said, "Fair enough, but there might be a connection to something that happened while Horse was in the Peace Corps."

Penny said, "If we can get back to those journals again, I would like to raise the point that the last entry in journal number three was written in November of 2009. Kristina arrived back in the United States in August of 2011. She was attacked in Guatemala and rescued by Horse shortly before she returned. Given that long time interval, there may be a fourth journal, and it may include information regarding the location of those flash drives that Carlos gave Kristina."

Irma said, "That's a possibility, but not very probable because Kristina wrote at the end of the third journal that she was afraid to write any more of her thoughts on paper. She was afraid that the people who killed Carlos Benitez would be after her next. You remember her comment, don't you, Arthur?"

"I do, and I agree with your thinking, but I'll have to ask why that group of men attacked her.

Guatemala is a primarily Catholic country, and most men would never mistreat a nun for fear of losing their chance at salvation. Wally, you've been there. What do you think?"

"It only makes sense if the gang suspected that Carlos had given her damning evidence before he died. If she had kept everything to herself, they may have decided to get rid of everyone who had anything to do with Carlos. Do you know about any other attacks on people who had known Carlos?"

Penny said, "We don't, but we can add that to the list of things to check down there. There is another possibility. The criminals may have paid off a priest to reveal what he heard in confession. There aren't many priests who would violate their vows like that, but if it happened, it probably would have been because they were blackmailing him due to something he had done."

Irma said, "You may be right, and it's worth investigating, but I'll stick with my view that Kristina planned to tell no one, not even her priest."

Arthur said, "Let's move on. We're making good progress. Wherever those three flash drives are, what do you think might be on them, and why are there three of them? Do you think there's a huge amount of data on a single subject that fills three drives, or do you think they cover three different databases? Steve, you do a lot of computer work in your investigations. Why don't you take this one?"

"Thanks, Arthur. My guess would be that they have data on at least three subjects unless they contain a huge number of photographs. Pictures are the only thing that would take up enough space to fill three drives. On the other hand, each drive might easily contain data on several different activities. Per the quotation you cited from the journal, it is likely that one file involves the details of illegal adoptions he

180

worked on. Carlos could have included many other files on three drives."

Irma said, "Your logic suggests that the gang would have been involved in many crimes if Carlos Benitez required three flash drives in his quest to get even with them."

Arthur said, "I'll speculate that the drives included past info including names and addresses for illegal adoptions, personnel rosters with locations for their organization, financial data with bank accounts, and legal connections for the U.S. end of the operation. I don't think that Carlos was high enough in the organization to know much about their future plans."

Jeremy had been writing feverishly on his yellow pad. "How do we find out what they're up to now?"

Arthur said, "That's why Joe Gonzalez isn't here. He's working undercover with the gang to see if we can get some direct evidence on their activities. This has been a valuable session, but the key to our success may be what we learn from Joe's efforts. I think you've all highlighted important avenues to explore, but evidence from field observations trumps speculation every time."

CHAPTER 53 – UNDERCOVER

Joe Gonzalez felt the pressure of maintaining his assumed Jose Lopez identity as he entered the McDonald's restaurant. Chet Quinto had been happy to exchange his old tools for the promise of new ones, and Chet's old set looked appropriate in the trunk of Jose's old but well-tuned car. John Samson had said he would be sitting at the closest table to the Men's Room, and Jose discovered a man who matched the description he had received from Marco in that spot. As he approached, the man extended his hand toward him.

"You must be Jose. Welcome, I'm John, and I'm looking forward to having you work with us."

"Thanks, John. I brought my tools. Do you want to eat something here, or are you ready to go somewhere else?"

"Unless you're hungry, we'll go. I have some errands to do later, and I'd like to get you introduced and settled soon."

"That's fine with me."

Jose followed John's car to a corrugated metal building set back from Flagg Road in a field. It looked like a farm outbuilding, and it was masked from the road by growing corn that appeared to fill the space between the building and the road, but which was actually a band only fifteen feet deep. Two smaller concrete block buildings were set a little farther back from Flagg Road, framed by two ancient-looking apple trees. Jose noticed several motorcycles in various states of disrepair behind the metal building. He got out of his car and walked to join John at the corrugated building. They entered through a small door to the right of a large sliding door. Inside, Jose saw four modern workbenches, a chain-link security room, and a hydraulic car lift mounted on a well-maintained concrete slab floor.

"John, this is a much better work area than I expected based on the outside appearance of the building. Is it weatherproof? That sliding door would leak a lot of cold air in the winter."

"We have overhead forced air heaters plus a second overhead garage door that we keep open during the warmer months. It's hidden by the closed sliding door that is only there to make the building look shabby."

"Where do I work, and what do you want me to do?"

"You'll be in charge of this building and will work here except when I have another job for you elsewhere. Leave two of the workbenches clear for other people who will be coming and going. The storage room belongs to someone else. You'll learn about that later. At times people will be making deliveries that will go into the storeroom, and at other times people will come in to have their cars or motorcycles fixed or to exchange vehicles. We have a bunch of cars and bikes, and we switch around."

"I saw some motorcycle pieces and wrecks out back. Do you want me to rebuild them and get at least a couple of bikes working from that pile?"

"Sure, do that in your spare time. I have a feeling that you won't be bored. I'll also ask you to make a few deliveries now and then. There's a gas pump out back, so you won't have to worry about using up all of your own fuel. That's about it; any questions?"

"For starters, do I have to be here full time and punch a clock, and do I work for anyone else beside you?"

"Good, you're thinking. Unless I have a specific job for you, all you have to do is to be sure this place

183

is neat and that the vehicles in it and out back are fueled and ready for use. I'll give you most of your instructions, but as time passes, I'll introduce you to others. When you meet them, I'll tell you how you'll interact with them. We have loose and easy-going relationships unless we get into a tight-schedule situation."

"What about Pedro Garcia? Will I be working with him in any way?"

"Pedro's like a personal assistant to me, but he never gets out here. He doesn't even know about this place. You'll see him once in a while, but only in passing."

"Are you saying that this place is a secret? Am I supposed to avoid talking about it?"

"That's good thinking, Jose. Let's just say that it's like that government need-to-know business. I'll tell you when someone is supposed to show up. If people come without advance notice, call me before letting them in."

"Are there identification cards or passwords or anything?"

"We haven't had to do that yet, but we may add something of that sort in the future. That's it for now. Here's the two thousand dollars I promised for the first month." John handed him a fat envelope. "I hope you don't mind cash; it avoids paperwork. I had the bank give it to me in twenties so that you could get change anywhere."

"Thanks, John, I appreciate it."

"I'll be back out here in three days. That should give you enough time to get your gear installed and to check a few of our vehicles. The next time we talk, I'll give you your first assignment."

CHAPTER 54 – THELMA LOU

Bobby and Renee returned to Dr. Kerski's waiting room with Thelma Lou, but this time they felt relaxed enough to enjoy watching the dozen or so fish in the aquarium while they waited. Bobby reflected that studies must have indicated that aquariums relax patients, because so many doctors' offices had them. This time Renee watched for the opening of the hidden door she had previously overlooked. She was rewarded after only eight minutes when the panel pivoted open to reveal the same nurse who had guided them through the examining room labyrinth on their previous visit. This time he escorted them to a slightly larger consulting room than before.

"Dr. Kerski will be with you in just a few minutes."

Bobby checked out the medical wall posters while Renee sat down with the baby. "Renee, in all the visits you've made to doctors, has any one of them used one of their standard anatomical posters to explain anything?"

"Now that you mention it, I don't think so."

"I think their only purpose is to give patients something to study while they wait. I'll bet the doctors wouldn't even notice if somebody took them down."

"Interesting idea, Bobby, but don't do it. We want a good relationship with Dr. Kerski."

As if on cue, they heard three taps on the door, and Dr. Kerski bounded in.

"Hello, you three. How's Thelma Lou today? Have you seen obvious progress? I predict you have; how about that?"

Renee stood up with the baby. "Thelma Lee hasn't had an apnea episode in two days, at least not one that we've observed. Does that mean she's cured?"

"Put her on the examination table here, and I'll listen to her heart and breathing...That's good; you can just rest your hand on her leg to be sure she doesn't move around too much."

Dr. Kerski listened to the baby's heart and lungs with his stethoscope and then probed gently at several points with his fingers.

"She's a very good patient and is responding well to the caffeine therapy. I don't want to stop it suddenly, so we'll taper it off over the next two weeks. If during that period she has no more episodes, we'll call her cured and just watch her for future developments. That would require one more visit and test here in six months, and then we'll have your local doctor continue to monitor her. If anything unusual occurs in the future, you're always welcome to come back or have your doctor consult with me."

Bobby said, "You're convinced the Apnea of Prematurity is cured?"

"If it isn't, it soon will be. She has made great progress, and you should expect a normal growth pattern in the future. She's had a slow start because of her prematurity and this condition, but I think you'll find that she'll tend to catch up with other children of her age. Sorry, Thelma Lou, I was talking about you when I should have been talking to you. You're going to be just fine, and probably the prettiest girl in your class at school."

Renee reached out and gave Dr. Kerski a one-armed hug. "Thank you, Doctor; you've brightened our outlook."

As they approached their car, Bobby hugged both Renee and the baby. "This calls for ice cream and some spirited duets as we drive home."

CHAPTER 55 – PENNY AND WALLY

Penny Gonzalez answered her telephone to find Wally Sanborn on the line. "What's up, Wally? Is it something new about the case?"

"Not exactly, Penny; I'd just like to discuss ways for me to get more involved in the investigation. I thought I had a role to play, escorting you as we tried to initiate an illegal international adoption, but now that we've concluded that this gang has phased into other schemes, I'm on the sidelines. I need a new assignment in order to feel that I'm part of the group."

"At this point, I'm also an observer and coordinator. You're a military man. Just think of both of us as being the fresh troops that are held in reserve for the final assault. Backup troops are an important ingredient for achieving a final victory. Stand by, and keep thinking about different aspects of the case. I'm sure we'll reach a point where we'll both make significant contributions."

"Thanks for the pep talk, Penny. I had hoped you'd have an immediate task for me, but I can live with the backup status. Please keep me posted. Bye for now."

Penny disconnected and set down the phone. She smiled as she realized that she had talked to Wally about a future active role with the idea of placating him, but her intuition convinced her that it would actually happen.

CHAPTER 56 – EVIDENCE ROOM

Chief Bobby Andrews faced the piles of papers on his desk and realized how long it had been since he had devoted all his capabilities to his job. He had operated at decreased efficiency while Renee had been in her final weeks of pregnancy, and he had devoted most of his time to Thelma Lou since her arrival. It was time for an effort to get current with this mess. It would take a major effort, but he felt ready for it now that the doctor had used the magic word *normal* in predicting his daughter's future. He began to read and sort papers.

Sergeant Gomez entered Bobby's office. "Chief, Pastor Blake's out front. He wants to know whether you have time to go over something with him. He told me to tell you that he'll come back later if you're busy."

"Send him in, Al. This jumble of papers can wait for one more day."

A few minutes later, Arthur entered and perched on the corner of the desk while Bobby completed an intervening phone call. As Bobby returned the phone to its cradle, Arthur stood and extended his hand toward his friend.

"Congratulations on your good news about Thelma Lou. You and Renee deserved that. We've all been praying for you, and maybe it helped."

"Whether it was the praying or the good doctor, my heart is grateful. I never anticipated the complexities of parenting, but I now appreciate the scope of the job."

"Memorize that lesson, Bobby. Complications are going to be woven into your life's fabric for a long time."

"Are you here as my pastor, Arthur, or are you working on one of your hunches for the current inquiry? How should I classify this case? It has local murder and assault aspects, international and Catholic Church connections, plus a sprinkle of child-trafficking."

"To answer your question, I came because of the case, but I'm pleased as your friend to see how refreshed you look now that your baby's health issue has been resolved. Regarding your second question, this investigation appears to be very complex, but I suspect that we'll soon discern its overall pattern."

"I like your optimism, but remember that I'm just a local cop. I can't get involved with all of this international stuff."

"You're already involved. Don't forget that we found Kristina's journals from Guatemala in the trunk of her car as we examined it in this very building."

"That's true; there can be local events affecting an international case. You've convinced me, Arthur; how else can the Parkville Police assist you?"

"I believe you have an evidence room?"

"We keep accumulated evidence in a locked unit at a storage warehouse. We don't have enough room here. What do you want to examine?"

"I think you have Kristina's belongings from her apartment."

"We do have them, but there's not much. Kristina's apartment turned out to be a single rented room. Her vow of poverty as a nun gave her a frugal lifestyle."

"I think we'll find her few belongings interesting. Let's go to your warehouse, but first I want to call Wally Sanborn and ask him to join us."

CHAPTER 57 – TRANSIENTS

Joe Gonzalez looked at his cell phone and read the incoming text message: *Jose - expect 3 visitors. They will leave cars. Need motorcycles. Confirm message received. John*

After a quick trip to the back of the building to select the best three bikes, he responded: *Message received. Have 3 ready to go. Jose*

Joe, in his guise as Jose, had installed the automotive tools acquired from Chet Quinto and had cleaned the work area. John Samson had not contacted him for several days, so he had used that time to tune the six motorcycles stored inside the building and two cars parked out back. During the process he had noted that a black Honda motorcycle had two different treads on the front and back tires. Just before he received John's text message, he had taken close-up photos of it. He made sure that it would not be claimed by one of today's visitors by burying it under the pile of broken and disassembled motorcycle parts outside. Later, he would transfer the bike pictures to his home computer and then email them to Bobby. He knew how easy it would be for the gang to check his phone use history. They might even have a device installed here to monitor his transmissions.

He had also taken a few pictures of the building and its surroundings, the license plates on the cars and motorcycles, plus close-ups of the locked fenced-in storage room. He had been careful to refrain from trying to gain access to it in case they had set traps to detect unauthorized entries. The combination padlock did not look unusually sophisticated. There would be time to try to open it after he knew the cage contained something worth his efforts.

Jose heard a car arrive, and walked outside to meet the first of the promised three arrivals. He rounded the corner of the building to see a tall thin man wearing blue jeans and a red plaid shirt climb out of a two-year-old black Jeep Wrangler. He approached the man being careful to maintain his slight Jose Lopez limp.

"Hi, I'm Jose Lopez, and I'm in charge of this place. Can I help you?"

"You're showing good caution, Jose; I'm Bill. John said you would loan me a motorcycle for a couple of days. I also have to leave a package in your storage room."

"That's fine with me, Bill. Glad to meet you. I can give you a Honda bike that runs well but has a few scratches. I don't have access to that caged area."

"No problem, Jose, I have the combination for the lock."

Bill removed a blue plastic bin from the Jeep. Jose could see it was heavy from the way Bill hoisted it, and the sounds of bumps and rattles told him that the bin contained multiple articles. The individual items sounded hard and relatively small. Jose followed Bill into the building and stayed by his workbench while Bill unlocked the fenced room, inserted his container, and relocked the door. Jose hid any outward sign of interest in Bill's mission because he wanted to maintain the appearance of being trustworthy and reliable. He had to learn a lot more before he did anything that might reveal any hidden motivations. Bill rejoined Jose after depositing his burden.

"Do you have anything to drink around here?"

"When John first gave me this job, I found that the old refrigerator over there was broken, but I've fixed it and stocked it with some soda pop and bottled water. Help yourself."

"Thanks, Jose, I appreciate your initiative. I'll take a bottle of water with me for the trip. Now which bike is mine?"

"You can take either the black or the red Honda. They're working a touch better than the Suzuki, so I'll save that one for later."

"Good enough, Jose, I'll go with black. That's my color. Is the tank full?"

"You're ready to go. Does your Jeep need any work while you're gone?"

"Nope, it's running real well. I'll be back for it in about three days. Nice meeting you..." Bill started his engine and eased the Honda out of the building and over to his Jeep where he retrieved a helmet and a backpack from the back seat. Then he accelerated down the driveway toward the road. Halfway down the drive he passed an incoming red Ford pickup truck and waved to the driver.

Jose could now confirm that these visitors knew each other and that the transfer to a motorcycle for an assignment was routine. He wondered whether the purpose was to go somewhere more accessible on two wheels, or to disguise the couriers by not using their personally registered vehicles. He stepped forward to greet his second visitor. He wondered why he was surprised to see that the pickup driver was a woman.

"Hello, I'm Jose Lopez."

"Hi, Jose, John said you would be here. I'm Barbara. I'll leave my truck here and take a motorcycle."

"Everything is ready for you. You can park your truck next to Bill's Jeep. Leave your key if you want me to clean it or do any work on it while you're gone."

"Thanks for the offer, but Rosie is in great shape. I always name my cars and trucks." Barbara drove to the parking area and got out of her truck carrying a helmet and a backpack that was a bit bigger than the one Bill had worn as he rode away.

"Do you want a cold drink, Barbara?"

"That's tempting, but I'll load up and get on the road."

Jose watched as she strode over to the caged room, unlocked the padlock, and transferred several items from Bill's plastic bin into her backpack. Then she replaced the lid on the bin and reset the padlock as she left the storage cage.

"You talked me into it, Jose; I'll take a cold drink with me." She went to the refrigerator, selected a bottle, and slid it into a compartment of her backpack.

"I'll take the red Honda if it's ready to go."

"It's all set – gas tank is full."

"Thanks. You're doing a good job. We'll have to get John to give you some extra assignments when things get slow here. I'll see you on the way back."

Barbara donned her helmet and backpack. She straddled the Honda and rode it out through the big door. Jose watched intently as she accelerated down the driveway and turned left at the road. *So she's higher in the organization than John. She can tell him to give me more assignments. If I can trace enough strands, I'll see the pattern.*

He had assumed that the activity pattern would be repeated, with the third visitor coming immediately after Barbara had left. In this he was mistaken. No one arrived until late afternoon, when an incoming vehicle disturbed the silence just as Jose was preparing to leave for the day.

Jose stood in front of the big open door and saw a black minivan approaching more rapidly than was reasonable on a driveway. The driver honked his horn twice. Jose wondered if he would have to jump out of the way, but the van screeched to a halt five feet shy of the doorway.

The driver, a stocky sandy-haired youth in his early twenties, turned off the ignition and approached Jose. "Sorry about my mad dash up the driveway, but I was delayed by an accident that tied up the interstate. I didn't know if you would still be here. I'm Larry."

"Welcome, Larry; another half hour and I might have given up on you, but there's no problem. I'm Jose, and everything is ready. You can park next to the red pickup and the Jeep."

Larry backed up and executed two tight left turns to pull in on the far side of Bill's Jeep. He walked back to the building carrying his backpack and helmet. "Do you have a good bike for me?"

"You're the last one in, so you don't get a choice, but this Suzuki should be fine for you. It's fueled and ready to go."

"Good; I'll just take care of loading up." Larry walked over to the storage cage, entered the combination to open the padlock, and transferred items from the plastic bin into his backpack. When he finished, he exited the room, and latched the padlock. Jose saw that the lid to the plastic bin lay on the floor beside the empty container. *So that's the process. Bill brings the goods in, keeps something in his own pack, and the others distribute what he leaves behind in the bin.*

"Want a drink for the road, Larry?"

"No, I'm fine. I've kept you late enough already. Let's both get out of here. I'll be back for my van in a few days." He started the Suzuki, revved it up a couple of times, and started his acceleration before the bike left the building.

That kid loves speed. Jose started the shut-down process. After turning out the lights he took a cold drink for his own drive home and locked the doors. As he walked toward his car he welcomed the prospect of once again becoming Joe Gonzalez and spending time at home this evening. His cell phone held photographs of the motorcycle with the mismatched front and rear tires, but even if it had been the one ridden by Horse's murderer, how would they identify the rider? *They all select bikes at random, and who knows how many other riders there are in this gang?*

CHAPTER 58 – REMNANTS

Wally Sanborn met Arthur and Chief Andrews near the side door of the warehouse containing the police department's evidence storage unit.

Arthur shook his hand. "Thanks for coming on short notice, Wally. Did you bring that logistics tool kit you told me about during one of our coffee sessions?"

"It's in my back pocket."

Bobby asked, "Is that what you used during your intelligence support work for the Army? It's pretty small."

"These tools have modified many everyday objects to include weapons, eavesdropping devices, and a few things that are still classified. They have to be small to keep the modifications from looking obvious. The kit also includes some lock picks in case I have to place an object within a locked room. What's our target today?"

Arthur said, "I'll explain it after we get inside. Show us the way to your evidence locker, Bobby."

When they approached the outer warehouse door, Bobby entered his code into the keypad alongside the entrance, and the lock released. Then he led them through a maze of hallways lined with identical doors until he came to one marked 293. He unlocked and removed the padlock, slid open the latching bar, and raised the roll-up door. They entered to find themselves in a double unit from which the dividing wall had been removed. One side was full of cartons stored on heavy-duty shelf units arranged like the letter E. The other side contained larger items and cartons on movable furniture dollies and a workbench with a swing-arm fluorescent lamp.

Wally said, "This looks very professional, Bobby. I see you even have a location index chart on that clipboard."

"You can credit Chet Quinto for that. We don't have enough work for him to be a full-time mechanic, so he appropriates other functions to keep busy. This evidence locker is one of them. He's a well-organized guy."

Arthur asked, "Does the chart show the location of Kristina's belongings, or will we have to read the labels on the boxes?"

Bobby studied the clipboard chart. "According to this, we're looking for cartons numbered twenty-three and twenty-four, and those cartons should be on the back shelf unit in the right-hand alcove." He walked over to that area. "Here they are on the third shelf. Chet has good records."

He removed the cartons from the shelf and set them on the workbench for Arthur and Wally to examine.

Arthur emptied the contents of the first carton onto the workbench. "You weren't exaggerating when you said she had few possessions." He sorted through the items, moving each from right to left after viewing it. "I think we're going to have to look in the second carton." He replaced the contents of the first carton and closed it.

Bobby said, "I can see you've had one of your hunches again. You know exactly what you're looking for."

"Yes, I do. Remember, when we examined Kristina's car and found the journals?"

"Sure."

"We took that car apart because it was one of the few things that uniquely belonged to Kristina and that she always would have had with her, no matter where she went."

Bobby said, "That's true."

"What was the first thing of hers we found in that car?"

"Joe found a magnetic box under the left front fender containing a car key on a chain with a crucifix."

Arthur said, "That wasn't just an object; it was a message. As a Catholic missionary, what would Sister Kristina always treasure and keep close to her?"

Wally said, "That's great logic, Arthur. She would never part with her crucifix. That keychain with the miniature crucifix was indicating that the key was the crucifix. If you're right, she left that message in case anything happened to her. Let's test your theory."

Wally opened the second carton, and slid the contents onto the flat surface. A twenty-four inch high alabaster and wood wall crucifix sat on the top of the pile, and a second smaller silver-on-wood pendant crucifix lay alongside it.

Wally said, "They're both well-made and artistic. The pendant looks old, so it was probably handed down for several generations, probably within the order. It's quite big for family use. I think the large wall crucifix is what we need to examine for treasure hunting. Sometimes the wooden cross on these things is relatively flat so that it doesn't protrude from the wall much. The legs of the cross on this one have more realistic square sections."

Bobby said, "Do you see anything unusual?"

"Let me adjust the lamp for better light. Oh, that's interesting. Either Kristina was a talented woodworker, or she knew someone who was. I had expected to find that someone had cut into the back of the cross to hide something and then covered it over. In this case the wood grain pattern is intact. The woodworker cut slices off both ends of the horizontal beam of the cross and also off the bottom of the vertical beam. Then the slices were replaced to match the grain pattern and glued. I suspect we'll find drilled cavities beneath these plugs. Whoever did it was a true craftsman."

Arthur took a closer look at the fine joint lines beneath the end caps. "Can you pry those ends off without damaging the cross? I have a few Catholic friends who might be interested in having this later."

Bobby said, "I'm afraid that would be much later, Arthur. We can't release evidence until all aspects of the legal process on the case have been completed."

"That's understood. I'm only requesting that we try to preserve the artistic quality of the piece."

Wally said, "I have a very thin, yet strong, knife blade that should do the trick. The big question is whether the glue they used will release as I work at it." He started with the cap at the bottom of the crucifix, assuming that his first attempt would be the most likely to cause damage and that the bottom of the cross would attract minimal attention. "These things are pretty tight. Bobby, look through your evidence listing to see if you have a case that involved a hair dryer. I think I need to apply heat to this joint."

"It so happens that I know we have evidence from such a case. Mrs. Bressling died when she was electrocuted by a hair dryer dropped into the bathtub with her. At first we considered it an accident, but over the course of time her husband made enough confusing and contradictory statements that we began to suspect he had caused the accident. He confessed after we advised him that we knew that his business was failing and that he had purchased a big life insurance policy on his wife two weeks before she died...Anyway, the index says that I should look in carton number sixteen." Bobby retrieved the carton, opened it and extracted an oversize hair blower. He gave it to Wally and replaced the carton in its original location.

Arthur said, "That hairdryer should still work after all the time it's had to dry out. It's a big one so you'll have lots of heat."

Wally set the dryer for its lowest heat setting and turned it on. The fan rattled a couple of times and then started to rotate smoothly. He tested the heat level with his hand and then applied it gradually to the bottom end of the crucifix. Wally transferred the blower to Arthur while he pried at the end cap junction. He could feel it start to move. Prying alternately on each side of the square beam, he eased the cap up until he could grab it with his fingers. As Wally slid the cap and its attached piloting dowel off, he signaled Arthur to stop the blower.

"That was the trick, Arthur. The person who modified this cross used hot- melt glue to seal it. He also used an unusually long dowel slid into the hole to make the assembly rigid. Now let's see what's in there." Wally used a long-nosed hemostat tool to reach into the cavity and clamp gently on the item inside. As he pulled on it, he realized that the hole had been drilled to match the object's width. Even without the end cap, the object would not have dropped out due to gravity. "Here it comes."

Arthur and Bobby watched intently as Wally extracted the computer flash drive from the base of the crucifix. Arthur gave a thumbs-up gesture as Wally laid it on the workbench. He said, "Well done; that's one down and two to go."

Bobby added, "This is the first case I've seen where all the key evidence was inside the Police Department for a long time before we found it. You've had good insights, Arthur."

"It was mostly a matter of trying to understand the victim and think like her."

Bobby worked with Wally to heat and pry open the two end caps on the horizontal bar of the cross. They succeeded, and soon they had three flash drives perched on the workbench.

Arthur said, "Now it's time to turn these over to Irma and Penny for analysis. They're appropriate candidates for retrieving all the stories these things have to tell."

CHAPTER 59 – IRMA AND PENNY

Penny opened her front door before Irma could ring the bell. "Come on in, Irma. Joe's catching a quick nap before he has to go back undercover as Jose Lopez. He's worn out due to having to be two different people for so long. I hope we make progress quickly so that we can pull him out of there."

"We'll soon see what's on those flash drives that Kristina brought back from Guatemala. With a little luck we'll begin to understand the scope of the organization that's employing Jose. I brought my computer with me so that we can have two work stations analyzing the data at the same time."

They set up their equipment on the dining room table, next to the pitcher of lemonade and glasses that Penny had set out for them.

Irma contributed three yellow pads of paper to the setting. "Call it habit, but I feel more comfortable if I back up the computer findings and printouts with notes on old-fashioned pads of paper. Each note I write tends to generate another observation that I could not have anticipated."

"I have my procedures too, Irma. That's why I asked you to join me here instead of working at your apartment. We don't know whether the organization we're investigating is sophisticated or not, but I don't like to take chances. I've repeatedly swept this house for any possible electronic bugs, and our wireless network is protected and encoded so that no one can intercept any meaningful data that our machines transmit."

"Working here is fine with me. I'm still focused on the day when Arthur and I get into a house of our own."

"Have the two of you talked about the details of the wedding?"

"He's still pretty skimpy with his time for socializing, but at least we've agreed that there will be a wedding and that the clock is counting down toward that event. We both know that it won't happen until we complete this investigation, so I would welcome a quick solution."

"That sounds like our cue to fire up the computers and examine these three flash drives. The guys had all the fun of finding them. Let's show them how well we can perform in analyzing their contents."

Irma laid the three thumb-sized drives on the table. "Note that they're all dissimilar designs from different manufacturers. That says to me that they were either loaded with data in three locations independently, or they contain a large amount of data generated at a single location but that the second and third drives were each purchased only after the preceding drive became fully loaded."

"We can test those observations by seeing whether the files in these things are similar in type."

The drives weren't numbered or otherwise identified, so Penny took one at random and plugged it into her computer. Then she explored its contents. "Let's mark this drive as number one. It lists three folders containing multiple files plus a few isolated files. They all appear to be documents."

"Open the first folder to show the individual files in it."

"They look like case files for adoptions. They have people's names for the titles, and they're American-sounding names; none of them are Hispanic. They also have pretty old dates."

Irma opened her briefcase and pulled out a copy of one of Kristina's journals. See if you have a file dated in 2008 or possibly earlier for Joshua and Isabelle Weadle. They were the couple mentioned by Kristina as potentially good adoptive parents."

Penny scrolled through the list of files. "Here it is. The file is called Weadle2007. They must use the year of first contact to name the files."

"Do you have a file for George and Mable Benton?"

"Here it is – Benton2006. Their case apparently took longer before they received a child."

"Based on Kristina's comments, they probably didn't push the process as hard as the Weadles would have. The Bentons were more interested in using the child than raising him...The journal says that his name was Pablo. The Bentons' case also probably took longer because they wouldn't have been willing to pay as much as the other couple."

"Anyway, we have confirmation that this flash drive contains records of illegal adoptions. The gang would certainly want to get those back. Even if the names of people involved in the negotiations aren't shown in those files, they have the adopting parents' names, and those people could supply the names of their contacts."

"That information could also be a roadmap for finding the children and returning them to their birth parents. How many adoption files of that type do you have?"

"I count twenty-six. Some of them are likely to have been kidnappings, and the rest probably involve payments made to unethical orphanages, even if the birth mothers gave up their children voluntarily – more evidence for criminal cases."

"That will require some legal opinions. The orphanages probably disguised the payments they received as placement or legal fees. They could even claim that they had been reimbursed for medical testing and documentation. A lot will depend on the ages of the children when they were adopted and the condition of their memories."

Penny opened the next folder to show the files inside it. "This is a more recent set of files. It has files with names that sound more like businesses."

Irma removed a second journal copy from her briefcase and skimmed its contents. "See if you have files marked Huehue Heights and Our Children Together."

Penny examined the list. "Yes, they're both here, but abbreviated a bit. I have *HuehueHtsHome2009* and *OCTogether2009*."

"See if any other names sound like orphanages."

"Some are in Spanish, but I have *ToddlersRest1* and *ToddlersRest2*. I also have a Spanish file called CasadeNinos3. None of those files ends with a year number. They must be from a different series."

"Well, whether we have one or two series, they seem to be children's homes or orphanages. There is a connection or pattern here. Open the third folder in that drive, Penny."

"This folder contains thirteen files, but their names don't tell me very much. They seem to be a combination of a person's last name and a code. I'm opening ramos269sw. I think the final two letters of the file name are compass directions. This file contains a map of parts of California, Arizona and New Mexico – southwestern states. There's a small circle around Ciudad Juarez at the border between New Mexico and Texas. That could indicate a point of entry from Mexico for traveling to destinations on this map."

"If you have a file that ends in *se*, check whether it contains a map that shows an entry point from Mexico and southeastern states."

"I have it. The file is called denton845se. It shows a circled entry point at Nuevo Laredo, and the map covers portions of Texas, Louisiana, Mississippi, and Alabama."

"The interesting thing about that one is the Denton part of the file name, suggesting that others beside Hispanics are involved in this enterprise."

"Looking further into that Denton pdf file, I see a name, Stan, and a telephone number. Presumably that would make the contact Stan Denton, and if we have a phone number, we should be able to trace him, even if it's a cell phone. What do you think about these files, Irma?"

"My guess is that they relate to couriers of some kind. The dispatchers call them when there is something for them to deliver in their territory."

"Now I'm going to play a hunch. I see a file that ends in *nc*. I think that means north central, and that might be the code for this area. Joe said that the name of the man who came to his building with a container full of small items was Bill. I'm opening the file labeled booker372nc. It has two maps, one of the Texas/Mexico border with Reynosa circled, and one showing parts of Michigan, Indiana, Illinois, Iowa, and Wisconsin. That would be a suitable area to be called north central. Looking for contact information, I come up with Bill and a telephone number. I think it's the same person. These folks are smuggling something across the Mexican border and distributing it to various points in the United States."

"That's good thinking, Penny. Now we have to determine what they are moving around and why."

"I don't think we're talking about drugs because Joe told me that the bin contained hard objects. He also said that Bill had the bin visible in his car. People who carry drugs try to hide them in case they are stopped and searched."

"Let's not play guessing games. We have two more flash drives that might give us answers. I'll mark this one number two and examine it."

Irma inserted the flash drive into her computer and looked at the contents listing. "This one is quite different. It has twelve folders each of which is called *church* followed by a number. I've opened the first folder, and I see that it contains a number of jpg files. These folders appear to be photograph albums from different churches."

"Can you tell where the churches are located from the pictures?"

"From their style, I would guess they're in Guatemala, but they could be in Mexico or Honduras also. It would take some research to identify them."

"Are they just exterior shots?"

"Some inside shots and some outside shots, but there are quite a few close-ups of architectural details and decorations. These churches look old, and they have pretty fancy carvings and statues everywhere."

"That sounds like Guatemala. The Indians there are Mayan descendants, and their people were big on carvings like that. Some say they're Catholic in name only. They still cling to their Mayan heritage, and it may be more important to them."

"Anyway, this flash drive is completely full of church pictures. Look at the third one, Penny."

"I think this one must be meant to go with all of those pictures. I see a list of churches in Guatemala and another file listing churches from various other locations. There's also a list labeled *brokers and auctions*. I'm beginning to see what they're doing."

"I see it too. They're stealing artifacts from old churches and selling them here in the art market.

They're probably going through many people and businesses across the country so that no one realizes how many items they have stolen. This is big business and much safer for them than drug trafficking."

"How does this tie in with the missing Guatemalan children?"

Irma thought for half a minute before speaking. "I would guess that they use the children to disguise what they are doing. If you were traveling in Mexico with a couple of Mayan Indian children, and the authorities found you had one or two church relics with you, the children could say that they were family heirlooms that their grandfather or great-grandfather had carved."

"They could also walk past official checkpoints with them because nobody keeps track of all the kids walking through the streets and alleys of Mexico."

"Penny, I think this is a big organization that looks small to the outsider. You had files on children's homes and orphanages. I'll guess that some of those places are in Mexico. Remember that Kristina wrote in her journals about the Mexican, Miguel, who wanted training procedures for children's homes. Suppose they set up a string of homes from Guatemala through Mexico to the border with Texas. The smuggling could be done under the guise of transferring children from one home to another. They wouldn't have to worry about the difficulty of completing adoptions, because these would be handled as transfers among temporary shelters for children. Nobody would be applying for adoptions. Neither Guatemala nor Mexico would interfere because somebody other than the state was caring for the children, and that saves the government money. These folks are smart."

"And Carlos Benitez knew he could destroy their operation when he gave these flash drives to Kristina. Thank God she kept them so well hidden."

CHAPTER 60 – STEVE DUBOIS

"Arthur, this is Steve DuBois calling. Penny briefed me on the analysis that she and Irma performed on the three flash drives. I assume that you've received the same information from Irma. She suggested that I contact you to generate a plan of action from this point forward. I'll be arriving in Parkville by noon. If your schedule is open, I'd like to meet with you at your church office."

"We should develop a plan of action, but if you don't mind, I'd rather have this meeting at Irma's apartment. She should be involved because she has seen the actual data files, and we'll have more privacy there. I'd also like to include Jeremy Hadley. He needs to get involved in more aspects of our investigations in order to gain confidence in his skills."

"That's fine. I'll meet you there around one o'clock. Joe will be back in his undercover role by that time, and Penny has to make some contacts regarding our other active cases at the agency. She'll be available by phone if we need her."

"I'll see you then, Steve. In the meantime Irma and I will formulate an agenda for the meeting."

CHAPTER 61 – OVERVIEW

They gathered at Irma's dining room table which doubled as the ABC Consultants conference table. Irma had the downloaded files from the flash drives in her computer. She had returned those drives to Chief Bobby Andrews on her way back from Penny's house. They would work with the file copies and safeguard the originals in the secure evidence locker.

Arthur took a swallow of coffee and started the session. "First, I want to state that Irma and Penny did a great job reviewing the data on those flash drives. Thanks to their efforts, we now have an overview of the activities of this international gang we're investigating. Jeremy, to bring you up to date, the data files suggest that these people are stealing artifacts from colonial-era churches in Guatemala and smuggling them to various art brokers and auction houses across the United States. They're sold in small batches as items from private collectors. The gang appears to be using the transfer of children and teenagers through a string of orphanages as a cover story to mask these operations. We have now plotted the locations of the children's homes documented in the flash drive files to show that they form a conduit for moving items from Guatemala through Mexico to Texas. American operatives then carry the items to their final destinations."

Irma said, "It's a well-conceived and elaborate distribution system. The only problem is that while we have information on geographic points on the network, we know nothing about the higher level people behind it. Do you have anything more for us, Steve?"

"That's exactly why I requested this meeting. We have enough information to put together a task force to close down most of the transfer points, but that wouldn't get us the senior management of this outfit. We don't want to let them know federal agents are watching them until we can locate the bosses and put them out of business too."

Arthur said, "We know that John Samson's man, Pedro Garcia, transports papers back and forth to one or more Chicago law firms. Have you identified them and found out what they are doing as part of this business?"

Steve said, "That's another chicken and egg situation. If we pick up Pedro and scare him, he'll give us that contact information, but that will tip off John Samson and the lawyers to the fact that they're under investigation. We're pretty sure that we know what they're doing anyway. In the past those lawyers probably handled documentation and negotiations for illegal adoptions. Under this new stolen art scheme, they're probably conjuring up bills of sale and other ownership documents for the *collectors* who are putting the church treasures up for sale."

Irma passed a tray of crackers and cheese slices around the table. "I doubt that the lawyers would even know who the top people are. The attorneys are acting as intermediaries, and they would want to protect themselves by being able to say that they provide legal services without knowing any more than necessary about the organization's business."

Arthur said, "The key to finding the bosses is to discover who makes the management decisions. Who decides what art objects and artifacts are to be stolen? Who tells the troops where to deliver them for sale?"

Irma opened the file of photographs on her computer. "I'll take that one step further, Arthur. Who took all of these photographs? I don't think they were taken by tourists. A lot of these pictures are shots of items stored in private parts of churches that tourists would never see. The person who took them had special access privileges."

Arthur said, "I'd like to compare those pictures to church art objects that have been recently sold at auctions. If we find some that match your photographs we'll know the entire route taken from church to sale and the timing of that journey. Steve, can your agency get records of art object sales with photographs?"

"I think we can, but let me check with Penny to be sure. Can we take a break while I call her?"

"Irma said, "Consider the meeting in recess. Let's give Steve some quiet for his call by adjourning to the kitchen for some refreshments. I have goodies all ready for you on the kitchen table."

They headed for the kitchen where Arthur and Irma shared some pecan pie while Jeremy made a ham and cheese sandwich. He explained that, as the baker's son, he couldn't get very excited about pastry.

A few minutes later Steve entered looking concerned. "I can't reach Penny on her home phone or on her personal or agency cell phones. I'm going to drive over there to check for a possible problem."

Jeremy said, "I'll go with you." They both hurried out.

CHAPTER 62 – WEDDING ISSUES

When they were alone, Irma gave Arthur a fresh mug of coffee and sat down across the table from him.

"While we wait for news about any possible problem at Penny's place, I need you to tell me you're committed to our wedding and to set some ground rules for it."

"I'm committed and enthusiastic about marrying you, but it's going to have to wait until after we've caught Horse's murderer and put this organization out of business."

"That could happen quickly, or it could take a long time. I think we should put a target date on the calendar or at least have a time limit so that we have some control over our wedding plans."

"You've been very patient with me, so I'll agree to the second or third weekend in October. Is that satisfactory?"

"I never know what to expect from you, Arthur. I'd expected you to procrastinate some more, and you came up with a date. Before you change your mind, I agree to the second weekend in October. Now I'll be able to work in a bit of planning around the edges of the investigation."

"My only conditions are that we have a fairly simple ceremony and reception and that we don't have hundreds of guests."

"Since you have only a few relatives and I have no close ones, I can live with your stipulations. Where should we go for a honeymoon?"

"You know my tendency to work things out without advance planning. Where do you want to go?"

"You'll probably think I'm weird, but we've been learning so much about Guatemala during this case that I think I'd like to go there."

"You're not weird at all. The same thought had crossed my mind. I'm all for it. Just don't look to adopt a child while you're down there. Remember that they've made that very difficult."

"I just want to go back to the Guatemalan consulate to make trip arrangements with a real wedding ring on my finger. That play-acting we did a while ago felt very good."

"Irma, you're as romantic as a teenager."

"What's wrong with that? Someone in this family has to be romantic. Life isn't only a matter of applying logic; you need some magic too."

"In that case, bring me the sugar bowl from your kitchen cabinet and a pair of chopsticks."

"I don't know what you're up to, Arthur, but it sounds intriguing." Irma set the sugar bowl and the chopsticks on the table between them. "What happens now?"

"Say the magic words *sweeten my life*, and stir the sugar with the chopsticks."

Irma picked up the chopsticks and said, "Sweeten my life." She stirred the sugar with the chopsticks and felt something hard in there. She probed around, grabbed something with the chopsticks and raised it slowly above the bowl.

"Oh, Arthur, that's a beautiful pearl necklace. You do have magic. How long has that been in there?"

"A magician never tells his secrets. It hasn't been sitting in there; you just created it by magic. We've agreed on our wedding plans. Let the magic begin."

CHAPTER 63 – NEWS

Steve DuBois and Jeremy Hadley approached the front door of the Gonzalez house and rang the doorbell. After receiving no response, Steve tried the doorknob and found that it turned. He opened the door and called, "Penny, are you here?" Again he received no response.

"Jeremy, you check the back yard to see if anything looks unusual. I'll look inside and then open the back door for you."

Steve checked the front rooms, found them neat except for some papers strewn on the floor beneath and around the dining room table. Then he headed for the kitchen. There he saw a dish with toast in it on the table alongside a cup of coffee and a cell phone. The light on the coffee maker indicated that it was keeping the coffee in the pot warm. Steve switched it off, pocketed the cell phone, and opened the back door for Jeremy.

"I haven't found Penny yet, but the coffee pot was set on the keep-warm setting."

"I checked the garage, Steve. A car is inside. If she's not in the house, she may have walked somewhere or left in someone else's car."

"Jeremy, you look upstairs while I check the basement. Be careful. If someone came in, they could still be here."

Steve headed downstairs, holding a small pistol that had been concealed in an inside jacket pocket. He heard Jeremy climbing the front stairs overhead. At the foot of the stairs he found a flashlight on a shelf and turned it on. As he walked around he directed the light beam toward all of the dark corners and shadows. He found nothing unusual except for an old school wall clock that Joe had left partially disassembled on his workbench. Steve headed back upstairs to see what Jeremy had discovered.

They met at the foot of the front stairs.

"Steve, nothing looks unusual upstairs. The bed's not made, but I don't know whether that's significant; would Penny leave without making the bed?"

"I think it would depend on the degree of urgency of her errand." He returned his pistol to his inner jacket pocket. "I don't see any signs of a struggle, but that doesn't tell us whether Penny left by herself, or if she was taken away by someone. I also don't know whether Joe has been driving from here in the car he uses as Jose Lopez, or if he drives his own car somewhere else to transfer to that one. We need more information to be able to answer our questions."

Steve took out his telephone and called Arthur. He explained the situation. "We're not sure whether Penny has been kidnapped by someone or if she left on her own. There are indications that she left in a hurry. There is some mess, but no signs of a struggle."

Arthur said, "I think we have to assume that someone took her away. When we finish this conversation, I'll alert Bobby to the possibility. This is his jurisdiction...One other thing, Steve; Irma wants to know whether you saw Penny's laptop computer anywhere."

Steve checked with Jeremy before responding. "No, Arthur; we found her cell phone, but neither one of us has seen her computer."

"That's too bad. That makes it all the more likely that someone kidnapped Penny and took her computer to check its contents for information about the state of our investigation. That suggests something even worse."

"What's that?"

217

"If they took Penny and her computer, they know about Joe's undercover work. They're both in danger. We'll have to move rapidly to save them."

CHAPTER 64 – ROCHELLE

Chief Bobby Andrews set down his telephone after speaking with Arthur. He knew it was time to call a friend for assistance. He looked up the number for Chief Wilson Bascker of the Rochelle Police Department and keyed it in.

"Hello, Wilson; this is Bobby Andrews. I need your help. I have a possible emergency that involves both of our jurisdictions. We've been working with a federal agency on local aspects of one of their interstate investigations. I just received word that one of their agents who has been working undercover in Rochelle may be in danger, as is his wife who may have been kidnapped in Parkville. The name of the fellow out your way is Joe Gonzalez, and he's been working on this case as Jose Lopez. He was in a corrugated garage building on Flagg Road near South Center Road. Are you familiar with that area?"

"Hi, Bobby; this must be a bad scene. You don't even have time to exchange pleasantries first. Sure, I know that area. There are two or three buildings that resemble the one you described. We'll check them out for you. You said this agent has been working undercover, so I'll just tell the boys his alias name. You said that was Jose Lopez, right?"

"That's it Wilson."

"We'll get right on it, but let's make an effort to meet for coffee or a beer midway between us within the next week or two. We have some catching up to do."

"That sounds good to me, and thanks for your help."

"Hold on a minute, Bobby...I think I'd better cover this one myself. I just got word that our fire department is responding to a 911 call up there. It may be the same building. I'll call you as soon as I have more information. Bye for now."

CHAPTER 65 – ON THE SCENE

Chief Wilson Bascker turned into the driveway to find two fire engines, an ambulance, and one of his patrol cars already on the scene. The building was burning intensely on one side, and it appeared to be spreading. He parked and hurried up to Captain Jim Riley of the Fire Department.

"Jim, did you check for occupants?"

"Hi, Wilson; we gave a quick check through a window and didn't see anyone."

"I'm afraid we're going to have to send someone inside. I received word that someone who works in there is a potential murder target, and this fire may have been set as the weapon to kill him.. I'll tell you more after we check it out."

Jim Riley radioed for two men with air tanks to go in through the small door and instructed the paramedics to stand by for possible victims. He and Chief Bascker watched as the two-man team smashed the lock on the door and entered. A few minutes later he received a report of a man inside who was unconscious and locked in a cage room. The firemen requested that someone bring them a bolt cutter so that they could cut the padlock on the door to that room. They also said that the fire was growing more intense and that it wouldn't be safe to stay inside much longer. Before Jim could select someone to deliver the bolt cutter, he saw Shirley Jackson run into the building with that tool. Shirley had been a member of his team for nineteen years, and she would soon be eligible for retirement.

Jim called for another tanker truck. They were too far out of town to have hydrants available, and he had to keep the fire away from the doorway so his people could get out. The building would be a total loss, so his concern was for his people and the victim trapped inside. He knew that Wilson Bascker and his police would soon be handling this case. Jim just wanted it to be classified as an attempted homicide and not a successful one.

Shirley's voice came over the radio. "We have him out. He's in bad shape but alive. Keep that fire away from the door, and have a stretcher for us. The roof is about to go.

Two minutes later, three figures appeared in the doorway carrying a fourth. They managed to get eight feet away from the building before the roof on the far end collapsed, followed by two of the side walls. The wall with the large and small doors remained erect, but they had become doors to nowhere. Twisted metal and charred equipment were all that remained on the other side.

The paramedics moved in to treat the victim and administer oxygen to the firefighters. Jim Riley directed his people to turn their attention to wetting down a gasoline storage tank behind the building, next to a pile of old motorcycle parts and a parked car.

Chief Bascker called his Parkville counterpart. "Bobby, someone locked your man inside that building and torched it to get rid of him. The firefighters got him out alive, but he'll be in the hospital for a while. There's not much left of the building, but we'll keep people away from it until the federal agents arrive to canvass the area for evidence. We'll help them in any way we can. I've seen a few blazes set to mask the way someone died, but this was an attempt to roast this guy alive. That makes me mad!"

CHAPTER 66 – PENNY

Bobby knocked on the door of Irma's apartment. When she opened it she saw the tension in his face. "Come on in, Bobby. Arthur's in the kitchen. Do you have news for us?"

At the sound of voices, Arthur returned to the front room with his coffee refill. He set it down on the dining room table and waited for Bobby's response.

"They tried to kill Joe by locking him inside the building and setting fire to it. He's alive and in the hospital in Rochelle. He has a concussion from when they knocked him out plus some smoke inhalation problems. At least the rescuers reached him before the fire did. He wasn't burned. Has Penny showed up yet? She'll want to get down there to be with him."

Arthur said, "Right now, we don't know where Penny is. She may have been kidnapped. Steve and Jeremy checked the house and found evidence that she had left in a hurry. Her computer was gone, and papers were all over the floor, but they didn't find signs of a struggle. My guess is that someone in the gang followed Jose Lopez home from work and found that his real name is Joe Gonzalez. They probably don't know much more than that, but they assumed he was some kind of a cop and went after him. They probably returned to the house to get Penny so that they could learn more about Joe's identity and organization."

Bobby said, "I'll ask Wilson Bascker to put someone on guard outside Joe's hospital room. I'll also ask him to spread the word that they weren't able to save the man in the building. If the gang finds out that he survived, they may go after him again. My detectives will take a closer look at the Gonzalez house and ask the neighbors what they saw. In a small town people know their neighbors and are suspicious of strangers."

Irma had been listening intently but now joined the conversation. "Bobby, did Chief Bascker say anything about cars on the property where the building was burned?"

"He said that there was one older car parked near a pile of motorcycle parts behind the building. Why?"

"That car would be the one that Joe drove as Jose Lopez. Steve and Jeremy found one car in the Gonzalez garage. That says that either there's a second car belonging to Penny and Joe that's parked on the street, or it was available for Penny to drive away in it. She may have left her house voluntarily."

"We'll check for a parked Gonzalez car right away. By the way, where are Steve and Jeremy?"

Irma said, "Steve is checking on their agency's other cases and alerting their people to the fact that Penny and Joe have been identified, and they are potentially in danger. I'll brief him on Joe's condition as soon as we finish here. We've assigned Jeremy to be our liaison to the agency for now, so he's with Steve. They work well together."

Bobby said, "That's probably because they're the youngest of all of us. We have to play the wisdom and stature cards to succeed as we grow older."

Arthur laughed and patted Bobby on the shoulder. "You have a long way to go before you worry about getting old. Your new daughter will keep you young...Right now our focus should be on Penny. We know that she's missing, and we're not sure whether she was kidnapped or if she's somewhere on her own. I think the thing to remember is that she's a well-trained manager and covert investigator. They probably went after her, thinking she was a conventional housewife. She's extremely capable, and

I wouldn't be at all surprised if the hunters have now become the hunted. Bobby, if you can confirm that her car is missing, I think we should give credence to the theory that Penny is tracking the people who came after her. Even if she was taken, we should be alert for some communication from her.

Irma said, "That's good positive thinking. I hope you're right.

CHAPTER 67 – NEXT STEPS

After Bobby left, Irma prepared to call Steve DuBois. "I'll bring him up to date on our discussion with Bobby and on our thinking that Penny may have escaped kidnapping and may now be tracking those who came after her. What else should I say?"

"Tell him that I'm going to the scene of the fire in Rochelle. I'm pretty sure there's important evidence there. He can meet me there or send someone from his agency to establish a federal jurisdiction on that site. John Samson told Joe that Jose Lopez would be working both in Rochelle and in Wheeling. With the Rochelle base gone, the gang might be working through the Wheeling location. Wheeling, Illinois is the site of the old Palwaukee Airport that's now called Chicago Executive Airport. My guess is that they used Rochelle as a base for distributing objects that come north over the roads and Wheeling for distributing items that arrive by air. If that's true, then their Wheeling base should be on or near the airport. Steve should have some of his agents try to locate that base. They should look for a building similar to the one in Rochelle, maybe even an aircraft hangar."

"What do you want me to do while you're gone?"

"Stand by for a possible message from Penny, and let us all know if you receive one. As a more active task, you might transfer the combined orphanage and distribution location information from those flash drives to a map so that we'll have a better feeling for the smuggling routes and the overall scope of this enterprise. That might also help if I'm wrong and Penny really was kidnapped. I would hope that they'd take her to Wheeling, because we'll be checking on that site, but there are many other places they could have her."

"So you're not quite as optimistic as you pretended to be?"

"What I said was logical, but it's also proper to cover all possible eventualities."

"Under that heading of looking at alternate possibilities, I have my recurring question."

"What's that?"

"Are you going to continue to be able to give your best efforts to being a pastor, when you are so devoted to pursuing investigations?"

"Ask me again after I become a married man with new responsibilities."

CHAPTER 68 – CRIME SCENE EVIDENCE

Arthur called Bobby from his car and asked him to contact Chief Bascker to authorize his presence at the Rochelle fire scene. He also asked whether the Parkville Police had located Penny's car parked near her house. When Bobby said they hadn't found the car, Arthur felt slightly more convinced that Penny had escaped her attackers. He knew that he had been optimistic in postulating that she was now in pursuit of them. In reality, he had no way of knowing where she was or whether she had been injured. His NASA problem-solving background and faith always prodded him to anticipate good results, even when the odds were heavily against that outcome.

After an uneventful drive, Arthur arrived at the burned-out building and identified himself to the Rochelle policeman on duty there. He drove to the rear of the property and parked outside the yellow-taped perimeter of the crime scene. He noted with relief that the firemen had kept the gasoline storage tank from burning or exploding. That additional conflagration would have greatly complicated his search for evidence.

Arthur knew exactly where to start his search. Joe had told him that he had concealed the motorcycle with two different tire treads beneath the pile of extra motorcycle parts. If the fire hadn't damaged that stack, he would have a significant trophy to take back to Parkville for comparison with the tread casts made at the site of Horse's murder. He had begun to remove the top few levels of motorcycle components when he heard a car approaching. He looked up to see Steve waving as he climbed out of a black Ford Expedition. He was wearing a black baseball cap with FBI on the front in gold letters.

"Hi, Steve, did you change agencies?"

"Hardly! We have an arrangement with the F.B.I. for situations like this. The public knows and respects their authority, so we use their identification in order to avoid publicizing our agency. Afterwards we document our field activities with them so that they'll be able to claim responsibility. Have you found something?"

"During Joe's first days undercover as Jose Lopez, he spotted a motorcycle that may have been used in the murder of Horse McCabe. He told me at that time that he had hidden it under a stack of old motorcycle parts behind the building. The fire didn't reach this point, so I'm about to find out if it's still here. You can help if you'd like."

Together they pulled motorcycle sections off of the pile and sorted them into smaller collections by size and type. Arthur was impressed by the number of assemblies on the new piles.

"There's enough stuff here to assemble at least another half dozen bikes."

"You're right, Arthur, and knowing Joe, that's exactly what he would have done with his spare time if he had continued undercover for a while. He would have found ways to combine parts from different brands even if it required making new steel adapter hardware."

They reached the bottom of the stack and found the complete motorcycle that Joe had described. Because it had been outside the building and at the bottom of the stack, it had been shielded from the fire. The tires were in good shape for Bobby's comparison with the tracks found at the earlier crime scene.

Steve said, "I'll tag it and document where we found it. Then I'll drop it off in Parkville for Bobby tomorrow. I don't think you have enough room for it in your Saturn Vue."

"That's fine, let's take a look at the old Chevy that Joe used as Jose. It wasn't damaged by the fire, and Joe may have left something useful in it."

Together, they hoisted the black motorcycle into the back of the big Ford and tied it in place so that it wouldn't shift position as Steve drove. Then they headed for the older car.

"Arthur, see if there is anything on top of the driver's sun visor. Joe has a habit of leaving keys there for cars that we share at the agency. This isn't his regular car, so he may have used the same trick on this one."

Arthur reached above the visor and pivoted it downward just enough to see whether anything was perched on top of it.

"Good thinking, Steve, the keys are here along with a small digital camera. Joe may have taken another batch of pictures before they slugged him and threw him in that cage. I'll unlock the trunk and check it while you see if there's anything of interest in the car."

Arthur opened the trunk and was disappointed to see that it was empty. He lifted the floor covering and found nothing there either. He shut the trunk and walked alongside the car to see how Steve was faring.

"I struck out, Steve. Did you find anything interesting?"

"So far I have fifty-three cents, two cigarette butts, and a hamburger wrapper. We can send them to the lab, but we got this car off of a used car lot, so any DNA on the cigarette butts or anything else is probably not important. I haven't seen anything that Joe would have considered important except for that camera you found above the sun visor."

"Wait a minute. I see something that's at least interesting."

"What's that?"

"There's a small crucifix hanging from the rear view mirror."

"That was probably part of Joe's undercover persona. They would have expected Jose Lopez to be Catholic. Even if it's not, it may have come with the used car when we bought it."

"I know that all crucifixes are pretty similar, but this one looks very much like the one we found on a keychain in Kristina's car. I'm going to tag it and take it for comparison with that one."

"That's an interesting observation. Let's look inside what used to be a building. Maybe something significant survived the fire. Tomorrow I'll have the car towed to Bobby's garage for more complete examination."

Steve returned to his car and retrieved two hard hats. He put one on, gave the other to Arthur along with a pair of surgical gloves and then led the way as they entered what remained of the building.

"Be very careful not to bump into the wall sections that are still standing. We don't know how stable they are."

Once inside, they separated, with Steve going over to the caged room area where Joe had been found unconscious while Arthur proceeded to the remains of the workbench and shop area.

Steve picked up and bagged something near the cage. "This is probably what they used to clobber Steve. It's a chrome plated pry bar, and it might be smooth enough to hold fingerprints. I'll have the lab folks check it."

Arthur found the tool box that had belonged to Chet Quinto. It had been hit by a falling steel beam and was dented so badly that he couldn't open it. He would take it back and let Chet see whether he could access it. Joe might have inserted something valuable inside. Arthur lifted each collapsed bench to see whether anything underneath it was worth examining. After finding nothing useful under the first two benches, he lifted the third to find two pieces of a broken wooden carving in a shallow undamaged metal box. The bench had collapsed on top of the box without even denting it.

"Steve, you had better come over and look at this."

"What did you find – a treasure?"

"You might say that in more senses than one. Look what's inside this metal box beneath the workbench."

"It's a broken carved wooden bird, and it has some old fading paint on it."

"To be more specific, it's a broken carving of a quetzal, painted green, white, and red. The quetzal is the national bird of Guatemala and also the name of its unit of currency. This proves that Penny and Irma were right in concluding that the gang is smuggling art and artifacts stolen from old churches. This one apparently dropped, breaking off the bird's long tail, and they threw it away. Joe retrieved it for evidence."

"Do you think that's why they decided to do away with him?"

"My guess is that they didn't know he took it out of the trash, or it wouldn't be here. I'll stand by my earlier theory that they decided to go after him when someone followed Jose Lopez home and found that Joe Gonzalez lived there."

CHAPTER 69 – TRACKING

Penny and her laptop computer made it out through the back door just before three tough-looking individuals entered her house through the front portal. Fortunately, she had responded to the sound of a van door slamming by leaving the kitchen and looking out the front window through the sheer curtains. Despite all of her security training, she had succumbed to the lure of small town living by leaving her front and rear doors unlocked for the past few days. The only positive aspect of this miscalculation was that she wouldn't have to repair a bashed-in front door.

She slipped out of her back yard through the side bushes and across Mrs. Finkle's yard to the side street where she had parked her black Ford Focus. It was small, dirty, black, and four years old, a combination which made it nearly invisible in traffic. Penny stashed her computer out of sight beneath the seat and moved to a new parking spot closer to the corner so that she could see the unmarked white van that had disgorged her would-be assailants. A neighbor seeing her reposition her car would mention it to the police if they inquired about her whereabouts. She wished she hadn't abandoned her cell phone in her haste to leave the house. She would have no ability to summon reinforcements during the chase.

Penny felt a slight surge of adrenaline as she contemplated the techniques she would use as she tailed the van. She'd done this before, but usually with Joe sitting beside her. He was off by himself in an undercover role, and she would likewise solo in a surreptitious road chase. She laughed to herself at the prospect of her shadowing the very people who had been unsuccessful in their efforts to harm her or take her away.

Penny watched as they came out of her house. One of the men was carrying a box of papers. Had she deposited all the critical documents into the secure cabinets? They never would have been able to gain access to those files; but had she left any revealing scraps or drafts on the table? She didn't think so, but could not be certain.

The van started to move, and she forced herself to count twelve seconds before she started her car. It was too easy to spot a following car if it moved in synchronization with you, even though they did that all the time in the movies. By the time she picked up speed, the van was two blocks ahead of her. She knew the Parkville streets better than they did, and she was confident that she wouldn't lose their trail. If this had been an organized agency pursuit, they would have multiple cars involved in order to vary the appearance of the immediate chase vehicle, but she didn't have that luxury and would have to settle for lane changes and intervening vehicles to disguise her pursuit.

As expected, the van headed in the general direction of Rochelle. Penny wondered whether they would lead her to the building where Joe had been working for them as Jose Lopez. She felt a touch of disappointment when they turned away from Rochelle and headed south on the highway toward Bloomington.

Ten minutes later the white van turned onto the eastbound tollway heading toward Chicago. Penny mentally prepared herself for the next stage of her pursuit by reviewing the tips she had learned for following cars in high speed heavy traffic. She was surprised a few minutes later to see the van turn onto the ramp for the Dekalb Oasis. *Perhaps they need gasoline.* Penny followed and watched as the van bypassed the gas station and the entrance leading to the restaurants. It headed for the parking area closest to the eastbound exit ramp. Penny pulled into a parking space near the restaurant entrance and watched.

The driver and the other two men got out of the van and stood talking to each other for a few minutes. Then the driver got back into the van and drove down the eastbound ramp back onto the tollway. *He was leaving them here. Should I follow the van or stay with the two men?* Penny made the quick decision to follow the two men into the building. The surprise came after they bought candy bars, when they walked out the other door of the oasis building into the westbound parking lot. When Penny saw the two men climbing into separate cars that would exit the oasis going westbound, she knew she was in trouble. She couldn't follow them, and the van had a big head start.

Reversing direction, Penny ran through the building, out into the parking lot, and back to her car. Then she drove toward the eastbound exit ramp. As she accelerated back onto the tollway, she realized that she had little hope of catching up with the white van unless he continued to drive straight toward Chicago and unless she drove through traffic faster than he did. As she wove through the four parallel streams of eastbound traffic she also discovered that there were many white vans on the road.

CHAPTER 70 – HOSPITAL

The ambulance had delivered Joe Gonzalez to the Emergency Room of Rochelle Community Hospital within ten minutes of its departure from the burning garage and shop building. Because of the relatively short distance to the hospital and en route radio alerts from the Emergency Medical Technicians in the ambulance, the ER doctors had positioned themselves to administer care as soon as the ambulance arrived. The EMT's had maintained Joe's airway open and had fitted him with an oxygen mask that was delivering the gas at the recommended volume of 15 L/min. Upon their arrival, the paramedics transferred Joe to the custody of the waiting medical team. The ER personnel then whisked him off for intensive care.

In the absence of Penny, whose condition and location were still unknown, Irma had headed for Rochelle and the hospital to give Joe whatever comfort and support she could. By the time she arrived, he had regained consciousness but was not yet fully aware of everything that had happened to him.

After conferring with the attending doctors, Irma entered Joe's curtained-off cubicle.

"Hi, Joe; you've been through a lot, but after some treatment and rest, you're going to be your normal self again."

"It's good to see you, Irma. Did you bring Penny with you?

"I'm afraid you'll have to settle for me right now. We think that Penny's off on a mission of her own."

"What do you mean by *think*? Don't you know for sure where she is?"

Irma patted his shoulder. "Ease up, Joe. This isn't the time for you to get stressed out. I promise I'll give you a complete summary of Penny's current circumstances as soon as you answer a few questions about your own experience."

"Go ahead. What do you want to know?"

"Do you know who hit you and knocked you out?"

"I'm sure it was John Samson, because he was the only one I saw before I blacked out. The problem is that I was hit from behind, so I didn't actually see my attacker."

"You were found locked in the cage room. Were you in there when you were hit?"

"I had managed to pick the lock on that cage, but I think I was outside the building when I was hit."

"You don't know for sure where you were when it happened? Had you left the cage door open?"

"I think I must have some memory missing. I saw John Samson coming up the driveway in his fancy red car, and I waved to him. He drove into the building. Then I went back to work on straightening out the fender on the Chevy I was driving. I don't even remember John coming out of the building. I remember trying to force that fender back into shape and then waking up here, but nothing in between."

"That lapse would be due to your concussion. You may remember more with the passage of time. John tried to kill you. He hit you on your head and dragged you into that cage room. Then he locked the cage and set fire to the building. If Bobby hadn't alerted Chief Bascker of the Rochelle Police that you might be in danger, the Fire Department wouldn't have even tried to rescue you. They thought the building was empty."

"Why did Bobby contact Chief Bascker? Why did he think I was in trouble?"

"Now you're ready for my story about Penny."

CHAPTER 71 – WHEELING

Steve DuBois had just pulled into a parking space by the main buildings at Chicago Executive Airport, formally known as Palwaukee Airport and still sporting signs displaying both names. His cell phone rang. He answered it to find Penny Gonzalez on the line.

"Penny, we've been looking all over for you. We thought you had been kidnapped."

"That was their intention, but I slipped out the back door before they entered the house. Then I started tracking them."

"Did you have any luck? Where are you now?"

"I'm in Wheeling, at the old Palwaukee Airport. I'll tell you the whole story later, but I finally tracked their white van to a construction area in a corner of the airport next to Palatine Road. They have a bunch of older construction trucks and bins of stone and paving materials here. The guy in the van headed directly for this area. I missed the turn, and I had to go way out of my way and take a bunch of turns to get back here. While I was doing all that backtracking, I watched him from a distance getting out of the van and into a red jeep. By the time I finally reached that corner of the airport he was gone. After a long chase, I lost him. At least I found a pay phone. Where are you?"

"I'm in the main parking lot at the same airport. John Samson told Joe when he first met him as Jose that he would sometimes work in Wheeling. Arthur figured that they would have their shop on or near this airport, so I came to check it out. I made some calls while driving here and learned that this airport is the Chicago distribution hub for Federal Express.

I'm sure that's the key. They use FedEx to send the rush items they're selling and either pick them up at the FedEx center here or are close enough to have an early delivery time. We'll have to have someone analyze the FedEx procedures and records to see whether we can identify their account and find their address."

Penny said, "Our both being at this airport reminds me of the old saying that all roads lead to Rome. My chase proves they have a connection with this place, even if it's just as a vehicle exchange point. We can install a surveillance camera to monitor the van and this parking lot. We can also attach a GPS tracking device to the van."

"Arthur also thought that they'd make Wheeling their main location now that the Rochelle facility is gone." Steve regretted his words as soon as they left his mouth.

"What do you mean by that? What happened to that facility? Is Joe all right?"

"I'm sorry, Penny, I forgot that you've been out of contact. They tried to get rid of Joe by knocking him out, locking him up, and setting the building on fire. Thanks to Bobby's friendship with the Rochelle Police Chief, the firefighters knew to search for him, and they got him out in time. He's at Rochelle Community Hospital with a concussion and some aftereffects of smoke inhalation. Irma has been with him there while we looked for you."

"I'll have to call him right away. You're sure he's going to recover fully?"

"That's what the doctors say, and if you want to call him, I have your abandoned cell phone in my pocket. There's a McDonalds right next to the airport. Let's meet there, and you can make your call. I'm so glad we didn't have to rescue you from kidnappers."

CHAPTER 72 – PLATES AND PICTURES

They spent the morning straightening up the parsonage after a large Bible study meeting the night before.

Irma looked up from smoothing the couch cover and said, "You do realize, don't you, that this place definitely needs a woman's touch?"

"If by that you mean cleanliness and neatness, I definitely agree. If you mean creative decorating, I'd like to reserve a say in the matter."

"Arthur, are you telling me that you don't trust my taste?"

"No, I'm just saying that I'd like to be sure the overall impact of your tasteful decorating is compatible with my thinking. I assume that you do want us to cooperate on projects."

"We've been doing that through our ABC Consultants investigations for quite a while now. I don't think our domestic life together will be much different."

"Speaking of the investigations side, have you downloaded the photos from the camera I found on top of Joe's visor to your computer?"

Irma stopped dusting the furniture and glared at him. "You can't keep the current case out of your mind, can you? Am I ever going to get you to concentrate on me for a while? Anyway, the answer is that I did download them, and I found that they were mostly pictures of license plates and one face photograph of a woman I don't know. That's either that Barbara woman in the gang, or Jose was having an undercover fling."

"Undercover is a good place to have a fling."

Arthur dodged the dust rag aimed at his head. "You have a strange habit of throwing things at me."

Irma said, "We're not having any undercover flings today. I already made the bed."

"Since we're not married yet, any liaison I had with you would qualify as a fling, as would all the objects you throw at me."

"To tell you the truth, when we work on fixing up this place rather than my apartment, I almost feel as though we are married...I did say almost. We still have to have the ceremony."

"Reverend and Mrs. Blake: how do you like the sound of that?"

"It's a little formal, but I do like it. Anyway, I transferred all of the license plate photos to a flash drive. When we finish here, we can take them to Bobby for him to run through the Police Department's computer. We'll soon have the names of these people unless they're driving stolen vehicles."

"Or unless they're driving their own vehicles with stolen plates. Anyway, I'll take you to lunch, Miss Cinderella, and then we'll visit Bobby and his computer."

"That sounds good to me, Prince Charming."

An hour later, they parked in front of the Parkville Police Station and carried two packages inside. When Sergeant Al Gomez greeted them in the front office, they placed their parcels on the table that displayed handout literature.

Irma said, "Hi, Al. We have a present for you and all of the troops. We brought ice cream and cones for you. Is Bobby busy?"

"Thanks for the treat. I'll see that everyone gets some. Bobby's in his office; He'll be glad to see you."

Arthur and Irma headed for Bobby's office as Al's voice resounded over the P.A. system announcing the availability of ice cream treats at the front desk. They

241

realized that Bobby would have already guessed their presence. When they entered his office, he was beaming at them."

"You guys sure know how to make a grand entrance. Anyway, I have good news. We compared the tire treads on that motorcycle that Steve brought in from the Rochelle fire scene, and it definitely is the one that Horse's murderer rode."

Irma said, "That confirms that the murderer was involved in this group, whatever it turns out to be, and that Horse was killed in connection with some of their criminal activities."

Arthur said, "It might also have been a personal grudge, but someone in the gang is the killer...Bobby, we have photos that Joe took of the license plates on the cars and motorcycles at the Rochelle facility. If you run them through your computer for ownership records, we may learn a lot more about these people."

"That sounds promising. Give them to me, and I'll get started right away."

Irma handed Bobby the flash drive. He inserted it into a socket on his computer and started to review the contents. "I'll start with the motorcycles. All of them may be registered to the same person or organization. If so, we'll learn who's in charge or what to call this group." He traced three of them and then smiled as he turned toward Irma and Arthur.

"The two Hondas and the Suzuki are registered to Guamexx Motorcycle Leasing. I also cross-checked that name, and I found that they have sixteen motorcycles registered in their name. It lists one address each in Illinois, Iowa, and Indiana."

Arthur said, "That's bad news and good news. We haven't identified the gang, but we can contact this Guamexx outfit to see who leased these particular motorcycles. There weren't any license plates on the murderer's motorcycle, but we can check the VIN number plate on it to see its history."

Bobby said, "That's a good idea, although criminals sometimes remove the VIN plate on stolen vehicles and others that they don't want traced. There may even be some VIN number plates on some of those partial assemblies of bikes behind the burned-out building."

Bobby examined Joe's photos on his screen, copied the license plate numbers onto a sheet of paper, and then entered them into his online tracing form. As each set of results appeared, he printed it. Within a few minutes he had the results ready for their analysis and discussion.

"Here we go again. John Samson's pride and joy Ferrari is leased from Guamexx Sports Leasing. Bill's Jeep is leased from Guamexx Adventure Leasing, as is Barbara's Ford pickup truck and Larry's Dodge minivan."

Arthur said, "They're smarter than I expected. They hide behind leasing companies to minimize the probability of a license plate check leading to their real names and addresses. They may even carry phony driver's licenses. What do you think of their smokescreen, Irma?"

"I'm not a betting person, but if I were, I'd wager that those addresses for Guamexx Leasing are also fakes. I think this company and its various divisions exist only on paper. Bobby, do an online search for any other companies with the Guamexx name."

"I come up with Guamexx Transfer Company and Guamexx Galleries."

Arthur patted Irma on the shoulder. "Bingo! You have the whole picture, Irma. This organization *is* Guamexx. They bring in the artifacts as Guamexx Transfer Company when they're shipping directly to a client who sells them on its own, and they use the

Galleries name when they're supplying an auction house or a private art collector. They're counting on simply disappearing if the authorities come down on them. If we didn't have all of that information from Kristina's flash drives, we'd never be able to locate the different parts of the organization."

Irma said, "We still don't have any names or addresses of the leaders or the local people here. As soon as we arrest any one individual, the rest will scatter. Don't you agree, Bobby?"

"It's time to get Penny's agency to take the lead in going after these folks. This is a federal project. We'd have to hit all of their locations at the same time to get a significant number of them."

Arthur shook his head. "We're not ready to sweep them up until we can identify some of their leaders. We're making progress, but we need a plan to catch the leaders. At least we now have the name they hide behind."

CHAPTER 73 – HOSPITAL CONFERENCE

They gathered in Joe's hospital room. Penny and Steve occupied the straight chairs the hospital provided for visitors, but Irma and Arthur sat in wheelchairs they had corralled from an alcove near the nurses' station.

Penny said, "I asked you to come here for this meeting because I want Joe to stay involved in things as he recuperates. He's been the one taking the risks on the front line."

Joe said, "I may not be completely back up to speed, and my head still hurts a bit, but I realize that she was taking a lot of risk during her high speed highway chase. Anyway, we know much more about these people than we did before. We even have detailed FedEx records of packages received by Guamexx Transfer and Guamexx Galleries in Wheeling. They have a small office just south of Palatine road for receipt of packages, and transfers to their distribution couriers."

Arthur said, "As I see it, we know where most of the transfer points throughout the network are, and you could close them down with a federal task force, but you still wouldn't know who the leaders are."

Penny shook her head. "John Samson has to be fairly high up, or at least the public face of the organization, or they wouldn't give him that Ferrari to drive."

Arthur said, "I agree, Penny, now that we know he didn't buy it himself. Do you think he would reveal the names of the other leaders if you interrogated him?"

"I doubt it. He's the kind of guy who prides himself on his toughness. Irma, do you think forensics will reveal the identity of the person who rode that murder motorcycle?"

"That bike has been through a lot, Penny. Fingerprints would be useless. There is a chance we could get DNA evidence from dried blood on it, but the results would only pay off if we had the DNA of a suspect with which we could compare it. Nevertheless, I'll work with Bobby to get what we can from that bike."

Steve said, "We've checked all our resources, and we have no legal records for Guamexx as a company. Either they made up the name without legal paperwork, or it's an entity formed in Mexico or some other external country."

Penny said, "This is a frustrating situation. The group is a network, not a company. We think we know what they do and how they do it, but we have very little information on the people involved. If we start to arrest the lower echelon people from the data Kristina left, we'll lose the top people because they'll just disappear. They'll also be very leery of accepting anyone new, who might be working undercover, because they already discovered an operative in their midst. Speaking of that, is Joe still in danger? Do you think they'll try to kill him again?"

Arthur said, "We think we've avoided that possibility. Chief Bascker of the Rochelle Police told the media that an unidentified body was found in the debris after the fire. The real danger is that they might make a second attempt to kidnap you, Penny. I think you should move in with Irma while Joe remains in the hospital."

"That's fine with me if Irma goes along with it. That should keep Joe from worrying about me. When would you like me to arrive, Irma?"

"My inn is open for business as of right now. You might have to share some of your recipes with me while you're there."

"That sounds like fun. Consider it a deal. Now, what's your proposal for catching these people, Arthur?"

"I have a couple of suggestions. First, I think the gang will be looking for Marco Fernandez because he introduced them to Jose Lopez. They don't know that we have Marco in jail. He played his part well before. I suggest that you may want to consider turning him into an operative. You'll have to be honest with him and tell him that he might be in danger if he accepts the job, but you might dangle some kind of career position in front of him. I think he'll take it, and it might improve his future. My second suggestion is that you get the local police to find a reason to arrest Pedro Garcia. It would have to be a charge totally removed from the activities of this gang. It would be hard on him because he's a family man, but he has worked with John Samson as a messenger for a long time, and he probably knows all the local connections of this enterprise and the people involved. If you could interrogate him without the gang getting suspicious, we might get information on the higher-ups."

Joe said, "You know, I have the feeling that Pedro would talk if we handled it properly. He's so devoted to his family that he might jump at the prospect of getting into the witness protection program. We could offer to transplant the entire family somewhere else and give them a better economic outlook. We might even be able to tempt him into some valuable conversations without having to arrest him."

Penny asked, "How would we use Marco to help find the leaders? They only brought him in as muscle before."

Arthur said, "It might be dangerous and tricky, but if you were invisible to them at Irma's place, he would be their only lead to the story of Joe Gonzalez. Don't forget, because you two are new in town, nobody here knows much about you. I assume you didn't broadcast your agency background story."

"Nope, we always play our cards close to the vest. Marco might be good bait for a trap or for a misinformation campaign. What did you think of him, Joe? Would he be useful?"

"He might work out well. I had the impression that he enjoyed working with me before. At least they would believe his reaction to a situation. If we used someone with special training, he or she might not know how to react under pressure. I don't think we have anything to lose, and he might take us several steps forward. Let's do it."

CHAPTER 74 – MARCO

Although Marco Fernandez was surprised when Sergeant Gomez opened his cell door and led him to the interview room, he refused to show his emotions. He figured he had an advantage in any confrontation when the opposition couldn't read his feelings. When he entered the room he found a man and a woman already sitting at the table. Al Gomez motioned for Marco to sit down and then left the room.

The woman was the first to speak. "Marco, I'm Penny Gonzalez, and I represent a federal agency, as does my colleague here, Steve DuBois." Steve nodded to Marco, and Penny continued. "You know my husband Joe, who is also in our agency, as Jose Lopez."

A look of recognition passed across Marco's face despite his resolve to hide his emotions. "Why isn't Jose, or Joe, here? He's an all right guy."

"He's not here because John Samson and his buddies tried to kill him by knocking him out, locking him in a cage, and then burning down the building that confined him. To be accurate, they think they succeeded in killing him, but they didn't."

Marco no longer tried to hide his feelings. "That's like putting a guy in jail and then burning down the prison. Burning someone alive is complete horse crap. We all know that our number will be up sometime, but that's not an acceptable ending. It's like throwing acid in a beautiful woman's face. It just shouldn't be done...Anyway; you said they didn't succeed, right? I like Jose. He was cool when we met with Pedro. He knew how to make Pedro get real interested in his deal."

Penny said, "Joe liked working with you too. He has to spend some time recovering, but he'll be fine. We hope that you'll be interested in working with us to get Samson and his crew out of circulation. If you help us, we might have more work for you in the future within our agency."

"Are you saying that you might have a federal job for a dumb piece of muscle like me? That doesn't sound likely."

"We don't all sit behind desks in offices. As you've seen with Joe's effort as Jose Lopez, there's lots of field work and infiltration of different groups. Steve here used to be part of a SWAT team."

"Now that's something that would be my kind of work. What do you want from me?" Marco leaned forward on his chair as he spoke.

Penny noticed Marco's change in posture. She leaned forward and spoke in a conspiratorial tone. "Samson will be looking for you because you're his only lead to the identity and background of Joe Gonzalez. He doesn't know that you've been in jail."

"You kept me here because you've been worried that I would tell Samson what's going on, and now you want me to do just that. What a weird development this is."

"We don't exactly want you to reveal who we are. We want you to find out more about Samson's associates so that we can identify them and get more details about how the gang works."

"Why would Samson lead me to them?"

"We think they'll come to you when you tell them you want to sell them information about others who have infiltrated their operations."

Marco stood up and started pacing back and forth. Steve mirrored his move by also standing up, in case Marco did something unexpected. "You guys want to dangle me out there as bait. We already know from that burning building that these folks play rough. Why should I do it, and how can I be sure I won't end up dead?"

"You'll be safe until you give them the information on other infiltrators, and we'll have armed people close by to support you."

"What if they take the news of more infiltrations as a signal that they should shut down the operation and disappear?"

"That's the chance we're taking. If they do that, we lose them, but we think their business is too lucrative for them to simply close up shop. Anyway, that's our proposal, Marco, will you work with us?"

"Do I get a badge and a long term job if we get these people?"

Penny noted with satisfaction that Marco had already made his decision. He had said *we* instead of *you* in connection with this mission. "You'll get them both."

"Then count me in."

CHAPTER 75 – PEDRO GARCIA

Per Joe's suggestion, Steve had checked for a military record on Pedro Garcia and had discovered that he had served in Iraq with the Illinois Army National Guard 1644th Transportation Company, based in Rock Falls, from October of 2004 until October of 2005. While he was there he had met his wife Carol who was also in the unit. They had avoided additional tours of duty because Pedro had developed a heart murmur, and his wife had lost part of her left foot in a roadside bomb explosion. This background gave Steve more understanding of Pedro's family commitment and would function as valuable ammunition for their discussions.

Steve called Pedro early in the morning and identified himself as Steve Murray, a benefits manager for the government's Department of Veterans Affairs. He requested a meeting to review Pedro's qualifications for possible additional benefits due to his and his wife's service-related health problems plus his family obligations. Steve suggested that Pedro come to meet with him at the VA offices on North Lake Street at one o'clock in the afternoon, having already made interagency arrangements for the temporary use of an office suite. Penny would be there acting as his supervisor in the next office.

Pedro Garcia arrived promptly at one o'clock, and, as instructed, the VA Benefits receptionist directed him to Steve's office.

"Mr. Murray, I'm Pedro Garcia, and I'm here for our appointment."

"Welcome, Pedro, you're very prompt. Please take a seat while I finish signing these papers." Steve signed his name on some stock forms and placed them in a file folder that he inserted into a drawer of his desk. Then he turned back to Pedro. "I understand that you are currently receiving some benefits from our department."

"Yes, my wife and I are both Iraq veterans with disabilities. She was wounded in an explosion, and I developed a heart murmur while I was over there. We also have two dependent children, and that affects the amount we receive."

"Are you employed?"

"I don't have a regular job, but I operate a contract messenger service."

"Does your service have many customers?"

"Actually, there's only one company I work for, but with the benefits I've been getting so far, we've managed. You indicated that additional benefits might be available for us?"

"I did say that, but first I have to ask a few more questions to see whether you qualify for them. Is your wife employed also?"

"No, she's a full-time housewife. We feel that kids get a better start on life when there's a parent at home with them."

"Have you ever been arrested and charged with a crime?"

Pedro twisted in his chair. "I once was present when someone else was arrested for stealing a car, but I wasn't arrested. I convinced the policeman that I had just arrived at this person's house and that I could prove I was working at my job when the car had been stolen."

This would be the tricky part of the interview. Steve fixed his stare on Pedro's eyes. "Do you consider yourself an honest man?"

"What kind of question is that? I was honorably discharged from the National Guard after developing my heart murmur. I became a U.S. citizen last year, and I'm a good husband and father. Of course I consider myself honest. Do you ask that of every applicant for benefits?"

Penny had walked in from the supervisor's office. She moved into Pedro's line of sight. "No, Pedro, we don't; but perhaps we should. In this case we know that your contract customers, John Samson and his associates, are definitely not honest, and we want to know whether you are part of their outfit or an innocent outsider."

"Who are you people? You don't sound like Veterans Affairs paper-pushers...And the answer to your question is that I'm always careful to stay within the law, even when I work with others who don't."

"Then you're aware that your customers are criminals?"

"I'll go so far as to say that I've had some suspicions, but I'm only running an honest messenger business."

Penny said, "You'd better be telling us the truth, or you could be held as an accessory to murder and a bunch of other crimes. In answer to your earlier question, the federal agency we represent has nothing to do with Veterans Affairs. We investigate interstate and international crimes that threaten the security and the economy of the United States. You're involved, however innocently, in the workings of a large criminal network. If you give us enough information about them and help us bring them down, you won't be prosecuted. Otherwise, you'll be taken from your family and put away for a long time."

"Hold on there. I told you the truth about how I operate. What do you need to know? If I have the information, I'll give it to you. I only know who gives me each package, and where I deliver it."

Steve said, "That's exactly what we need to know."

CHAPTER 76 – REACTIONS AND SUSPICIONS

John Samson sat across the picnic table from Barbara, nursing his beer as he talked. He'd already finished his steak, but she was still working on her salad. "This barbecue session was a good idea. It gives us a chance to talk without anyone else around. What bugs me is that I really liked that Jose Lopez guy, and then he turned out to be an impostor – I assume some kind of cop, but I don't know much more."

Barbara looked up from her salad. "Don't you think it would have been smarter to question him before you killed him? He's not going to tell you anything now."

"We hoped to get his wife at that house we found when we followed him home, but no one was there. I've had someone watching the place ever since, but she hasn't turned up. Maybe they were separated or divorced."

"We'll have to get a new place for the overland deliveries. Wheeling is too far out of the way. You're like that guy who burned down barns to roast the pigs inside. You could have eliminated him without burning down the building."

"I agree. I was so angry about his abusing my trust that I wanted to make his death extra painful. I'll bet he woke up at the peak of the fire and suffered for a long time."

"Who was listed as the owner of that building? Was there insurance coverage?"

John looked a little sheepish. "We lost out on that one. There was no insurance because we didn't bother about permits or codes when we erected the building. We paid some supplier in cash to put it up over his vacation. I think he stole most of the materials from his boss, but I'm not sure. The land was a parcel that had been tied up in an estate dispute for years, and we just squatted on it. We won't be going back there again, so no problems about someone tracing us."

"That's especially true since you drive such an inconspicuous car. I told you to get rid of that Ferrari. I'm not comfortable with that degree of ostentation. At least use it only for pleasure trips."

"It was a pleasure trip. I stopped in unannounced, drove into the building, and found that he had opened the cage room."

"Did you remove the merchandise before you started the fire?"

"That I did. By the way, we may have to lean on Miguel to speed up the transfer of merchandise to the border. We almost missed an auction last month."

Barbara pushed her empty salad bowl aside. "I'll take care of that. It may be time to look at his operation for possible spies down there. The Zetas are getting aggressive. As long as they think we're just moving kids around, they won't bother us, but if they get wind of our artifact profits, they may try to take over. Miguel is supposed to pay them protection money. I'll make sure it's enough to keep them happy."

"What's the status of our couriers on the east and west coasts? Have you heard anything about new people who, like Jose Lopez, might not be trustworthy?"

"He really got to you, didn't he? Our other areas haven't added any new people for a long time, so you don't have to worry. I think you're mostly mad at yourself because you brought Lopez into the business. Don't worry about it. We all make mistakes sometime.

He may have been a con man rather than a cop, just trying to get a piece of our action."

"Do you really think so?"

"I don't know anything for sure, but we'll keep our eyes open to see if there's anyone else looking over our shoulders. I think he was a lone wolf trying to get a piece of the killing we're making."

"Good wording; he got a bit of killing, all right."

CHAPTER 77 – LOOKING BACKWARD

Arthur sat at his desk in his church office staring at nothing in particular. Irma caught him in this pose as she entered.

"I'm trying to interpret your distant stare. Some would think you're just daydreaming, but I think I know you well enough to say that you're chewing on a problem. It's probably meatier than writer's block for your next sermon, so I'm going to guess it has something to do with our current investigation. Do I win a prize?"

"Yes, but I could be mean and ask you to be more specific."

"That's not a problem; I know you better than you think I do. You're chewing over something we've already discussed because you think there's something more to be extracted from it."

Arthur got up and gave her a hug. "You're good at both investigating cases and seeing into my mind. Remind me to never try to hide anything from you."

"That's a given. We have to share our thinking or we'll both get into trouble. Now let me help you analyze your current problem."

"I think that we can learn a lot more about the roots of this case from Kristina's journals. We read them and learned quite a bit, but then we set them aside. Now that we know the contents of the flash drives that Carlos gave her, and given the fact that we're beginning to understand the gang's operations, we should go back and study what Kristina observed, whether she realized its significance or not."

"I think that's a brilliant idea, and I thoroughly agree. Remember those words later. I may not always play the student, hanging on your every word and thought."

"I hope not. I'm smart enough to realize that you grasp new insights at least as firmly as I do. Anyway, do you have the journals with you?"

"In a manner of speaking I do. I have scanned versions on a flash drive in my briefcase. I sent the originals back to Bobby for his evidence locker."

"So you also thought we'd want to revisit those journals?"

"They gave us the starting point for learning what was behind the murder and the attack on you. I knew that we would want to take another look at them sometime."

"Let's do it. Pull up a chair, and pull up the files for the first and third journals. I'm looking for information about what Horse McCabe was doing before he worked in Santiago Atitlan and about the ministries of the Maryknoll Sisters before Sister Kristina arrived."

Irma looked at Arthur as though he was crazy. "Those things won't be in the journals."

"I think we'll find enough in the journals to tell us where else we should look."

CHAPTER 78 – MARCO RETURNS

John Samson answered his phone and heard an unexpected voice.

"John, this is Marco Fernandez calling. Can we get together? You owe me some money for that job I did for you."

"My memory is that you would only get the second payment if you got those journals out of the guy. However, I'm in a generous mood. I'll pay you, but you're going to have to give me some information I need. I'll meet you at O'Brien's Tap in Schaumburg."

"John, don't take this the wrong way, but I'd like it to be a more public place. It's just a phobia I have about meetings in dark secluded spots I know nothing about. My dad died in that kind of meeting. How about meeting in downtown Chicago at Buckingham Fountain? We'll be outside, so nobody will be able to overhear us, and we'll look like a couple of tourists."

"That's a bit out of my way, but it's a nice day, so I'll go along with it. Let's meet at two o'clock. That should avoid the rush hour."

John disconnected and pocketed his phone. *He should be worried. If I find out he knew Lopez was a fake when he brought him to my attention, Marco will have an accident. It's interesting that his father irritated someone enough to get bumped off. Maybe stupidity runs in their family.*

A few hours later John walked toward Buckingham Fountain after parking a few blocks away. He found himself enjoying the park scenery and the view of the many boats on Lake Michigan. He had to agree with Marco that this would be a good place to discuss private matters. There were so many tourists and family groups that no one would pay much attention to two old friends greeting each other and walking in the sunshine. As he approached the fountain he spotted Marco on the lake side of the fountain talking with a young African-American woman. John felt a slight kinship with Marco in that they both liked to connect with pretty females.

As John appeared in the distance, Bonnie Thomas placed her hand on Marco's shoulder affectionately and said to him and to all others on her radio frequency, "Samson has arrived. Be prepared to move in if Marco has a problem. Start your recording now." She gave Marco a quick kiss on his left cheek, and walked away toward Michigan Avenue. He smiled in response and watched her energetic retreat from the fountain scene. *I think I'm going to like being part of this organization.*

On other sides of the fountain plaza a balloon vendor made a present of his last red balloon to a small blond girl; an electrician climbed down his ladder from a light pole; and a photographer and his brunette model walked closer to Marco's position for their next series of glamour shots.

John approached Marco, oblivious to the significance of anyone around them. "Hey, my friend, I saw you talking with that chick. I guess you handle yourself all right with the women. She looked as though she wanted some more time with you."

"She'll be spending more time with me real soon. This place is a magnet for women of all ages. There's even a model posing for pictures taken with the fountain as background."

"When she finishes, maybe I'll offer her a ride in my chariot. That Ferrari is something special for most women."

"Did you bring my money, John?"

John passed an envelope to Marco. "Here it is, as promised. Just don't rush off with it. I want to discuss a few things with you."

"Sure; go ahead."

"Through Pedro you introduced me to Jose Lopez. How did you first get to know him?"

"I met him through my lawyer. Jose was another one of his clients. The three of us had a few beers together and went to a couple of Cubs games."

"Where did you get the money for a fancy lawyer?"

"That wasn't a problem. He's a young guy, Manny Jacobs, and he works for the Legal Aid Society. I got involved with him when my girl friend of the moment accused me of beating her. I hadn't touched her, but she tried to get me in trouble with the law when I left her for someone else. Manny got me off by proving that her scratches and bruises were self-inflicted. He's a good guy to know when you have a legal problem. You might want to look him up. Someday he'll be a big wheel."

"Don't worry, Marco, I have lawyers who are already big wheels that come running when I call. What was Manny doing for Jose?"

"I don't remember. We were drinking buddies. Your lawyer could probably check with the cops and find out. Why all this interest in Jose's background? Just ask him."

Samson debated how much he should tell Marco. Then he said, "I'm curious about his background because he died in an accident, and I wanted to send a sympathy note to his family."

"I didn't know he was dead. Man, that's tough. He seemed like a good guy to me, and now he's gone. You never know when your time is coming."

"Actually, Marco, there was a problem with Jose. From our dealings so far, I think I can trust you to keep what I say to yourself."

Marco tried to keep tension out of his voice. This part of their talk would determine his future. "Sure, John, if it's confidential, I won't repeat it. What's up?"

"The truth is that Jose Lopez was an assumed name. I think he was actually someone else, and he was spying on me and my operation. I don't know whether he was a cop or from some other group."

"Wow, that's a shocker. He said he had come in from Mexico a while before I met him. Maybe he was with one of the cartels down there."

This time it was John who looked shocked. He hadn't thought of that possibility. Miguel had said that he was paying off the Zetas to keep them away from his orphanages. He didn't like the sound of Marco's speculation. Aloud he said, "Do you know much about the Mexican cartels, Marco?"

"I hear some whispers about their activities now and then, but I know people who have connections down there. I keep myself out of anything involving the cartels, but I have ways of finding information about them. Is there something specific you want to know? For a price, I could start some inquiries. It would be expensive, because I'd have to pay off a few middle men, but I'm pretty sure I could get answers for you."

"Just hold that thought for a while, Marco. I want to check with a few of my associates, and then I may take you up on that offer. I didn't realize you were so well connected."

"I don't advertize everything. It's fine with me if people think that I can only supply muscle to a project. If people underestimate you, you have an advantage."

John reached out and shook Marco's hand. "I came here expecting a much different conversation. I guess I'm one of those who saw only the muscle part. I'll be back to you within the week with a proposition that will benefit both of us." He walked away in the direction of his car, and Marco walked toward Michigan Avenue. John didn't see that several other people followed Marco.

CHAPTER 79 – ROOMMATES

Penny and Irma discovered that they enjoyed each other's companionship even more without their men around. Joe had moved from the hospital in Rochelle to a rehabilitation facility, and while Penny lived with Irma, Arthur spent most of his time at the church and parsonage. This temporary living arrangement had been set up for Penny's protection against another kidnapping attempt, but she and Irma enjoyed being roommates.

Breakfast became a time for indulging in special cuisine. They finished off *Penny's Famous Chocolate Swirl Pancakes* accompanied by a pot of *Irma's Honey Cinnamon Tea*, and collapsed on a matched pair of reclining chairs.

Irma said, "This was a great meal, but too many like it will keep me from ever fitting into my wedding dress."

"You talk as though you've already purchased it. Is that true, and if so, does Arthur know about it?"

"Yes, it's true, and no, he doesn't know I bought it. He'd probably be all upset again about the degree to which I plan ahead. When the time comes, I might have to imply that I borrowed it from a friend or relative."

Penny laughed and reclined her chair to the second position. "You're free to say that you're wearing my dress. Joe would never remember what I wore."

"Thanks for volunteering, but if Joe looked at your wedding album we'd be caught in a lie. I was kidding about making up a story. Given Arthur's profession, I'll have to be honest and say I bought a dress, but if he fails to ask the key question, I won't have to tell him when I bought it. I'll keep the dress hidden until we firm up our plans. It has simple styling because it suits our personalities. I'd show it to you, but after all this time waiting to get married, I don't want to do anything that might jinx the event. I've become superstitious."

"That's understandable, Irma. I'd feel the same way."

"I hate to change the subject, because my wedding plans are very important to me, but I think I should tell you about a conversation I had with Arthur. We were discussing ways to identify the leadership of this organization and put them out of business."

Penny brought her reclining chair to the upright position. "I've been puzzling over that one myself. I feel limited without having Joe handy for this kind of conversation. Did you come up with something?"

"Not yet, but we think the answer lies in the way this group and scheme were developed in the first place. We're going to analyze the material in Kristina's journals again and then do some follow-up work on any theories we generate. Arthur and I both believe that if we can find the beginnings of this conspiracy, we'll learn enough to understand its current scope."

"That sounds good to me. If you and Arthur take that approach, we'll have at least three separate but coordinated efforts to wrap this up. We're also going to check out all of the delivery contacts that Pedro Garcia has given us, and confuse our opponents with misinformation that will be planted by Marco Fernandez. If we get them bothered enough, they won't be able to disappear before we shut them down. As I see it, the weakness of this art smuggling organization is that it involves too many people in too many places. Once we gather them up, someone will start talking, and we'll see the entire picture."

CHAPTER 80 – JOURNALS REVISITED

Arthur, Irma, Wally Sanborn and Jeremy Hadley clustered around the large church library conference table, which was adorned with yellow lined pads of paper and a laptop computer. Arthur had suggested they reexamine the journals in this more formal atmosphere rather than Irma's apartment, believing that they would have fewer distractions as they sought to extrapolate insights from Kristina's brief passages.

Arthur finished his mug of coffee and opened their discussions. "Jeremy, I'm looking to you for suggestions as we review the journals. Peace Corps volunteers tend to be young and adventurous, two qualities that I also see in you. As we discuss events that Sister Kristina documented, try to react to them as if you were a volunteer on the scene in Guatemala. Wally, you'll be our expert on Peace Corps procedures, based on experiences in your youth."

Irma placed her computer so that everyone could view the screen. "I've scanned the contents of the three journals into my laptop, and we have paper printouts of the three notebooks on the table also. Using the paper printouts plus the screen display, we'll be able to examine several sections of these materials at the same time."

Arthur held up one of the printed copies. "Our task today is twofold. We will try to examine specific details in the notebooks that we might have overlooked during our earlier readings of these materials, and we will attempt to put the journals into context and postulate what else might have occurred down there. Irma and I will be revisiting the journals while you, Wally and Jeremy, will bring fresh eyes to this effort since you have only heard about these documents but have not previously seen them."

Wally nodded and made a couple of preliminary notes on his pad of paper. "To avoid going over everything, let's start at the beginning, and then we can jump to sections that Arthur and Irma found particularly significant. Jeremy and I should be able to keep up without having to reread every chapter and verse."

Arthur said, "That's the way many in this church approach the Bible, absorbing the gist of things without reading it completely. Irma, summarize the beginning."

"Kristina starts her journals shortly after arriving in Guatemala where she has been assigned to a home for orphans and unwanted children in Jacaltenango in the western highlands of Guatemala. She joined the Maryknoll Sisters, in part to get away from a bad environment at home where her stepfather, Rodrigo, whipped her because she was too independent for his taste. She does appreciate the fact that she learned Spanish from him. Shortly after beginning her assignment in Guatemala, she and two other sisters travel to Antigua with a priest named Father McShane. That trip is described in glowing terms."

Wally looked up from his notes and made a hand gesture. "Let me jump in with some information I researched. Antigua is the headquarters city for the Peace Corps in Guatemala. It's possible that Kristina and the other nuns met some of the Peace Corps volunteers there, perhaps even Horse McCabe. His name suggests that he was Catholic, and they might have met at a church there."

Arthur wrote something on his pad. "That's a good point, Wally. I also wonder if we know anything about the other nuns who went with Kristina, or if she had close friends among the nuns. How did she relate to Father McShane?"

Irma scrolled through the material on her screen. "Father McShane was older, and Kristina did not agree with many of his traditional outlooks. She thought he was a bit stodgy and out of touch. She would not have been close to him. She doesn't say anything about the other nuns who made the Antigua trip, but I get the impression that they were also relatively young and new to their assignments. She did mention that she met some Peace Corps people in Antigua. Kristina mentions a few other sisters and indicates that she likes to be independent when she works. Consider this passage:

There are just a few of us from the U.S.A. Sister Patrice is quite a bit older and from somewhere in Texas. Sister Michelle is from Pittsburgh; she is just a little older than I am but very timid and a by-the-book type. Sister Monica is from Boston and will be returning to the States next week. As long as I do my work well, I don't have to worry about close oversight, and that suits me fine. I am properly devoted to our Lord, but I am not an organization person."

Jeremy turned his chair to face Irma. "I'm a bit younger than the age Kristina would have been then, but I get the impression that she may have been divided in her outlook. She says that she is properly religious, but she also looks down on a nun who does everything according to the rules, and she is pleased that she will be able to work at her assignment without close supervision. She sounds as though she doesn't like rules and will follow her own conscience in all matters."

Wally said, "Those are very good observations, Jeremy. I'll add the fact that young Peace Corps workers tend to party when they get back to a city where they have friends. Their parties in Antigua may have involved one or more of the younger sisters. Young nuns frequently like to see the reaction they get at a social event when they identify themselves with their religious calling."

Irma said, "I can also certify that young female doctors like to deflate aggressive young men at a party who are puffed up with feelings of self-importance. That wouldn't apply to you, of course, Arthur."

"Thanks, but I like your lines of thinking. Don't forget that much later, Kristina turned her back on church rules and married Horace, or Horse, McCabe. There might have been some relationships at those Antigua parties that would have been costly for one or more sisters."

Wally said, "That's an interesting speculation, Arthur, but we could never prove it, and I don't see how it would relate to this case. You told me about the men who later tried to kill Kristina. You said that she escaped only because Horse rescued her. Is there anything in the journals that gives us the names of her attackers or their motives?"

Irma scrolled through the page images on her computer screen. "Here are the final three entries in her third journal. Kristina wrote them after Carlos Benitez had been murdered and after she had received the flash drives from him and had hidden them. Those events influenced her frame of mind when she wrote:

September 3, 2009 – I met Horse during a walk this morning. He joined me for about half a mile. Then the rains started up again and we had to take shelter in a cave we found. It was one of the most pleasant sojourns I have had. I know that I will have to leave this place soon. Change is coming.

October 23, 2009 – I reread my journals this morning, and I now realize that I will soon have to stop recording my thoughts. If anyone read them I could be in danger.

I will start to think about a good hiding place for them. Neither the other sisters nor outsiders should be able to find them.

November 7, 2009 – That Mexican, Miguel, is back in town, and he must be suspicious of me. I've noticed two of his men taking turns following me whenever I leave the orphanage and other church facilities. Like many farmers and other Guatemalan men they carry machetes that could cut people to pieces. Sometimes I get nervous when I see so many men with machetes. At one point this afternoon I decided to try to slip away from Miguel's men and visit Horse. I managed to take a series of quick turns in the town and then get on a bus without their seeing me. Imagine my disappointment after all that effort when Horse wasn't even home. Then on the way back I walked through some thick bushes and scratched my hand badly. I have made a mess of this page with my blood. At least I proved to myself that I can elude my followers when it is necessary."

Arthur wrote several lines on his yellow pad of paper. "Those passages suggest a relationship with Horse before Kristina was attacked. They also suggest that the danger to her was based on suspicion by Miguel or someone else in this criminal outfit that Benitez had told her more than she should know. Finally, they state that she had been followed by Miguel's men and that they had carried machetes."

Jeremy raised his hand as he would in school. Then he sheepishly lowered it. "I understand that almost all farmers down there carry machetes. Would people take notice of outsiders carrying them?"

"Miguel's men weren't farmers, but they could pass as farm laborers or people who had to chop their way through overgrown trails in the surrounding forests. Because of that, no one would think twice about their machetes.

'The importance of the machetes may lie in the fact that Kristina died from a rabies infection of the cut on her leg. Irma, you examined her body in the hospital morgue. Would you like to guess at the weapon that cut her leg?"

"The wound was consistent with having been made by a machete."

"Therefore, it's a good bet that she was attacked by Miguel's men, and Miguel runs the chain of orphanages used to smuggle Guatemalan colonial church artifacts through Mexico and into the United States. Directly or indirectly, the smuggling organization caused her death."

CHAPTER 81 – LAWYERS

Penny and Steve entered the law offices of Bexley and Josiah, identified by Pedro as one of his regular pickup and delivery points. Their North Michigan Avenue address and conservative-sounding name added prestige to the firm, but Penny doubted that either of the named partners had ever existed. As they entered, a man came out of one of the private offices surrounding an open, stylishly decorated seating area.

"May I assist you? I'm John Krimmens, one of the senior attorneys here."

Steve took the lead as they shook hands with John. "Hello, John; I'm Steve Devens, and this is Penny Josephs. We're from the Knackmeister Art Museum in Mt. Morris, Illinois. It's a small museum affiliated with the United Methodist Church, and we feature historically significant art and artifacts of a religious nature. One of the auction houses we deal with referred us to Miriam Gilbus from your firm. Is she in?"

"I'm afraid you'll have to settle for me today. Miriam is on vacation this week and next. We do sometimes represent sellers of the type of items you mentioned. Are you in the market for anything specific? If you are, I could pass your request to one or more of our clients."

Steve glanced at Penny; she nodded slightly and stepped forward. "We're particularly interested in religious art and objects from North or South America. Too many museums have concentrated on European items and have driven their prices out of reach. We now plan to sell our European collection and concentrate on art from the Americas."

273

John's smile showed his interest. "Mrs. Josephs, I believe we would be able to assist you in two ways. We have clients who specialize in Central American art of extraordinary quality, and we would like to discuss the possibility of representing your museum in selling your European art. As you indicated, prices for European items are quite high and continuing to rise."

Penny removed a file folder from her briefcase, but did not reveal its contents. "That might be a convenient arrangement, but first we would require specific information on the contacts you would use to dispose of our collection. We're talking about major pieces and a few with slightly clouded historical backgrounds. This is not a project for amateurs."

"I understand completely, Mrs. Josephs. As an indication of my interest and good faith, I am prepared to show you our confidential listing of dealers and individuals with whom we have done business on similar art sales in the past."

"That would be a nice gesture on your part, but I'm afraid that Steve and I cannot make such decisions on our own. We would have to have a copy of your distribution credentials and documentation to bring before our Board of Directors."

John Krimmens hesitated. *Miriam usually deals with potential clients. Why did she pick this time to be gone? Should I let them take it or not?* After a brief internal debate he said, "I wouldn't be able to let you take any documents from our offices without consulting with Miriam Gilbus, and I won't be able to contact her for another week and a half."

Steve said, "From that statement I gather that she is the senior party here, and that we should be discussing any possible involvement of your firm in our project with her rather than with you." He backed away from John and left no doubt that he was prepared to depart.

John's hand shook slightly. "No, we each have the authority to act independently. What I can do is to give you the distribution information for a half hour in an office and let you make written notes to aid you in your presentation to your Board of Directors. That time period should allow you to leave with adequate information, while not physically removing our documents."

Penny said, "That's a reasonable arrangement, John. Steve will make notes while we discuss other aspects of the project. I'd also like to enjoy the view from your windows over Lake Michigan."

"That's one of my favorite ways to relax. Our view isn't completely unobstructed by other buildings, but it is beautiful, especially when you watch it as the seasons change." He went back into his office and returned with a spiral-bound book.

"Steve, make your notes; you can use the second office from the front door."

Steve took the book into the office as John and Penny headed toward the large windows. Once in the office, Steve wrote rapidly on the first few pages of a lined pad of paper. Then he opened the bound document and started to photograph the pages with his cell phone camera. *The logical flaw in people of John's age is that they overlook technological shortcuts.* When he finished photographing the entire book, he sat down and pretended to continue making detailed notes from the first few pages of the book.

While Steve was working, Penny and John admired the view of Chicago and Lake Michigan. Penny rattled on about the Knackmeister Museum and the beauty of small-town Illinois. After she was sure that John was completely relaxed, she worked a small bombshell into the conversation to gauge his reaction.

"John, I was just thinking about your name. Krimmens is rather unusual. Some friends of mine adopted a girl from Guatemala some years ago. They mentioned that their lawyer's name was Krimmens. These folks are Joshua and Isabelle Weadle, and their daughter's name is Jane. You wouldn't be the lawyer they worked through, would you?"

John, who had been gazing out the window with a smile on his face, coughed several times in succession. "Forgive me, I swallowed my mint. I don't recall your friends, but there was a time when we helped families with international adoptions. I hope that they and their daughter are doing well. We are no longer involved in such matters."

Penny pressed the discussion forward. "Did you enjoy working on adoptions?"

"To tell you the truth, it bothered me a bit, because some adoptions worked out well while others led to family breakups and abandoned children. I was happy to put that part of our business behind me...I'm going to have to end our conversation for now. I have an appointment shortly. We'll be pleased to work with your museum if the Board approves it. Now I'll have to retrieve our records from Mr. Devens."

They found Steve putting his pad of paper into his briefcase, and exchanged their goodbyes. Penny and Steve headed out of the office suite toward the elevator. As they entered that cubicle Penny said, "I think we've just located the weak link in the chain of this enterprise. We should try to take action before Miriam Gilbus returns and realizes how much we've learned from John."

CHAPTER 82 – BEGINNINGS

Irma had been at the library, browsing for wedding planning ideas. On her way home, she stopped at Parkville UMC to see how Arthur's morning had progressed. She entered his office as he returned his telephone to its cradle.

"Good morning, Arthur. I see you're deeply involved in church work. That makes me feel better, per our earlier discussions."

"If you call conversations between clerics church work, then you might feel pleased. As it happens, this conversation was with Father Patrick O'Connell who worked in conjunction with the Maryknoll Sisters and Father McShane in Guatemala. He retired a while back, and I tracked him down to a small town in Ohio. I'm feeling pleased because I learned many useful things from a priest who was on the scene during the period before Sister Kristina arrived and who remained there for five months after she returned to the United States."

Irma sat on Arthur's reclining chair. "What did you think of him? Is he a valuable resource?"

"He has clear memories of everything that went on during that period, and spent many hours exchanging stories with Father McShane in restaurants and taverns. He looked up to Father McShane for having developed close contacts with people in the military and the government down there. O'Connell said that he always had trouble relating to members of the secular power structures. Comparing his and Kristina's perspectives adds more depth to the picture. It's too bad that Horse was murdered before we knew enough to question him about what happened in Guatemala...You look cheerful. What's your project for the day?"

"I've been gathering ideas for the wedding, and since you're also in a positive mood, I'll let you take me out to lunch so that I can tell you about them. You may also fill me in on Father O'Connell's story while we're eating."

"The lunch idea sounds good. When I get enthusiastic I get hungry, and I do want to be involved in your wedding planning. However, I'll hold back on what I learned from Father O'Connell until I mesh it with other information I expect to get from some follow-up calls."

CHAPTER 83 – JOHN SAMSON

Marco Fernandez answered his phone to hear John Samson's somewhat worried voice.

"Marco, I need to get some information. What do you know about the Zetas? Have you had contact with them in the past?"

"I didn't want to get into details when we were at Buckingham Fountain, but I know a few people in their cartel. A few years ago, I was deported back to Guatemala, and I paid some Zetas to help get me back here. Most people think they only operate in Mexico, but they move back and forth across the U.S. border without difficulty. They usually stay pretty close to Mexico and let others do their dirty work farther into the United States. They feel safer that way."

"Do you think that Jose Lopez might have been one of their people?"

"I don't know. He knew a lot about cars and engines, and he said he serviced cars in big Mexican road races, so he probably made contact with some important people down there. Why do you ask?"

"I want to set up a meeting between the organization I represent and the Zetas. My people think we can help each other. Can you arrange a gathering to meet and negotiate? We can meet anywhere."

"I might have the contacts to set it up. What's in it for me? I recall that I had to come after you to get paid the last time. How about ten thousand up front? I'll bill you for any travel expenses later."

"Agreed...I'll get cash for you this morning. Where do you want it delivered?"

"Leave it with Anton, the bartender at Lefke's Tavern, the place where you first hired me and Gus Savage. I'll tell Anton to be looking for it. Make sure it goes to him personally; I don't trust the bartenders on the other shifts."

"No problem, Marco; you're important to us now, and we don't want to screw things up."

Marco disconnected and keyed in the special number he had been given. A familiar voice answered. "Greetings, Marco...Joe Gonzalez here; your call must mean that they've taken the bait."

CHAPTER 84 – JOHN KRIMMENS

John Krimmens stared out his window, studying the storm clouds moving in over Lake Michigan while wondering about the people who had visited him two days earlier. He had not previously heard of the Knackmeister Museum, but he knew that there were many small art museums, some of which were only occasionally open to the public. There were also private collectors who operated a nonprofit museum for tax purposes. Such museums were set up by law firms similar to his own.

Bexley and Josiah was an awesome name for this firm, implying both British and American Bible Belt origins. It also gave them the stature that comes with conservative outlook and age. The firm name would have been even more awesome if Messrs. Bexley and Josiah had actually existed. He felt proud that he had contributed the Josiah portion as an improvement on the original *Bexley and Company*. John would also feel proud if he generated a substantial amount of new billings from selling the items in the Knackmeister Museum European collection. He wouldn't have to share credit for that with Miriam Know-it-all Gilbus. She always thought she was better than he was, but he knew that she really didn't care about anyone other than herself, and that made him a much better person.

The telephone rang, jarring John out of his reverie.

"Bexley and Josiah, John Krimmens speaking."

"Hello, John, this is Penny Josephs from the Knackmeister Museum. I wanted to let you know that our Board of Directors has approved our engaging you to assist with disposition of our European collection.

They also agreed to have you introduce us to your clients who are a source for art objects from the Americas."

"That's very good news, Penny...Is it alright for me to be so familiar?"

"Of course it is, John. If you don't mind, I'll visit you in an hour, and you can give me some of the contact information for your clients. I do hope they have the types of historically-significant art that we are seeking."

"I'm quite sure they will have important additions for your museum. I'll break for lunch now, so as to return before you arrive. Will you be bringing Mr. Devens?"

"Steve will be coming in a little later. He has an appointment that requires his attention first."

John returned from lunch and immediately began arranging for his Knackmeister meeting. He connected the conference room projector to his computer and selected the appropriate file for his presentation. Then he positioned several pads of paper and pens around the table. He had just finished placing three file folders in front of his chair when Penny Josephs arrived. At the sound of the chime on the outer door he went to greet her.

"Hello, Penny, I do appreciate a client or a visitor who is prompt. Younger folks tend to show no discipline in adhering to their time schedules."

"Thank you for the compliment, John. I assume it means that you have everything prepared for our meeting."

"I've just finished arranging everything. I have photographs of many of the art pieces we've already delivered, along with contact information for you to use in arranging future transactions. I also have coffee brewed, along with hot water for tea."

"You're a good host, John. I'll have some black coffee. I used to take it with cream and sugar, but a close friend has extolled the virtues of black coffee for so long that I've switched over to it."

They settled into their seats at the conference table, and John initiated a Power Point presentation showing many of the art pieces they had sold for their client who imported such items from Guatemala. Penny could hardly believe what she was viewing. John had included a much larger assortment of pieces than she had expected. This organization had been essentially raping the colonial churches of Guatemala without stimulating a loud outcry from authorities there. Either this huge display represented a very small fraction of the available church treasures there, or colonial art carried a much lower valuation in Guatemala than it did in the United States. Penny suspected that some Guatemalan art experts and historians had voiced alarms, but that their voices had been ignored by the government.

"John, some of those pieces would be perfect additions to our collection. I notice that you have a number shown at the lower right hand corner of each image. What does that signify?"

"That indicates the customer or auction house to which the piece was sold."

"Would we be able to work through you to purchase some of these pieces from those parties as well as to purchase new items from your supplier?"

"I don't see why not, Penny. We might have to charge a higher commission for transactions on individual items like that than we would for items from our supplier where we have a single source for multiple pieces."

"That's quite understandable, and we would agree to such an arrangement. What about the contact information you promised for your suppliers?"

"Our supplier is Guamexx Transfer Company and its subsidiary, Guamexx Galleries. They have offices around the country, but their principals are based in the Chicago area."

Penny could hardly believe how indiscrete John was with his client's information. He had revealed that the local members of the gang were its leaders. Either he was an honest middle man, unaware of his criminal connections, or she had succeeded in offering him so large a piece of potential business that he didn't care about consequences. "You do realize that we will have to check on the reputations of these principals. Many museums have purchased artwork such as items that were stolen by the Nazis during World War II, and have later lost their investments by having to return them to the original owners. We don't want to get involved with artwork that does not have ownership documentation."

"That's good conservative thinking, Penny. We supply documentation with every piece we sell. In some cases we can trace the history of a piece through several possessors, but we can always validate the sale to our supplier from the previous owner."

"Are most of these parties in Guatemala?"

"Some are, but more of them are in Mexico."

Penny realized that Miguel's homes for orphans in Mexico had a second function. They added multiple documentable owners to each art object in order to increase the difficulty of tracing its origin.

"How do you calculate your asking prices?"

"We work through a trusted appraiser at a Chicago branch of a New York auction house. She should be considered reliable because we usually obtain a price very close to her appraisal point."

"Has this appraiser evaluated all the pieces shown in your presentation?"

284

"Yes, she handled all of those lots, and she was quite impressed with their quality."

That comment told Penny that the appraiser had to be getting a payoff, because many of the items she had viewed should have aroused suspicion that they had been stolen. Penny would immediately initiate an investigation of the appraiser and the auction house she represented.

John and Penny heard the chime announcing the opening of the front door of the office suite followed by the voices of two people talking in the lobby. John left the conference room to greet the newcomers, but Penny relaxed in the knowledge that the visitors represented the second wave of their assault on John Krimmens.

She heard John say, "Welcome, Mr. Devens; Mrs. Josephs indicated that you would be joining us. Would you introduce me to your associate?"

John's remark was Penny's cue to join the group in the lobby. As she approached them she watched carefully for John's reaction to Steve's response."

Steve gestured toward his teenage male companion. "John, I'd like you to meet Pablo Benton. You processed the paperwork for his adoption from Guatemala when he was eight years old. He had been placed in the temporary custody of an orphanage in Guatemala while his parents had economic problems, but without their permission he was delivered to adopting parents in New York City. Four months after his arrival in the United States Pablo was sold to a street gang. They used him as an underage drug courier and, more recently, as a male prostitute. We tracked him down and rescued him. We're now making arrangements to return him to his birth parents in Guatemala."

John looked deflated and confused. "Mr. Devens, you don't sound like a museum representative. Who are you? Is Mrs. Josephs also someone other than the person she claims to be?"

Penny stepped forward. "John, we work for a federal agency that is looking into illegal international adoptions and art smuggling. You have been deeply involved in these activities, and we want to determine whether you have been a primary initiator of these crimes or a peripheral participant. What is your role?"

"I've never been more than a go-between. In the years when we were enabling international adoptions, I was bothered by what we were doing. I knew in my heart that there had to have been cases like Pablo's where children were snatched or swindled away from their birth parents, but Miriam always convinced me that I worried too much. I probably would have left the firm if we hadn't changed over to processing sales of artwork. It didn't bother me as much to deal with objects instead of people. I rationalized that increasing the economic values of these items made my efforts defensible, but I knew that our resale activities were wrong and illegal. I've subconsciously been hoping for this business to fall apart. Is there anything I can do to make amends for my participation?"

Penny moved in for the kill, choosing her words carefully. "John, meaning well is no defense. You will be facing jail time for your part in this operation. The amount of time you'll have to serve will depend on the degree of your cooperation with us to eliminate this gang and its operations. Will you assist us by telling us everything you know about the organization you've represented? You can't withhold any information if you want any legal support from us."

Pablo Benton interrupted. "And make sure you reveal where other Guatemalan children were placed. We all deserve to go home to our families!"

John had moisture in his eyes now. Pablo's exclamation had crystallized his guilt. He remembered how he had entered the legal profession with high ideals, but also how he had gradually come to place a premium on money and prestige. "I should have talked to people like you a long time ago. I'll tell you everything I know, but it isn't very much. They compartmentalize the organization so that most people only know about their own areas of responsibility."

Penny said, "Thank you for your cooperation. Start by telling us who is in charge of this enterprise and whether your firm specified art objects for them to obtain, or only disposed of objects they brought to you."

"Let me start with the second question first. We did understand that these pieces originated in old Guatemalan churches. We had no definite knowledge of whether the group stole them or purchased them from others who had stolen them. If we had a customer requesting an item that one might expect to find in an old church, we could request it. With regard to the structure of the organization, we dealt through John Samson. My guess is that there are only a few people higher in the group than he is, although I might be wrong. Miriam Gilbus is my unofficial boss, not by seniority, but because Samson and the others trust her more than me. She's a bit sarcastic and domineering." He winced at his current situation and said, "I had wanted the Knackmeister Museum project to be successful so that I could prove to them all that I had the brains to manage this firm. Miriam will be looking down on me again after this failure."

Steve said, "Miriam will be making her comments from behind bars. We've already located her vacation cruise, and she will be greeted by police officials at her next port."

John looked impressed. "What do you want from me right now?"

Penny said, "We'll be taking all of your presentation materials about the artwork and the organization as evidence. How do you contact the higher-ups if you have a request for them?"

"Miriam handles that, using a contact file in her computer. I think she contacts them by email and inserts code phrases into her messages in case any message goes astray."

"In that case, we'll be taking Miriam's computer for study by our experts. For now, we want you to call John Samson and tell him that you're planning to go out on your own to work with a small museum that wants to sell part of its collection. You don't have to identify Knackmeister, but tell Samson that you'll be leaving the firm as soon as Miriam returns."

"Won't he be apt to send people to punish me for wanting to leave?"

Penny used her calmest tone of voice to reassure Krimmens. "We'll have people on alert to intercept anyone who tries to pressure you. We want Samson and his associates to sense disruptions to their normal routines and procedures so that they'll take steps that will reveal their identities. They're certain to react to your call, but we'll protect you from any possible harm."

CHAPTER 85 – CARTELS

John Samson terminated his phone conversation with John Krimmens and immediately hit a memory key to dial a special number. "That paper-pushing lawyer, Krimmens, wants out. He's latched onto his own cash cow client, and he doesn't think he needs us and our *shady* business any more. Can you believe that? After all these years that he's been cheerfully accepting our money, he calls us shady. I don't know many lawyers who haven't interpreted the law to their own advantage, and he has the nerve to call us shady."

The voice he heard through his phone said, "Well, take care of him. We've had to remove rebellious staff members before. Why are you involving me?"

The problem is that I'm on the verge of meeting with the Zetas to make an arrangement that will keep our Mexican operations running efficiently. If you want, I can let you handle that while I drop everything to handle Krimmens."

"Your birth name is Juan Samosa, John, and that makes you better suited to deal with the Zetas than I am. I'll cover the Krimmens matter for you. Based on all your past comments about him being a paper-shuffling wimp, I'm surprised he's acted up at all. Perhaps you're slipping in your ability to judge people. We'll have another conversation about that soon."

Samson disconnected and leaned back in his chair. Why did so many unexpected crises have to occur at the same time? He'd learned that Miguel had turned greedy and withheld the Zetas payoff money for his own use. Now Samson would have to try to negotiate a new relationship with them. What if Jose Lopez had been a Zeta, sent to check up on his group? The cartel had better not learn who killed Lopez. Just in case, he'd better have a Plan B for disappearing from everyone. He knew that he'd already accumulated more money than he could ever spend. The problem was that he also knew, as would Mr. Krimmens, that the organization frowned on people who abandoned their assignments or, even worse, went out on their own.

CHAPTER 86 – ARTHUR AND JOE

Arthur escorted Joe out of the Branchout Rehabilitation Center, looking for any residual health problems. Joe spoke and breathed well, unencumbered by the smoke damage he had suffered to his lungs. He also displayed no physical impairments to his head, limbs, or balance.

"Joe, do you feel as well as you look. I'm impressed by the speed of your recovery. Should we gradually ease you back into investigations, or are you truly fit again?"

"I'm the original me once more, Arthur, but I will hang back out of the limelight for a while. We have the gang believing that they killed me, and I wouldn't want to disrupt their sense of security on the matter."

They climbed into Arthur's car and headed for Chicago. Traffic was unusually light for mid-morning, and they parked in a garage less than one block from the Law Offices of Bexley and Josiah. As they entered the elevator in the building that housed those offices, Joe gave a very slight nod to the janitor who was polishing the brass trim in the lobby.

On the eighth floor, they entered the Bexley front office. Steve motioned Joe to the conference room where Penny awaited him, and then approached Arthur.

"What do you think, Arthur, is Joe ready for some action?"

"I studied him pretty well during the trip over here. He's both ready and antsy to get back to work after all of the time he spent on the sidelines. How's the lawyer Krimmens doing?"

"He wants to make amends for past sins, so he has been both helpful and cool."

"Will he be able to act out his part?"

"I think so, but we'll have to caution him about overacting."

Penny and Joe came out of the private office and approached Steve and Arthur.

Penny said, "We're going to find a place to stay since they're still watching our house. We'll make our temporary quarters a downtown hotel where we can have a change of scene. On the way, we'll discuss things that happened while Joe was out of circulation. Arthur, will you assist Steve while we're gone?"

"You two don't have to rush back. Steve and I will watch for new developments. I caught Joe's signal to the janitor downstairs when we came up. I'm pretty sure you've already arranged for backups."

Joe said, "I am rusty. That shouldn't have been obvious. Steve, what's the profile on support troops?"

"In addition to that janitor, we have a receptionist in a formerly vacant office across from the elevator who will warn us of new arrivals. Her boss and his assistant in that office are from one of our SWAT teams, and the mail girl for this floor is an electronics specialist who is recording everything we say on equipment hidden in her mail cart."

Arthur said, "You sound well-prepared indeed. Why don't I play the part of John's legal client?"

Joe said, "I'm not sure that would be smart. They've had contacts with your church. We don't know how many of their people have been to Parkville UMC and might recognize you."

"In answer to that point, I could be a client on the phone with John from one of the other offices. That would keep me concealed but still let me coach him if he gets nervous."

Penny said, "Fair enough, Arthur; we'll relieve you folks in a couple of hours if nothing develops by then."

As Joe and Penny left, Steve and Arthur exchanged glances that said they expected action soon.

CHAPTER 87 – ZETAS

John Samson had expected that the Zetas would want to meet with him and his people in Texas or Mexico. When Marco called him and said that the meeting was set for tomorrow evening at a hotel near Chicago's O'Hare Airport, he felt surprised and relieved. At least they wouldn't be able to bring a ton of armaments through the airport for the session. The problem would be to keep the Mexicans from getting angry during the discussions. Their violent reputation made John nervous. He would arrange for five people to back him up in his delegation. A smaller number of people would suggest weakness; a larger number would threaten confrontation.

At seven-thirty the next evening John Samson's red sports car followed by two silver utility vehicles with hidden weapons compartments arrived at the appointed hotel on Mannheim Road. The six occupants of those vehicles entered the hotel to find Marco Fernandez awaiting them in the lobby. He shook hands with John Samson and led their party to a banquet hall he had reserved. As the group entered the hall, they noted that eight people in suits and sunglasses were standing in positions spaced around the periphery of the room. John motioned for his people to spread out also. It would be a bad tactic to have a compact group of people facing a widely spread delegation whose members just happened to be standing next to substantial furniture pieces and structural support columns that would offer cover should gunfire erupt.

John remained calm and asked Marco to introduce him to the leader of the Zeta group. He expected that person to be the tall, athletic man standing slightly to their left. As Marco approached an overweight man sitting at a table to their right, Samson realized too late that he had let his surprise show on his face. He tried to reestablish a neutral expression without success. He began to sweat.

Marco said to the seated individual, "Raoul Herreros, allow me to present John Samson who wants to discuss an arrangement with you."

"Senor Samson, you appear to be Latino, but your name does not reflect it."

"It was originally Juan Samosa, but I modified it after becoming a United States citizen."

"Are you not proud of your heritage?"

"My heritage has nothing to do with our discussions today. I wish to petition your organization for safe passage for any merchandise we bring through Mexico from Guatemala. We are, of course, willing to pay for this favor so long as the fee is within our means."

Raoul stood and surprised Samson by his height. Again, John displayed his miscalculation in his facial expression. Herreros snarled his response. "To the contrary, your heritage should make you ashamed of stealing from the Church. My brother is a priest in Guatemala, and he has told me of colonial era churches that have been stripped of all their symbols and holy objects. You do not have to be an angel to respect a house of God."

John felt his sweating increase. This was not going well. "We do not touch the major churches, only the little ones away from the cities."

"You mean the oldest churches with the most valuable objects. Do you rob grave sites as well? You are pathetic. Why should we help you?"

Samson looked to Marco for help, but could not determine his loyalties from his stoic expression. Samson's followers appeared to have retreated a bit behind him. To Raoul he said, "You should help us because we pay well and because we do not get involved in any of your businesses. We are not competition to your organization."

Raoul said, "Do you realize how easy it would be for us to put you out of business. We know the stations on your smuggling routes. We could destroy them and let the authorities mop up the rest of your group. You have offended us and the Church and the governments of several countries. What do you say to persuade us to leave your business alone?"

"I cannot speak for everyone in our group, but we might be willing to share our profits."

"That is far from enough. You obviously are not high enough in your organization to speak for it. Give me the names of your superiors, and I will speak with them."

"I can't do that. I would be killed."

Raoul said, "You can do that, or you will be killed for remaining silent." He turned to his men positioned around the room. "Seize them all!"

John panicked and ran for the door, pushing aside anyone who blocked his path, including his own supporters. He heard fighting and shouts behind him as he reached the outer lobby. He knew that this was the day he would celebrate the speed of his car.

John shoved the hotel valets out of the way as he sprinted for the Ferrari. Jumping in, he turned the key, and gloried in the roar of the engine. So far no one was following him. Once down the long driveway he would merge into the airport traffic and disappear. They would never be able to catch him. He accelerated down the hotel driveway toward freedom.

Samson didn't see the bulldozer moving in from his right to block the driveway until it was too late. He felt the shock of an accelerating sports car impacting an immovable object. The door flew open. He and the car flew upward in two separate trajectories. His flight seemed to last forever.

CHAPTER 88 – BEXLEY AND JOSIAH

Steve's phone rang. He listened and responded briefly, a slight increase in his muscle tension betraying the message's content. "Places everyone – it's show time. Our receptionist friend says that a man and a woman are heading our way. John, go to your office and phone Arthur in the extra private office. Arthur – close your door, and speak to him softly so that they don't realize you are talking from within the suite. I'll step into the conference room to make the calls that will cut off their retreat after they arrive."

Arthur's desk phone buzzed. "I'm here, John. Just start a normal conversation about providing legal assistance to Parkville United Methodist Church, and give me your best sales pitch about what your firm can do for us. That conversation will keep your tone normal, and our church might actually be in the market for legal support, so try to close the sale."

"Good morning, Pastor. I've always been amazed by the lack of attention of churches to legal matters. In this day and age you are exposed to liabilities all the time...Yes, I understand that you carry liability insurance, but do you realize that you could be sued for many interactions with your congregants and the public that are not covered by insurance?"

A tall, thin man and an athletic-looking woman had entered the front office very quietly. They could hear every word of John's telephone pitch for new business. It reinforced Samson's message that John Krimmens planned to leave their organization and start his own law firm. They approached his office doorway from the side in order to surprise him as soon as the conversation ended.

"That's my story, Pastor. I plan to be in your area next Tuesday, and I'd appreciate the opportunity to discuss this with you in person. Would two o'clock suit your schedule? That's fine; I'll see you then."

As Krimmens replaced the telephone on its cradle, Bill and Barbara stepped into his office. Barbara seated herself on his guest chair and took the lead, while Bill towered silently behind her.

"I haven't seen you for quite a while, John. You communicate with us through Samson and his messengers. How are you?"

"Hello, Barbara; I didn't hear you come in. I'm fine, but I don't know your associate."

"I brought Bill with me in case you choose to make this meeting difficult. Samson tells me that you want to leave Bexley and Josiah to start your own law firm. While initiative and enterprise are normally praiseworthy traits, we can't allow your move in this situation."

"What do you mean?"

"I mean that you have been exposed to transactions and business practices that we consider proprietary and that we would not like you to share with anyone else."

"You can always rely on attorney-client privilege to restrict such discussions."

"John, you know very well that our business requires loyalty that goes beyond the normal attorney relationship."

"That would be because your business goes beyond legal and ethical activities."

Barbara sat a bit straighter in her chair, and Bill took half a step forward. "John, I'm trying to remain civil with you, but you're in danger of crossing a dangerous line."

John stood up and stared at them. "Thanks to you and your organization, I've violated all of my personal ethics for years. There are limits to my willingness to rationalize it. Taking children away from their birth parents and stealing church treasures are not the careers my parents expected me to pursue. I'll have no more of them."

Barbara stood and found that she was looking upward into John Krimmens' eyes. She had always thought of him as a little twerp, but he seemed taller today. "That does it, John. We will have to ask you to accompany us. We can't tolerate your loose cannon behavior that could sink our operation."

"You mean your criminal and despicable operation, Barbara."

"I mean the business from which you have accepted large sums of money for many years. It's a little late to play the angel part."

"I agree that I have been weak and unethical. That's why it's time for me to change. Leave now and I won't press charges against you for intimidation and attempted kidnapping."

Bill removed a pistol from his pocket. "Cut the fancy talk Krimmens. You're coming with us. Say goodbye to this place. I don't think you'll be seeing it again."

John just smiled and looked over the heads of his visitors. Before they could turn around to share his vision, Barbara and Bill had their arms pinned to their sides by the two SWAT members in business suits. Steve then stepped into the office and wrenched Bill's gun from his hand.

"You won't need this where you're going." Steve announced that he and his associates were federal agents and that Barbara and Bill were under arrest.

Barbara began to protest that they had only discussed business matters with their attorney and that Bill had a license to carry the pistol for her protection. She claimed that Bill had only shown the weapon after John had threatened her.

Steve said, "That's a very good story, Barbara, However, you may have noticed the mail girl and her cart in the hallway as you entered this suite. She has a recording of all your words and actions since you arrived. This office has two hidden video cameras that have monitored everything, included your attempt to kidnap John Krimmens."

CHAPTER 89 – SORTING IT OUT

Jeremy enjoyed being included in the group meeting in the Parkville Police Department. Based on his assignments during this case, he felt equal in stature with the others rather than merely a rookie observer. Jeremy had requested that Chief Andrews let him be the first to speak, and he readily responded to the policeman's nod.

"This has been the summer of my dreams, working with all of you on this case. I especially appreciated the opportunity to be one of your Zetas when we rounded up most of the Midwest part of the gang. I was afraid we were going to have a shootout when Raoul Herreros confronted Samson. I didn't expect John to panic and run the way he did. Anyway, thank you for welcoming me into this amazing crew of investigators."

Penny said, "You've handled your assignments well, Jeremy, and you've accepted the tradition of trainees being asked to do a wide variety of things. I agree with your endorsement of the role that Raoul Herreros played. That is his actual name, by the way. It was so perfect for his part that we had to use it. In real life he's one of our software specialists and rarely gets to go on a field assignment. We had hoped that John Samson would surrender peacefully, but kept that bulldozer ready, just in case."

Arthur said, "God rest his soul. He who lives by the performance car, dies by the performance car. Joe, how do you feel about Samson's death? He did try to kill you, and he thought he had succeeded."

"As a professional in law enforcement, I can set aside the personal implications of his death. However,

I have to admit that if I were a civilian I might be a tiny bit glad to see him get what he wanted for me."

"I'll enter that as somewhat less than *an eye for an eye*. How about you, Penny; do you feel better now that it's safe for the two of you to go home?"

"I do, but I'll miss rooming with Irma. She's a great roommate and will take good care of you, Arthur."

Irma said, "You owe me five dollars, Penny. I told you he'd blush if you said anything like that."

Everyone laughed until Chief Bobby Andrews called the meeting back to order. "It's nice to hear laughter in this room where we're usually stressed out by serious events. As your host, I'll have to get us back on track. From my jurisdictional point of view, I need the identity of Horse McCabe's killer. Irma, do you have lab results on that motorcycle?"

"The motorcycle had been left exposed to the elements for quite a while, but Joe's protection of it while he was undercover as Jose helped quite a bit. Now that we have many of the gang members in custody, we have their DNA samples for comparison. The results are that DNA under the motorcycle seat matches with a blood smear on the glove compartment door of Kristina's car, and they both match with the DNA of Barbara McCabe."

Bobby said, "Are you saying that she is related to Horse?"

Irma smiled. "Even Arthur doesn't know this part. I've been busy while you folks have been doing field work. Horse McCabe was Barbara's brother. She killed her own brother rather than let him expose her secret criminal enterprise. We should check her torso for evidence of one or more bullet wounds from Horse's gun."

Arthur said, "How did she feel when Horse spoke in our church as Ted Karga and said he was Kristina's brother?"

Bobby said, "The answer to that one is that she felt mad enough to run out after him and kill him. All of our witnesses stated that a man dressed in black chased after Ted, but it was Barbara with her hair pinned tight to her head to fit inside her motorcycle helmet. Did you see her leave, Arthur?"

"There was so much commotion after Ted, or Horse, shouted out against God that I was just scanning the faces of our members for their reactions. I didn't see her leave, but she may have taken his outcry against God as her signal to be the avenging angel."

Jeremy said, "There was nothing angelic about her. She probably wasn't even religious. What do you think, Pastor Blake?"

"Most people don't wear their religions on their sleeves. It's usually hard to discern a person's belief system, but not in Barbara's case. Some of you read Sister Kristina's journals. Barbara is in there, as Sister Monica, the nun who left Guatemala shortly after Kristina arrived. Joe aroused my suspicions of her when he found a crucifix identical to Kristina's in the garage building in Rochelle and suspended it from his car's rear view mirror. I checked her real name with Sister Rosemary Dawes at the Maryknoll Sisters headquarters last week. Some sisters use their real names and some, like Barbara, use the names of patron saints. I'm sorry about spoiling your surprise, Irma, but I did know her name is Barbara McCabe. Not only that, but I learned that Barbara and Horse had the same father but different mothers. Once her mother died, and her father remarried, she turned to church service as a way out of a troubled home life."

"Rats! You are going to be hard to live with – but I'll get used to it eventually. I should have noticed that Barbara and Horse had enough DNA differences to suggest only one common parent. I suppose she and he crossed paths in Antigua, Guatemala."

"They did. Horse spoke out against God in our church, but although he had a brief spiritual awakening after his parents died in a plane crash, he had never been very religious. Once Barbara joined the Maryknoll Sisters, he deliberately lost track of her, and she didn't follow his exploits either. They both must have been shocked when Sister Monica met the Peace Corps worker in Antigua."

Bobby said, "Joe, I assume that your people have been dismantling Miguel's chain of orphanages in Mexico. How has that gone so far?"

"We've been working through the Mexican Government on that one. They are a little slower in their operations than we would be, but it's their turf, and they're appropriately in charge. We don't really have to rush things, because everyone down there thinks that the Midwest organization was shut down by the Zetas and not by federal agents. Miguel's people are sitting quietly waiting to hear from the Zeta cartel. In the meantime, we've shut down the east and west coast branches of the operation in our country."

"That sounds good, Joe, but are we ready to close this case? Have we all concluded that Barbara McCabe, aka Sister Monica, was the head of the organization?"

"I'll yield to Arthur on that question, Bobby."

"Thanks, Joe; I was going to bring up the hierarchy of the organization after you finished. Barbara was the second-in-command of the outfit, supervising John Samson and through him the various couriers, attorneys, and art marketers. She also kept an eye on Miguel and the Mexican art pipeline. However, the originator of this scheme remained in Guatemala. I pointed out during some past discussions that there had to be someone with access to all of those colonial churches who would select the items to be taken. That same someone would have to be in a position to persuade the Catholic Church and the Guatemalan government agencies that the losses were random and not due to a single organization that should be pursued and destroyed. Kristina identified that person without realizing it in her journals. I confirmed it in recent telephone conversations with him when he deftly moved to redirect my attention elsewhere. Those discussions did succeed in making him nervous, and he has taken actions that will help us to arrest him."

Irma said, "I think I can identify him. From what you said, it can only be Father McShane."

"Right you are, Irma. The local churches appreciate visits from an American missionary priest, and they try to impress him by showing off their treasures. He tested the outlooks of the sisters who arrived for Guatemalan assignments during his trips with them to Antigua and other religious and tourist sites. McShane found the partner he sought in Sister Monica. He worked out the overall plan of the art-smuggling enterprise and prepared her for working with tough male subordinates by arranging for her to be trained in military special operations skills by an elite Guatemalan Kaibil veteran. That training gave her the skills she used to murder her half-brother. Father O'Connell alerted me to McShane's relationships with members of the Guatemalan military. By the way, O'Connell smokes cigars, so he may have been the man with Guatemalan connections in the back seat of Kristina's car. When McShane and Sister Monica felt the scheme was ready for activation, she petitioned to go home to the United

States because of a feigned health problem. The Maryknoll Sisters understood Kristina's fear of being found by assailants after her return to the States, but they never did discover why Sister Monica returned to being Barbara McCabe and broke off contact with them. My guess is that they chalked it up to her having insufficient faith for her calling."

Bobby said, "You suggested that Father McShane will soon be arrested. How do you know this?"

"Father McShane, since attracting my attention and sensing disruptions to the organization, has requested that he be allowed to retire and return to the United States. He hopes to fade out of sight after his return, but Joe and Penny's agency has advised Homeland Security that they have applied for warrants for his arrest. He will be detained as soon as he reaches an American airport."

Penny said, "It's difficult for me to understand his motives. Perhaps he was rebelling against the vow of poverty that he had been required to make. Hopefully he will tell us more when he arrives."

Jeremy looked a bit uneasy as he said, "I'm young enough to still want to hold onto my ideals. I can see a priest getting greedy and stealing items from churches, but was he involved in the gang's original trafficking in children as well?"

Arthur said, "As far as I can determine, neither Father McShane nor Sister Monica were involved in the illegal adoptions racket. Father McShane became a confidant to Kristina because he knew she was fighting child-trafficking. He kept track of the people she was watching and meeting. Once Kristina began to identify the members of the trafficking outfit, McShane realized that he had a ready-made organization he could usurp for the Central American end of things, especially when his interest coincided with the timing of the government's ban on international adoptions. He may have even rationalized that he was steering these people away from a more sinful type of crime."

Bobby said, "Pardon my policeman's hunger for details, but I want to know whether Samson and his people knew about McShane."

Joe responded, "I'll pick up on that one, Bobby. While I was undercover as Jose Lopez, I formed the definite impression that at that time Larry and Bill thought that John Samson was the boss of the outfit. Samson was quite willing to maintain that fiction, both in person and during telephone conversations. He turned noticeably more subservient when Barbara was mentioned. She definitely conveyed the impression to me that she could tell Samson what duties I should have. The question in my mind during that period was whether Barbara was the leader of the organization or if there was someone directing her. McShane stayed hidden and let Barbara run the operation, but he was in charge. We'll give him a thorough grilling to find his motives once he returns to the States. Then he'll retire to a federal prison instead of a church home for old clergy."

Arthur said, "Perhaps he'll find a new calling ministering to his fellow inmates."

Penny laughed. "My guess is that he'll find something valuable to steal from the prison."

CHAPTER 90 – FAMILY THOUGHTS

"Irma, you look troubled. Are you still concerned that I won't go through with our marriage?"

Since the conclusion of the case that had started with Kristina Karga's attendance at Parkville United Methodist Church, Irma had abandoned cautions as to public perceptions and had moved in with Arthur at the church parsonage. This morning they had followed an old-fashioned hearty breakfast with a period of relaxed sprawling on two well-worn couches.

"You can't fool me anymore. Teasing is no longer successful. I finally realized that you've been enjoying our premarital conflicts just as much as I have. I now count you as hooked and ready for me to officially pull out of the bachelor pool at our wedding. My thoughtfulness is due to internal torments rather than to your reluctant bachelor antics."

"That sounds intriguing. Spill your thoughts so that we can discuss them together."

"My story is that for quite a while I've been trying to visualize our family life together. I told you earlier of my daydream when I was shopping in the mall with our two children. They were the right ages to have been in elementary school. We had a son who looked Middle Eastern and an oriental ancestry daughter. To make that scene happen, we might have arranged two international adoptions. Now that we have completed this case and seen the potential perils of such procedures, I wonder if my vision could ever come true."

"Irma, I'm not sure that I believe in visions as much as you do, but even if we assume that your daydream was completely accurate, how do you know that we aren't slated to adopt American children of international descent? International adoptions may make sense when there are large numbers of children without parents in a specific country, and people adopt them to save them from terrible lives as orphans. Our country has large numbers of children with backgrounds from all over the world who need homes. Why not adopt them here instead of bringing in children from somewhere else?"

"You're right, Arthur, I have no way of knowing from my vision whether those children would have come from American or international sources. I just worried about it because of the child-trafficking aspects of this last case. We'll worry about children after we get well-settled together...What are your thoughts on children?"

"That was a long pause between those two thoughts. I do like children, and your vision family sounds fine to me. Let me know when you learn their names. Seriously, I'd love to have children, but given our age at marriage, probably not large numbers of them."

"I think that Bobby and Renee will have a great family life with Thelma Lou in their midst."

"Irma, they showed their family values when they welcomed and loved Thelma Lou even when it wasn't clear whether she would be healthy or would even survive. They welcomed the gift that God had given them despite the fact that it might have been a temporary gift. Contrast that with Horse's outrage with God after Kristina's early death."

"Have you always been satisfied with God's actions?"

"I don't think we have the right to object to them, except as a matter of temporary emotional release. Our job is to do the best we can with what we've got, under all circumstances."

"You'll get an 'Amen!' from me on that one, preacher. Now seeing as you're the one I've got, let's see how well I can do with you."

CHAPTER 91 – POLICE MATTERS

Arthur answered his telephone to find Bobby Andrews on the line. "Hi, Bobby, what can I do for you?"

"If you're not too busy, come down to the police station to help me sort out the handling of Gus Savage and Marco Fernandez. We still have them both charged with assaulting you at your church."

"I thought you had released Marco into Joe's custody."

"I did, but Joe brought him back today. He says that we have to clean up the ambiguities of their cases, and you're the one who filed the charges against them."

"Fair enough; I'll be there in thirty minutes."

When Arthur arrived at the Parkville Police Department, he had Irma with him. He was surprised to see Penny drive into the parking lot as they entered the building. She soon joined them in Bobby's office.

Arthur said, "I'm not quite sure what's going on here. Irma wanted to come along to meet Gus and Marco. Are you here for the same purpose, Penny?"

"Don't look now, Arthur, but you've been conned. I'm here because Irma and I are going shopping for my Maid of Honor dress while you guys handle the legal business. You're on final countdown, NASA-man, Shirley Hadley is handling final church arrangements, and your wedding is scheduled in two weeks. Angela King is available for that date to perform the ceremony. We moved the date up due to solving our case earlier than expected. Bobby and Joe flipped a coin to see who will be Best Man, and Bobby won."

Arthur looked at all of their faces and realized that they were serious. "I'm prepared for launch into the marriage orbit, but I refuse to wear a tuxedo. If you want me, you'll have to settle for a suit."

Penny groaned, but Irma nodded in agreement. "We've discussed this before. As long as he's only casual about his clothing and not our relationship, it's fine with me."

The women left for their shopping spree after Irma relieved Arthur of his credit card. The others returned to their legal issue.

Bobby showed Arthur a set of papers. "I had you fill out the complaint form a while back so that we could hold Gus and Marco while Joe did his undercover work. Since they've been formally charged, I have to ask you whether you wish to withdraw your complaint so that we can ask the judge to dismiss the charges."

"I definitely want to withdraw my complaint. Marco has been a big help during the investigation. I just wonder whether Gus will feel he's had a raw deal. Gus has been in jail ever since they assaulted me, while Marco has been out on interesting assignments twice. What do you think, Bobby?"

"Gus doesn't know about any of that. When we decided that Marco might be useful to us on the case, I separated them. Marco remained in their original cell here, while I transferred Gus to a cell at the Sheriff's Department. I told the two of them that the move was necessary because we had only one cell, and health rules require that we not have two prisoners in a single cell for more than a few days. Gus knows nothing about any activities in this building since his transfer. Marco will have to decide whether he wants his friend to know what happened."

Joe said, "Good thinking, Bobby. I may have to limit how much he tells Gus. Marco accepted our offer

313

to work for our agency. He'll be more valuable to us if no one knows about his new career."

Arthur withdrew his pen from his pocket. "Give me the new forms, and I'll withdraw my complaints against the two of them. Jesus said that I should forgive people who harm me, and they actually helped the case by introducing us to John Samson and his associates." He signed the two forms with an extra flourish on each signature. Then he stared alternately at Bobby and Joe. "You are two of my best friends, and you've pinned me down to a wedding date that's looming up in the near future. Do you want to say anything to defend your actions?"

Joe said, "For a guy who's so adept at analyzing a criminal enterprise, you're a bit of a wimp at making major decisions. We decided that you needed a push. You can't keep dipping your toes into the water; it's time to dive into the pool."

Bobby added, "As one of your fringe benefits, you and Irma will have the privilege of babysitting for Thelma Lou from time to time. How does that sound, Arthur?"

"That sounds fine, but I suspect that Joe and Penny may want to assist you with the baby too. I had actually committed to Irma quite a while ago that I would get serious about the wedding date as soon as this case was closed. Your conspiracy will add some fun to the event. I extend my sincere thanks to all of you. Just let Irma think that I'm submitting under protest. She likes to play the conqueror."

CHAPTER 92 – GUS AND MARCO

Sally, the waitress at Lefke's Tavern brought two beers to Marco and Gus and added a basket of onion rings in the middle of their round table. "The onion rings are free. We haven't seen you guys for a while; consider them a welcome back present." She used her slinkiest walk when she left their table, knowing they would be watching her.

Gus said, "Marc, look at the swing on that back porch. Sally sure knows how to turn it on for guys."

"Maybe you'll want to get extra friendly with her. She was giving you the eye."

"Really? I might have to see whether she's serious. Thanks, Marc; I usually feel that we're competing for women. You're willing to step aside on Sally?"

"Sure, Gus; if Sally likes you, she's all yours. I may have to be out of town for a while anyway. Maybe you two will be an item by the time I get back. You can consider her your prize for doing such good legal thinking when we were in jail. You said that we should just wait out the situation, and it worked. That preacher guy withdrew his complaint, and they had to let us go. Preachers are all softies. You can tell from their sermons."

"Thanks, Marc; I guess you're finally admitting that I'm the smart one. I didn't realize you went to church though."

"You should try it some time. It's a great place to meet classy chicks. Anyway, you win the smartness contest. Before I leave town I have to figure out whether I'm smart enough to smooth out my relationship with an angry lady named Estella. Keep my seat warm for me, Gus."

"Sure, Marc, I'll be here when you get back."

Richard Davidson

-END-

ABOUT THE AUTHOR

Richard Davidson is the author of the self-help guidebook: *DECISION TIME! Better Decisions for a Better Life*. He has written four novels: *Lead Us Not into Temptation*, *Give Us this Day our Daily Bread*, *Forgive Us Our Trespasses*, and *Thy Will Be Done*, which are the first four volumes of the planned five-volume Lord's Prayer Mystery Series. He is Past President of Off-Campus Writers' Workshop, the oldest ongoing group of its kind in the U.S. and the founder of the ReadWorthy Books Book Review Blog. He is also the founder of the Independent Mystery Publishing Society (IMPS). Mr. Davidson is a Certified Lay Speaker and a former Lay Leader in the United Methodist Church. He is also an aeronautical & astronautical engineer and a businessman.

OTHER WORKS BY THIS AUTHOR

NONFICTION:
DECISION TIME! Better Decisions for a Better Life, VBW Publishing, Inc.
ISBN 978-1-60264-063-4 (soft cover)
ISBN 978-1-60264-064-1 (hard cover)
ISBN 978-1-4581-8395-8 (Smashwords Edition eBook)
ASIN B0052GOZEO (Kindle Edition eBook)
Where you are in life today is the result of all of the past decisions you have made or which have been made for you in response to the various situations and events that have impacted your life. The decisions that you will make from this point forward will determine the degree to which your future will be positive or negative. *DECISION TIME!* gives you insight into the subjective decision-making process as applied to both small and large choices you will face.

It includes dynamic aspects, cultural effects, and morality as applied to decision-making for individuals, teams, corporations, and societies. *DECISION TIME!* prepares you to face the continuous impacts of decision situations confidently and without hesitation.

FICTION:
Lead Us Not into Temptation (The Lord's Prayer Mystery Series, Volume I),
VBW Publishing, Inc.
ISBN 978-1-60264-407-6 (soft cover)
ISBN 978-1-4581-7381-2 (Smashwords Edition eBook)
ASIN B0052MGI6Q (Kindle Edition eBook)
Arthur Blake, former NASA engineer turned minister, receives an emergency appointment to be pastor of the United Methodist Church in Parkville, a distant suburb of Chicago, following the bizarre sudden death of the church's unusual former pastor. Pastor Blake's attempts to unravel the mystery that shrouds his predecessor become involved with tracking the child of a possibly bigamous soldier in World War II England, art and jewelry treasures plundered by the Nazis and their sympathizers, and the eventual results of childhood sibling conflicts in combined families. Arthur's allies in his investigation include Parkville Police Chief Bobby Andrews, County Medical Examiner Irma Custis, and the married team of Penny and Joe Gonzalez who work for a clandestine government agency. During the course of *Lead Us Not into Temptation,* the reader discovers how seemingly minor historical events lead to major present-day dislocations in church, village, and family relationships.

Give Us this Day Our Daily Bread (The Lord's Prayer Mystery Series, Volume II)

RADMAR Publishing Group
ISBN 978-0-9829160-0-1 (soft cover)
ISBN 978-1-4580-6717-3 (Smashwords Edition eBook)
ASIN B0052MQI66 (Kindle Edition eBook)
Arthur Blake, Pastor of Parkville United Methodist Church, has to deal with the aftereffects of a traumatic communion incident. He works to assist the authorities in investigating the cause while doing his best to convince members of his congregation that it is safe to return to church. Working with the police and federal agencies, he discovers that the terror of the initial event is minor compared with the potential chaotic impact of future disasters being planned by the perpetrator. The investigation is interwoven with several relationship situations that affect the final outcome.

Forgive Us Our Trespasses (The Lord's Prayer Mystery Series, Volume III)
RADMAR Publishing Group
ISBN 978-0-9829160-1-8 (soft cover)
ISBN 978-1-4657-3739-7 (Smashwords Edition eBook)
ASIN B005SULQ6Y (Kindle Edition eBook)
Arthur Blake, Pastor of Parkville United Methodist Church, tries to assist his father to resolve his trauma after learning that his best friend, recently killed in a car accident, may have been an imposter with a heinous background. The investigation reveals that the presumed accident was but one link in a chain of murders. Blake works to determine the true identity of his father's friend, while also discovering the man's past activities and affiliations. Arthur works to solve the murders in conjunction with his colleagues at ABC Consultants. He also draws on assistance from associates at a covert government agency with which

he has worked before. The coordinated effort to solve the puzzle examines incidents that span the period between World War II and the present in order to defuse the personal, national, and international dangers resulting from them.

Learn more about the writings and random thoughts of Richard Davidson at: davidsonbooks.blogspot.com davidsonbookshelf.com
betterlifedecisions.blogspot.com
Like him on Facebook at https://www.facebook.com/pages/Richard-Davidson-Author/211578652220873?ref=hl Follow him on Twitter @mysteryimp